Precious Atonement

Melissa Maygrove

Truelove Press

Precious Atonement

Copyright © 2015 Melissa Maygrove

All rights reserved. No part of this publication may be reproduced, distributed, or transmitted in any form or by any means, including photocopying, recording, or other electronic or mechanical methods, without the prior written permission of the publisher, except in the case of brief quotations embodied in critical reviews and certain other noncommercial uses permitted by copyright law. For permission requests, please contact the publisher.

Truelove Press
Houston, Texas
www.truelovepress.com

This is a work of fiction. Names, characters, businesses, places, events, and incidents are either the products of the author's imagination or used in a fictitious manner. Any resemblance of characters to actual persons, living or dead, is purely coincidental.

First Edition
ISBN-13: 978-0-9960-397-3-4

Cover design by Carrie Butler, Forward Authority Design Services
Cover photo (couple) by RomanceNovelCovers.com
Cover photo (landscape) by amedvedev
Formatting by L. Diane Wolfe

Attributions
The poetry quotes in this novel were taken from:
"To Autumn" by John Keats
"She Walks in Beauty" by Lord Byron

Precious Atonement

*Ruined women don't hope,
killers don't dream,
and the dead don't feel pain.*

Chapter One

July 1849
Wood Creek, Ohio

Tragedy had found Rachel Emerson again, and fear cut deep.

Her father would be forced to hire new help for the farm. Three years ago, it had been due to deception and desertion. This time, death.

The man he'd trusted with his land and his family had lost his footing while patching the roof. Emmett Weeks might have lived, had a broken arm been his only injury, had his head missed the rock. Now another stranger would come.

Would the new man be honorable, like Emmett? Or would he corner her in the barn and rape her?

The thick summer heat coated Rachel's clammy skin, making her nauseous. She wrapped her arms around herself and stared at the shrouded corpse in the back of the undertaker's wagon. Her bones ached as the solemn conveyance rattled down the road and carried her safety away.

Her father lifted his head and replaced his hat. "If I believed in such things, I'd swear this family is cursed."

He cut his eyes to her, lashes lowered in apology, and she managed a small smile that was part forgiveness, part agreement.

Rachel stared at the shrinking wagon and sensed a fleeting pang of envy.

At least the dead can't feel pain.

Her mother's cooking could win a blue ribbon on a bad day, but that didn't help. It rarely did.

Rachel nudged the mound of scrambled eggs on her plate and forced herself to take another bite. She could feel her parents watching.

They were always watching. Watching and worrying that she wasn't eating enough, or that she wasn't sleeping enough, or that she wasn't talking enough. They meant well, but they made her feel like an insect under glass.

How was she supposed to feel normal again if they refused to treat her as such?

They did have reason to be cautious. After she was attacked, she'd refused food and water until she was so near death, the doctor told her pa to ready wood for her casket—but that was three years ago, and she had changed.

Her brother, Seth, had been put in charge of her safety, and even at fifteen, he felt responsible. Making him watch her die after he'd been forced to watch her raped was a cruelty she couldn't inflict. She'd begun drinking and eating for his sake.

Unfortunately, her feeble rally came too late.

Instead of fighting to live, she'd given up, and she'd lost her only brother because of it.

Rachel sighed and nibbled the corner of her toast. She still held out hope for Seth's return, but she had firmly accepted that she was a ruined woman. Living as a spinster wasn't the way she'd dreamed her life would be, but her circumstances left her no other choice.

Her ma lifted the napkin from her lap with slender fingers and dabbed her mouth with innate grace. "Lawrence, have you had any luck?"

He met his wife's expectant gaze, his empty fork hovering midway to his plate. "I've interviewed six men, but..." His eyes shifted in Rachel's direction, then lowered again. "No," he said as he speared a chunk of gravy-soaked biscuit, "I haven't hired anyone."

A grateful breath left Rachel's chest. It was selfish to be glad—her father looked haggard from doing the work of two men—but his poor luck meant no new stranger.

"I've got another interview scheduled for Friday," he continued between bites. "We'll see how that goes."

Rachel knew what her mother was thinking, even though the keen, discreet woman would never give it voice. Her pa had turned overly cautious when it came to hiring, and there weren't many men left to choose from. He'd run out of candidates soon.

"The apples are doing well this year," her ma said with a pleasant smile.

"Yes, they are," her pa agreed.

Rachel took another bite of toast. She felt them watching her again. They were probably hoping she would join in the conversation, but she rarely had anything to say. The only newsworthy thing in her life was that Emmett's death had resurrected her nightmares. She doubted Lawrence and Abigail Emerson wanted to hear vivid details of their only daughter's brutalization over coffee.

When enough ticks of the mantel clock and clinks of silver on china had sounded to thicken the air and make it clear she wasn't going to speak, her ma did what she always did and carried the conversation.

"It looks to be a mild day today," Abigail said to her husband. "I thought Rachel and I might pack lunch and eat with you in the field."

He paused, then nodded. "That would be welcome. I'll be working in the far pasture today. It'll save me some time."

After breakfast was over and the dishes were done, Rachel excused herself to go work in the garden. Planting and tending the vegetables was one of few things that brought her peace. The earthy scents calmed her, and watching the plants grow and bring forth their fruits made her feel optimistic.

She dug some potatoes, enough to fill the bottom of her basket, then moved to the beans. Beginning at the top of the shoulder-high plants, Rachel plucked pod after pod, lifting the leaves so the sun could reveal the stragglers. She set the basket down and knelt next to the row, inching her way along and gathering the ones on the bottom.

Her ma was right about the weather—the air was cooler and lighter than it had been in weeks. Still, the bright morning sun heated her clothes and caused little drops of sweat to bead between her shoulders and trickle down the center of her back.

The space where she knelt went dark, and Rachel welcomed the coolness of the shade. She stopped picking and dabbed her brow with her sleeve, waiting for the cloud to pass. But the light didn't return.

She straightened up to see what was blocking the sun. Before she could turn around, she froze. Icy blood stung her veins as her eyes traced the outline of the shadow. Even with the slant of the sun distorting the size and shape of the object, the being standing behind her couldn't be human. It could only be a bear, and it was huge. How had she not heard it approach?

Her heart pounded furiously in her chest as she held completely still. The bear was behind her, blocking the open gate, and the house was to her left. The fence surrounding the rest of the garden was too tall to climb. She was trapped.

Rachel's flesh prickled and her mind raced. Her father was too far away to come to her aid—he wouldn't even hear her cry for help. Without moving her head, she cast a sideways glance at the window of his office. It was open a couple of inches. Maybe if she yelled loudly enough, her mother would hear.

The shadow shifted as the bear lumbered toward her and raised one of his huge paws in the air.

Rachel spun around and scooted backward, the toes of her boots snagging the hem of her skirt and her heels digging for purchase. She couldn't make out the animal's features with the sun behind him, but he was even bigger than she'd imagined. Fear had her throat in such a grip, she couldn't utter a sound. The bear would kill her for sure.

He took another step forward, and she scrambled back again, terrified.

"Miss," he growled.

Rachel blinked.

"Sorry I startled you, Miss," he said in a low, rumbling voice that vibrated every bone in her body. The bear-man stepped toward her and extended his hand to help her up.

Rachel rose without his aid and backed away.

He lowered his arm, his massive shoulders drooping slightly. The bear-man took a few steps back and to the side, standing well clear of the exit. When he did, light chased away the shadows. He was tall and broad and musclebound, but he was just a man.

Still tingling with abating terror, Rachel eased out of the open gate and put more distance between them. "Who are you?" she asked bluntly. It had taken every bit of mettle she had to keep the tremors shaking her body from doing the same thing to her voice.

The man removed his hat with a beefy paw. Sunlight gleamed off his dark hair and lit his eyes, turning the beady orbs a deep sapphire. "Forgive my manners. My name is Jacob Evans. I came to speak with Lawrence Emerson."

She eyed him up and down. Thick hairy arms protruded from

rolled up sleeves, and suspenders drew twin lines from worn work pants, up over shoulders so broad, she wondered how he fit through the frames of doors.

Rachel returned her attention to his face, her neck bent at a sharp angle to make up for their difference in height. "He's not expecting you."

The bear-man stood, shoulders rounded, both hands gripping the brim of his hat. "No, Miss. He's not."

She looked him over again. Whatever business he might or might not have with her father, she doubted their meeting would lead to anything good. One thing was sure; she didn't want the mountainous *Jacob Evans* anywhere near her on a regular basis, or any other basis, for that matter. If he'd come to ask for a job, she'd best thwart that ambition now.

Ignoring the bats flapping around in her middle and her heart pounding like a chorus of wood axes in her chest, Rachel squared her shoulders and looked the giant interloper square in the eye. "My father can't see you, Mr. Evans. Please leave."

The bear-man blinked a few times and frowned. With a smoothing brow and a sigh, he put his hat back on his head and walked away.

Chapter Two

Rachel paused as she passed by the door of her father's office. The rumble of male voices inside set her on edge. The seventh man was already here for his interview.

Cursing her timing, she lifted her basket from its place by the door and hurried around to the garden. The soft, cool earth did little to calm her today. Under the pretense of tending her plants, she knelt near the open window and listened.

"I must say, I was surprised when you first contacted me," her father said, his words paired with the creak of his chair. "And, if I can be blunt, a bit skeptical."

A second chair creaked louder, followed by a pause. "If the tables were turned, I'd feel the same," the stranger said, his rugged, deep voice reverberating off the walls and echoing from the room.

Rachel shivered.

"I do have a homestead of my own in Millhousen," he continued, "but I left the fields fallow this year."

"Why fallow?"

"The land needed a rest, and so did I."

Her father's chair creaked again, the way it always did when he leaned forward. "So why take a job?"

The room fell silent. A breeze ruffled Rachel's skirt and teased the wispy tendrils that had come loose from her bun. She pictured the stranger squirming in his chair.

"You're in a bind," he finally said, "and I could use a change of scenery... Besides, the pick of laborers around these parts leaves a bit to be desired."

A thumping sound came from inside—her father's thumb tapping the arm of the chair, no doubt. He often did that when he was faced with a dilemma, debating.

The thumping stopped. "Won't your wife object to you working on another man's farm?"

"That won't be a problem," the man said with an odd flatness to his voice. "My wife is dead."

"I'm sorry." Her pa sighed. "I need a hand who can put in a full day, not someone who has to split his time between my farm and his. I'd like to hire you, but I'm not sure you're the best man for the job."

"I have a few responsibilities at home, but I've sold most of my livestock."

"Are you planning to sell? To move?"

"I'm considering it. I haven't made up my mind."

Her father grunted—not scoffing, just a masculine sound of acknowledgement.

"My point is, I wouldn't need to spend much time there. And the money I'd earn would increase my options. All things considered, I think we'd both be better off."

Rachel tensed as her heart pounded out the seconds. *Say no. Say no.*

"The job pays a dollar a day, meals included, and we work six days a week."

"If you'd allow me to board my cow here and give me an occasional Saturday off, I could manage it. I'd be willing to bring my hens, too. Your missus could have all they make, sell the extra butter and eggs in town if she wished."

Her pa tapped his thumb again. "If you agree to work for me, it will be on a trial basis for a time, no guarantees."

"Understood."

Boots shifted and chair legs scraped the floor. "Be here by seven on Monday and the job's yours."

A shiver worked its way up Rachel's spine as a tight ball of dread lodged in the pit of her stomach. The new hand seemed ethical. But so had the one who'd attacked her.

The men left the house and started walking her way. She moved on shaky limbs to another part of the garden, to shield her eavesdropping.

"Thank you for seeing me," the stranger said, his rich words wafting by on the warm breeze, no longer distorted from bouncing around a hollow space.

Rachel paused. *That voice...*

"I came by earlier this week," he said to her pa.

"Oh?"

What! Rachel looked over her shoulder and gasped. It was him! Her pa had just hired the bear-man!

Jacob settled his hat on his head and lowered his massive arm to his side. "I had left my horse with Simon Ledbetter to be shod. I decided to take a chance and call on you early, while I was close by."

"Close? Ledbetter's place is nearly five miles away. You walked?"

Jacob nodded.

"I never knew you were here."

He shrugged. "I came unannounced, and your daughter said you were busy."

Both men looked her way.

Rachel jerked her attention back to the pepper bush in front of her. Her cheeks burned as hot as its fiery fruit.

Jacob Evans shifted, and his massive shadow engulfed her. Her embarrassment instantly cooled as icy fingers of fear punctured her chest and curled around her soul.

Chapter Three

Rough hands grabbed her by the arm and shoved her to the ground. The hard-packed earth struck her hip and her shoulder, sending pain shrieking through her bones.

Rachel raised her arms to fight and coiled her legs to kick, but the cold eyes staring back at her stole her breath and her bravado. A sliver of sun shining through the cracked barn door glinted off steel and drew her startled focus from the man to his knife.

"If you fight or scream, I'll kill you." His deep, growling voice was so maniacal, it could have come from Satan himself. How could this be? All the times he'd spoken to her before, he seemed so nice.

Rachel blinked back tears of terror as he shoved her skirts high and yanked her drawers so hard, the laces cut into her skin. She closed her eyes as the man's hot breath coated her face and his cold knife pressed into the tender flesh of her neck.

"Your pa's not as smart as he thinks he is," the traitor said as he shoved his way between her legs. "Good thing, 'cause you're gonna be sweeter than anything I ever had before." His grimy hand fumbled about, then he thrust himself into her, tearing her flesh.

Rachel gritted her teeth against the pain. She couldn't scream. Would—not—scream. Her life depended on it. Hot tears rolled down her face, and bitter sobs lodged in her throat as he pounded into her over and over.

An anguished wail began as a groan in the back of her throat, rolling and churning, trying to burst free. *No!* Rachel came up gasping. Had she screamed?

Chest heaving with ragged, labored breaths, pulse throbbing in her ears, she stared into the darkness. The man was gone. She was sitting on something soft. Warm, wet cotton clung to her body like a second skin—her gown. She wasn't in the barn. She was in her room, in her bed.

Did I scream?

Rachel froze and listened for the trod of anxious footsteps in the hall.

Nothing. Silence. Thank goodness she hadn't disturbed her parents.

The cool night breeze wafting in through her window blew across her sweat-soaked gown, chilling her. Rachel sat on the edge of the bed until her heart stopped racing and her legs regained enough strength to hold her up. She stood and peeled the damp, sticky garment over her head, then pressed a cloth to her face and neck to blot away the perspiration.

A subtle, pre-dawn glow trimmed the edge of the horizon. She might as well dress for the day. There'd be no more sleep for her tonight.

She adjusted the flame of her bedside lamp until she could see well enough to dress. Silently, she freshened herself with water from her basin, then opened her wardrobe and chose the most colorless outfit she owned. She'd never be invisible, no matter how hard she tried, but she'd become a master at disappearing. The slate-colored skirt and plain gray blouse would help her fade into the background.

She twisted her hair into a tight bun and stared at herself in the mirror. She'd lost the bright eyes and round face of her youth when her attacker stole her innocence, but the restless hours she'd spent fighting him in her dreams had given her a haggard look.

And the worst part was that her dream had changed. This time, the image of her rapist had mutated into that of the bear-man. Now she'd face a huge, flesh-and-blood version the monster in her nightmares every day.

Jacob unhitched his team and turned them out into the paddock. He'd left at first light and arrived at the Emersons' early so he could get his cow moved in before breakfast. The crated hens in the bed of his wagon would have to be settled in later. And carefully, lest the rank-minded creatures fight so fiercely they kill each other.

A humble log cabin shared the yard with the main house, making the home's painted clapboard walls and generous porch look regal in comparison. The family that occupied it seemed the same—a mixture of the cultured East and the practical West.

Jacob climbed the steps and drew in a breath. He'd needed a change, and this seemed as good as any. He hoped he'd made the right choice.

Lawrence opened the door, lamp light outlining his lean muscular body and muting the tiny patches of gray at his temples. Jacob's new employer welcomed him and showed him to the dining room. The furnishings were nicer than most, though not ostentatious. And—thanks be to God—the chairs were not only large enough to hold him but appeared sturdy enough to support him.

A fair-haired, willowy woman, carrying steaming bowls of food, swept into the room and greeted them. She was tall, and though she didn't strike him as one to put on airs, she looked better suited to polite society than the hard work and indignities of farm life.

Jacob exchanged the appropriate pleasantries when Lawrence introduced his missus, hoping his rusty manners would suffice. He took his seat when the lady took hers and glanced around. Where was the daughter? The Emersons didn't act as though anything was amiss.

"We observe farm manners, except on Sundays and special occasions," Lawrence remarked.

With a mental shrug, Jacob sipped his coffee, then served his plate and tucked into his food.

Mrs. Emerson—*Abigail*, if he wasn't mistaken—dabbed the corner of her mouth daintily and turned a pleasant smile in his direction. "Lawrence says you're from Millhousen, Mr. Evans. Have you lived there long?"

Jacob hurried to swallow the mouthful of sausage he was chewing. He blotted his lips, too, though the motion wasn't nearly as refined as it would have been a few years ago. He'd left his gentility behind in his home state of New Hampshire.

No. That wasn't true. He'd buried it with his wife. "Just a little over two years, ma'am, since the summer of '47."

She paused politely, but, uncultured hermit that he'd become, he did nothing to aid the conversation.

"I'm surprised we haven't crossed paths," Abigail continued. "Well," she amended with splotches of peachy pink dotting her cheeks, "you and Lawrence, I mean."

Jacob dug for his manners, unearthing more pain while he was at it. "My wife died a few months after we moved to Ohio. I haven't done much socializing since I lost her."

Her face fell, and her peachy cheeks blanched. "Yes, of course. Please accept my condolence."

"Thank you."

The missing girl emerged from the kitchen, dressed in clothes the color of a rain cloud, and slipped into the chair across from him. The sad, slight creature didn't speak, didn't look up, save for a timid glance in his direction as she spooned a small bit of eggs onto her plate. After placing her napkin in her lap, she sat motionless for so long, he wondered whether she was going to eat her food or simply watch it grow cold. Her chest finally rose with a discernable breath, and she picked up her fork.

Jacob frowned. The young lady sitting before him was undoubtedly Emerson's daughter, but this was not the same bold miss who'd curtly sent him away the week before.

It had been clear from her father's expression that he would have conducted the interview early—that she'd acted on her own authority. Ever since, Jacob had looked forward to bringing the incident up and watching the little mutineer squirm. But now his desire for good-natured revenge was gone. All he felt was concern.

What had caused such a shift in her demeanor? He'd startled the dainty miss in the garden—literally petrified her at first—but she'd squared her shoulders and stood up to him as if she were his physical equal. Even with her head tilted back like a child's, she'd glared at him in a way that made him think twice about crossing her.

A sudden chill tightened his chest. Had her father gotten his own revenge? There were no marks on the young lady's skin that he could see, and Lawrence didn't impress him as overly harsh, but... Jacob clenched his throat against a roiling of his stomach. What else could explain her cowed behavior and the dark circles under her eyes?

A masculine throat cleared to his right.

Jacob jerked his eyes to his employer and felt his cheeks warm—he'd been staring.

Lawrence smiled at him. Polite. Strained. "More eggs?"

"Yes, thank you. I'll take more biscuits, too. They're very good."

"That's kind of you," Abigail said, passing him the pan. "Rachel made them."

Rachel.

Jacob chanced another look in her direction. His heart swelled when her haunted eyes met his.

Don't be afraid. I'll protect you.

Determined to make a good impression, Jacob worked as though the hounds of hell were at his heels and breathed a little easier when Lawrence seemed pleased. He couldn't let himself fail. Something greater than pride drove him to succeed at this job. And something far more important depended on it.

Rachel's bleak demeanor changed from meal to meal. By the end of the day, she looked completely beaten—not by fists, but possibly by the fear of them.

Jacob cursed his situation when it came time to leave. Lawrence had warned him never to be alone with the women. The rule was understandable, but it was also a vexing blockade. How could he question Rachel without a private audience? And, even more vexing, how could he ensure her safety at night from twelve miles away?

Jacob's tired back was grateful for his bed, but sleep was slow to come. After two long years, a new woman consumed his thoughts and invaded his dreams.

Frustration gnawed at Jacob the rest of the week. Rachel's bearing improved, but she was obviously troubled. He did the only thing he could—work hard, with his mouth shut and his eyes open, hoping he might get a chance to speak with her. Of course, what good was it when he spent most of his time in the fields?

Much to his relief the following Monday, things changed. While he'd been home, sitting and stewing on Sunday, some rails on the far side of Lawrence's corral had been knocked down. Jacob would never wish the man ill, but he was glad to be working nearer the house.

He loaded the new beam, then boosted himself onto the back of Lawrence's wagon and rode with his legs hanging off as it jostled across the bumpy sod. In the distance, the fabric of Rachel's skirt rippled in the morning breeze. She bound her hair tightly, but the red and gold strands still gleamed like copper in the sunlight. Her auburn-capped head disappeared and reappeared again as she wove her way through the trees in the apple orchard.

Lawrence reined the team to a stop near the break in the fence.

Pulling his attention from Rachel, Jacob shoved off the wagon and grabbed the beam. He laid it on the ground near the breach and eyed the damage—one cracked rail and two more intact but knocked clean out of the mortises. "Your bull musta got enthusiastic with his belly rubbing. How many head did you lose?"

"Not many. Amos..." Lawrence grunted as he wiggled the cracked rail loose. "Amos Everhart owns the land that adjoins my pastures. He found all six."

Jacob helped remove the pieces. He hoisted the replacement and held it steady while Lawrence guided the tenons, then did the same with the next.

"You've taken quite an interest in my daughter."

Jacob's heart kicked him in the chest. He raised his brows in mock surprise, too startled to speak and not sure what to say if he could.

Emerson's lips pursed slightly, but with their edges turned up like a cat with a cornered mouse. "You watch her. Often."

Shit. "I meant no offense. I, uh..." He scrubbed a hand across his jaw. "Frankly, I worry about her. Is she well?"

The smugness faltered. "Physically, yes. She– Her brother left home rather abruptly, and Rachel hasn't taken it well."

Jacob feigned nonchalance and grabbed the last beam. "Wanderlust...? Your boy?"

Emerson frowned. "Something like that."

It was something *more* than that, but Jacob kept his counsel. He'd get to the bottom of things eventually. Discreetly.

Jacob kept his distance from Rachel and—save appropriate courtesies— forced himself not to look at her. It pained him to do so, but, with Lawrence scrutinizing his every move, he had no choice. He'd bide his time until an opportunity presented itself and pray she'd be safe until then.

Finally, nearly three weeks later, he was working near the house again. Lawrence had asked him to replace some rotten boards on the fence surrounding the garden, and Jacob managed to time things so that he began the job just after Rachel arrived to do her daily harvest.

She watched him through the narrow spaces when he carried the new boards and placed them just outside.

He pretended he didn't know she was there.

Lawrence, who was repairing the latch on the paddock gate, watched him, too. But Jacob gave him the very same treatment—went about his task as if it were his sole focus.

Please, Jacob pleaded with his maker, *distract him so I can see to her safety.* He didn't fear discovery so much as he feared that Lawrence's meddling would waste what might be his only chance to speak to Rachel for another whole month. Hell, if the man kept hovering, he might be forced to sneak back after dark and toss pebbles at her window.

Working as slowly as he could without raising suspicion, Jacob wiggled the rotten boards loose and began affixing new pickets in their places. Rachel eventually went back to her weeding and picking. He kept replacing boards, but his heart began to sink as he neared the last few. Her father hadn't moved.

Jacob sighed. He kept working and unobtrusively watching, but he'd fairly given up.

A muttered curse came from the paddock.

Jacob glanced up to see Lawrence set his tools down and disappear into the barn.

Finally!

He turned his head and located Rachel. He didn't have much time.

She was kneeling by the fence a few feet away.

He crept closer until he could see her face through the hole left by one of the missing boards.

"Miss Emerson," he said in a harsh whisper.

Her head jerked up, and her eyes flared wide.

"Are you safe here?"

She continued staring at him, but she didn't respond.

"Is someone hurting you?" he pressed. He refrained from naming her father, on the small chance he was wrong.

Rachel's brows dipped in a look of confusion. "No," she whispered back. "I'm... fine."

The barn door opened.

Jacob lifted the new board into place, sealing the delicate woman inside.

Rachel Emerson was not—by any stretch of nature, truth, or sensibility—*fine*. But, Jacob frowned, neither was she lying. He'd surprised her, he'd shocked her, and he'd most assuredly confounded her. But nowhere in her reaction had he detected an ounce of deceit.

Perhaps it was as her father had said. Perhaps she was simply missing her brother.

Rachel seemed oddly afflicted for such as that, but maybe she felt responsible. If something had passed between the two of them, if she had said something harsh that caused him to leave, it could explain the depth of her misery.

As Jacob knew all too well, guilt was a cruel motivator, and remorse, a vicious companion.

Chapter Four

Rachel lifted a damp bed sheet from the basket at her feet and clipped it to the line. Concealed by the growing curtain of laundry, she watched her father's new hand as cool wet cotton rippled and flapped against the side of her face.

Mr. Evans positioned a round of oak, then swung the ax and split the log in two with a single strike. He righted the halves and swung again. Muscles bulged with exertion. Patches of sweat and dirt stained his shirt. Each sharp blow echoed over the land and galvanized the part of her that registered threat. Jacob Evans was a dangerous man.

At least he could be if he wanted to.

But—and this was the thing that puzzled her without end—for all the hulking, dreadfully strong being he was, this bear of a man had a gentle spirit about him. He spoke ably enough and he worked hard, very hard. Yet in spite of that, he possessed a quiet humility like someone with a simple mind. Maybe he was dull-witted. Perhaps he'd sold his stock and left his fields lying fallow because he didn't have the necessary faculties to manage a farm.

Mr. Evans wouldn't be the first man whose wife quietly managed things for a less-than-savvy mate. And she had died.

"You're staring."

Rachel turned to find her ma staring, too. At her.

She blushed.

Her ma peeked through a gap in the sheets. "That man easily puts two commandments to test. Three, if he weren't such a gentleman and I weren't such a devoted wife."

Rachel gaped. "*Ma.*" But she had to bite her lip not to smile. She recognized her mother's scandalous comment for what it was, an effort to treat her like a daughter—*just* a daughter—and Rachel loved her for it.

"Oh, come now. Don't tell me you haven't noticed those handsome blue eyes and that sturdy physique."

Rachel feigned shock. "Have you no fear of your maker?"

Her ma bumped shoulders with her and retrieved another sheet. "My maker put beautiful things on this earth to be enjoyed. I plan to feast my eyes on all I can before my mind deserts me and my senses fail."

The rest of the wash was hung amid shameless talk and stifled, girlish giggles.

Rachel hoisted the empty basket onto her hip and chanced one more look between the flapping panels of cotton.

The sharp echoes of the ax had gone silent. Mr. Evans leaned the tool against the chopping stump and stood motionless, staring in the direction of the road.

Boots thumped the ground to her right as her pa passed by. He said something to Mr. Evans, then stood a few feet in front of him with the same alert bearing.

Rachel exchanged a glance with her ma.

Two men on horseback approached at a casual pace.

"Looks like the Grimes brothers," her ma said as they reached the edge of the yard.

Rachel muttered an agreement. Those rangy frames and narrow faces set the brothers apart from most everyone else around. Their tattered hats and clothes, too.

She'd known Earl and Edgar since childhood. They'd attended school with her until their mother died the winter of their eighth and tenth years. Their father kept them home and put them to work after that. It was no loss for the younger brother, Earl—he'd nearly drowned as a child and couldn't learn letters or figures, no matter how he was taught. But Edgar had a sharp mind, and cleaned up, he wasn't bad looking. He could have made something of himself.

Edgar swung down off his horse, causing the leather of his saddle to creak. Above a week-old beard, clear green eyes flashed in her direction.

A strange ache pinched Rachel deep in the chest. Supposedly, Edgar had taken a notion to court her. But that was before... If he had, he'd never approached her pa. And then she'd shut him out along with the rest of the town.

Whether Edgar had given up on her or given up on himself, she'd probably never know.

He dropped the reins and took a few steps toward her pa.

Earl remained mounted, his expression flat, literally. The brim of his hat was permanently creased and stuck straight up in front, as though he'd smacked face-first into a wall. It matched his planar features and didn't do much for his looks or his perceived intellect.

"Mr. Emerson," Edgar greeted with a slight dip of his head.

"Edgar. What can I do for you?"

"I heard you were in need of a hand."

"I was. I filled the position."

Edgar glanced at Jacob. "Any chance you'd hire me and Earl for harvest?"

"The oats and wheat are in."

"Understood, but you still have corn and hay and apples, and hogs to butcher."

"What about your pa? Doesn't he need you?"

Edgar's shoulders rounded slightly. "He, uh... Things have been rough. He couldn't plant this year."

Her father lifted his chin in acknowledgement. "I'll keep you boys in mind for the hogs, but if you get a better offer before then, take it."

"That's a load a—"

"*Earl.*" Edgar's chide held both compassion and warning. He faced her pa again. "Thank you. We'll call on you again closer to hog time."

Out the corner of his eye, Jacob watched Rachel dry dishes through the doorway of the dining room. Tension had been the main course at supper, tension and cross patriarchal expressions.

Lawrence crumpled his napkin and tossed it onto the table. "I hope those two get another job before butchering time."

Jacob lifted his coffee and peered over the rim of his cup. "Wouldn't hurt to have some extra help with the hogs."

"True. But not them. Not Earl, anyway."

"So just hire Edgar." A month ago, he wouldn't have voiced such a frank suggestion, but things had changed. He felt more like a partner and less like a hired hand.

"I suppose I could. Though I doubt that would sit well with either brother."

Jacob shrugged. "It's your call."

Lawrence plucked at the wadded clump of linen before him, then snatched it up and half-heartedly chucked it again. "Those boys should be working their father's farm, providing for themselves and storing up an inheritance." His lips twisted into a scowl. "'Couldn't plant this year.' That's a steaming load of muck. Grimes *could* if he'd stay sober and stop wasting his money on cards and loose women."

Jacob's gaze shot to Rachel, who stood across the room, returning silver to the sideboard.

"I beg your pardon," Lawrence said to her as she ducked back out. "Damn," he muttered. "She's so quiet, I sometimes forget she's there."

Jacob sipped his coffee and focused on Lawrence again. The man was awfully wrought over men he was reluctant to hire. "Why don't those boys set out on their own? Surely they could do better than scraping by on odd jobs."

Lawrence sighed. "Earl is feeble-minded. He's capable of work, but I doubt he could survive on his own. Edgar looks out for him." He folded his hands around his cup. "I know the charitable thing would be to hire them, but..."

Jacob waited expectantly.

"They aren't exactly blameless," Lawrence finally said. "Earl has taken after his pa. Edgar, to some extent, too. They haven't exactly done the most with their assets."

Jacob grunted his concession.

Lawrence tapped his thumb on the handle of his cup, then met Jacob's gaze with kindled eyes. "I want to move west."

That mentally sat him back. "You're serious."

Lawrence nodded. "If I do, I'll need to be frugal, save as much as I can by spring—both money and rations."

"I wondered why you planted so generously. Where will you settle?"

"California. But not by way of a grant." He leaned closer. Despite his discreet posture, his whole expression took on a fervent gleam. "I've been corresponding with a distant cousin who's already there. He's located a thousand-acre spread, and he's arranging the sale for me. He assures me it's fertile with an abundance of grass for pasture."

Jacob glanced at the ladies still working in the kitchen. "Does your missus know?"

"She and Rachel know I want to move, but they're not privy to the details. I felt it best not to worry them unless it comes to pass." The spark dimmed a bit. "I've located a reliable guide, and my cousin is prepared to close the sale, but I can't go through with any of it until I find a buyer for the farm."

"Hm." Jacob casually saluted with his cup. "I'll let you know if I hear of anyone looking to buy."

Emerson's missus entered the room carrying the coffee pitcher. "Shall I freshen your cups?"

Lawrence smiled up at her like a smitten youth. "Yes, please." Recent conversation had brightened the man, but it was clear to any fool with half a brain and two eyes that the Emersons' alliance was a love match, and one that hadn't waned with time.

Jacob drained his cup and swallowed back the miserable mire of envy his heart yearned to wallow in, then eyed the space between the drapes. Dusk was quickly approaching. He shoved his chair back and rose. "None for me, thank you. I'd best get going."

Chapter Five

An odd sight caught Rachel's eye as she stepped off the porch on her way to the garden. Booted feet were turned toe-down, digging into the ground as if to gain traction. She set aside her basket and walked closer. As she rounded the corner of the steps, large trouser-covered legs came into view and masculine grunts and muffled curses grew louder.

The legs belonged to Mr. Evans, who was attempting to belly-crawl his way under her house. As if he'd fit.

The grunting and grumbling stopped. He reversed his movements and wriggled out enough to lift his head and look up at her. "Good morning, Miss Emerson. Are you here to help or simply stare at my fundament?"

Rachel's mouth fell open with an affronted gasp.

The vulgar brute had the good sense to blush. "Forgive me. I shouldn't have said that to you." He sighed. "I slept poorly last night, and the lack of rest has left me cantankerous."

Rachel pursed her lips and pondered how sharply she should scold him as she studied the smudges beneath his eyes. "I am a lady, Mr. Evans. I do not stare at–" Merciful heavens, she was staring! Rachel jerked her gaze back to his face and waved in the general direction of his– his *fundament*. "–at... at... *I do not stare."* She crossed her arms and dropped them to her ribs with abashed, indignant force. "I came out, I saw your boots, and I walked over to see what you were doing on the ground." She frowned. "What *are* you doing on the ground?"

He propped up on his elbows. "One of the barn cats birthed her litter under here. She's got them fairly sheltered from predators, but the nights are getting cold. I'm moving them to the barn." He squinted and peered under the house. "That is, if I can retrieve them."

Mr. Evans was wallowing in dirt over a litter of kittens. Rachel's heart softened on the spot. "I'm smaller than you. I could get them."

He glanced up at her. "Nah. No sense us both getting filthy. I can reach them. I just need someone to hand them to so I don't have to keep crawling in and out. Here." He shoved a straw-lined wooden box her way. "Take them from me as I hand them out and put them in there."

She knelt on a patch of grass and waited while he squirmed his way back under the house. After several huffs and grunts, he withdrew his arm and extended it in her direction.

Rachel stared at the furry orange ball in his half-closed fist. She'd have to touch that fist to scoop out the infant cat. And she'd have to get within grabbing distance of the bear-man to do so without harming the creature.

"Miss Emerson...? Are you there?"

"Yes." She couldn't make herself move.

"Miss Emerson." The muffled voice now had a longsuffering edge. "I don't bite, and neither do these kittens. Yet."

Yet? He'd meant the kittens. Surely he'd meant the kittens.

Rachel lifted the wooden box that could easily double as a club with one hand and edged forward on her knees. Making as little contact as possible with the prickly Mr. Evans, she curled her fingers around the warm soft kitten and—loss of weaponry considered and promptly dismissed—nested it temporarily in her lap.

Mr. Evans reached back under the house and retrieved another.

Touching him was easier this time, but Rachel didn't lower the box. She placed the tiny gray feline next to its orange sibling, then did the same with the third—another orange.

Mr. Evans suddenly floundered his way out, and Rachel longed to scoot away. But she would dislodge sightless, helpless kittens if she did. She was once again cornered and at this man's mercy.

The bear-man swiveled around and sat with his back to the house and a fourth kitten in his hand. He stared at the uplifted box, then at the squirming creatures in her lap, then her. He raised a brow.

Rachel swallowed with a parched throat that was as dry from embarrassment as it was from apprehension. She lowered the box and set it between them.

"You don't think very highly of me, do you, Miss Emerson?"

"I don't know you well enough to form an opinion, Mr. Evans."

He glanced at the box. *'Yet you were ready to knock me over the head with a wooden box,'* his expression said. A kitten box.

The phlegmatic man sat with a puff of calico fur cradled against his chest, stroking the wee cat with the index finger of his other beefy paw.

Rachel cringed and waited for a high-pitched howl of pain or the snapping of delicate bones, but the kitten merely slept. And contentedly so, it appeared.

"Perhaps it would help if you called me Jacob instead of *Mr. Evans.*" He'd stated his name with such mocking formality, she wanted to both laugh and clobber him with the box.

"I don't think that's a good idea."

Jacob frowned. His brow smoothed and he resumed petting the kitten. "How long did Mr. Weeks work for your father?"

"Three years."

He narrowed his piercing blue eyes. "Did you still call him Mr.

Weeks?"

"Yes." *Insolent man.*

The dark rings that encircled his irises seemed to lighten. "Do you miss him?"

Rachel stared at her lap. The abrupt shift from self-assured petulance to soft-spoken sincerity had caught her off guard.

She lifted her head and nodded. "He was like a grandfather to me. Not so much in age; in that, he was more like an uncle. But the way he treated me reminded me of Papa Emerson."

"He was good to you, then."

"Yes, he was." She had cried when Mr. Weeks died, and now she fought the urge again. Stating her feelings out loud gave them a sharp realness that only thinking them had kept dull.

Jacob looked past her shoulder and lifted his chin. "She's watching us."

"Who?" Rachel turned her head. A lean orange tiger studied them as she stalked the perimeter of the yard. "Oh." She faced the bear-man again. Mother cats could be fierce, but he was the greater threat.

Jacob shoved himself to his feet and gestured at the empty box. "Put the kittens inside. We need to move them while she's watching."

Rachel did as he said, then rose and held out the box to him.

"You're not coming with me?"

She glanced at the barn and suffered another dry swallow. "No."

―――⚮―――

Rachel carried a basket full of onions and potatoes into the kitchen and hefted it onto the dry sink. "Ma?"

No answer.

She washed her hands and sighed. Everyone's routine had been upended. Apple harvest started in days, which meant double the cooking and chores until then. It was times like this she wished Seth was still–

She closed her eyes as understanding dawned and a heavy wave of regret broke over her heart.

Rachel climbed the stairs and paused at the sight of her brother's bedroom door standing ajar. Talk of moving west—talk her father thought they couldn't overhear—always sent her mother here. She eased in.

Her ma sat on the edge of Seth's unused bed, tears wetting her lashes and one of his old work shirts clutched to her chest. A pained smile wavered on her lips. "He's eighteen now. I wonder how big he's grown." She laid the shirt on the quilt and smoothed it as if it were made of fine silk. "I bet this wouldn't even span his shoulders."

"Ma." Rachel joined her mother on the bed.

"I want to believe he's all right," she said, hugging the shirt to her chest and dipping her head to breathe its scent. "But he... It's been so long. *If he'd just send word.*"

Rachel placed a calming hand on her mother's arm, but she felt powerless. How could she reassure anyone when she had the very same doubts?

"Your pa–" Her mother's chest seized. She regained control of herself, but her whole face contorted with anguish. "What if Seth comes back and we're not here?"

"It'll be all right. *We'll* leave word. If Seth comes looking for us, there will be a whole town full of people who can tell him where we went."

"But what if he can't afford to follow?"

Rachel's next breath grated over her throat and caused her chest to ache. That, she had no answer for. Not the one her ma wanted, anyway—the one they both wanted. "One of them would get a letter to us. You know they would." *Then at least we'd know he was alive.*

"Come back downstairs," Rachel said, rising and urging her ma to do likewise. "We have to get ready for the apples."

"Are you ready for this?"

Jacob looked over at Lawrence. The ever-pensive man was actually smiling.

"I'm warning you," he said as he guided the buckboard filled with ladders, crates and baskets toward the orchard, "those women will work circles around us and dictate our every move in the process."

"I can take it," Jacob replied. Ha. Watching quiet, little Rachel take charge? He would revel in it, in fact.

"Perhaps." Lawrence set the break and dismounted. "But the real question is, can you take a steady diet of apples cooked in every possible way, shape, and form for the next few weeks?"

Emerson's wry smile was contagious. "I'm sure I can manage. Neither your wife nor your daughter has made a single thing I couldn't eat yet." Jacob planted his hands on his hips and gazed at the rows and rows of fruit-laden trees. "How long do you think it'll take us?"

Lawrence handed him a stack of baskets and turned back to grab more. "Roughly six days, but we spread them out. We'll pick for three, then you and I will start on the hay. That'll give the ladies a chance to put up the haul from the first round." He started unloading the ladders. "When they're done with that, we'll come back and pick for three more days." At Jacob's raised brows, he added, "I know it's odd, but doing it this way gives the women a rest and gives the first cut of hay time to dry."

Jacob grinned. "I dare you to say that to their faces."

"What?"

"That storing, peeling, drying, and canning apples is *rest*."

Lawrence let out a short chuckle that was more of a grunt. He hoisted himself into the wagon bed and shoved one of two wooden contraptions to the end. They were special, short ladders for the women that resembled a narrow porch with solid, stair-like steps and a rail around three sides. The platforms allowed the ladies to pick the lower-hanging fruit without much chance of falling and yet put them high enough to take the filled gathering bags from him and Lawrence without the men having to climb down.

They positioned the ladders and platforms around the first two trees as the sound of feminine voices drifted in on the brisk morning breeze.

Abigail and Rachel walked up, wearing faded muslin work dresses and each carrying an armload of cloth gathering bags.

Jacob tipped his hat. "Good morning, ladies."

They replied in kind, though Rachel's greeting was soft and subdued.

Emerson's missus deposited her cargo into a basket near one of the platforms. "Take care not to bruise the fruit," she said, tossing bags to the men, "or you'll spend the winter eating sauce instead of pies."

Lawrence slipped the cloth handle over his head and hung the bag around his neck. "Yes ma'am." His lips twitched and his eyes twinkled as he scrambled up the ladder.

Jacob followed suit and got to picking—that was easy. Keeping his mind on his work was not. His gaze kept wandering from the glossy apples hanging all around him to the redhead standing three feet down and to his right. The higher the sun rose in the sky, the brighter her hair gleamed, an appealing blend of brown and red and gold.

She looked up and caught him staring.

In an impulsive move to save face, Jacob polished the piece of fruit in his hand against his shirt and took a bite.

Rachel frowned.

"Mwhat?" he mumbled.

"You're supposed to be picking them, not eating them."

Jacob finished chewing and swallowed. "My salary includes meals."

She pressed her lips into a firm line and went back to picking.

He grinned and finished his snack. Rachel might be shy, but there was a wide streak of stubbornness under that mousy façade. Teasing her was going to be fun.

Jacob filched so many snacks during the six days they were picking, Rachel actually scowled at him a time or two. At one point, he almost blurted out, 'What are you frowning for? I'm saving you work.' Instead, he just smiled and took a big, juicy bite.

She probably despised him, but he'd gained respect for her—for both women. Their strength and stamina were in complete conflict with their thin frames and delicate looks.

Best of all, he'd felt a sense of peace as he worked alongside Rachel. He was... happy. And, when he wasn't taunting her, it seemed she was, too.

Jacob cut a swath of hay and winced. Harvesting the orchard had left him with scraped skin and painful spasms running the length of his back and his limbs. He was no sluggard, but when Lawrence waved at him from across the field and pointed toward a cluster of shade trees at its edge, Jacob laid his scythe aside without argument.

They'd no sooner entered the welcome circle of shade when Emerson's missus strode up with lunch. She set the basket on the ground and handed them big jars of cool tea.

"Thank you, sweetheart," Lawrence said as he removed his hat and mopped his brow.

"Yes. Thank you," Jacob echoed. He tipped back his tea and downed half the jar in one long series of swallows.

"I packed plenty of roast beef sandwiches. There's sliced cheese and apples, too."

Lawrence slid him a look, then smiled sweetly at his wife. "Will you and Rachel be joining us?"

"Heavens, no. There's too much work to do."

Jacob slid Lawrence a look.

"You're free of females till supper," Abigail tossed over her shoulder as she turned to leave. "Air your shirts if you like."

Lawrence removed his and spread it across a nearby bush. Jacob waited until the lady was out of sight, then did the same. The men settled themselves at the base of the tree and began pulling food from the depths of the basket.

Jacob bit into a thick sandwich and relished the calm breeze as it drifted past and dried the moisture from his skin.

"Care for an apple?" Lawrence had asked it with a straight face, but his eyes twinkled like a school boy up to no good.

Jacob grimaced as he chewed. "Mm. Maybe later." *Maybe never.* Six days of taunting Rachel in the orchard had backfired. Literally.

Lawrence stretched out his legs and sipped his tea. He rubbed his right shoulder and grimaced. "I'm beginning to regret my ambitious seeding."

Jacob nodded. They had weeks of work ahead of them, and the days were getting shorter. They'd be lucky to get the corn in before the first snow and the hogs butchered by Christmas. "I wish I lived closer. I could work longer days if I didn't have to waste so much daylight traveling to and from home."

"Would you consider staying here overnight during the next few weeks? I could loan you the cabin. You could still go home on Sundays."

Jacob shrugged. "I could." He drained his jug and set it aside. "Rachel said the cabin belonged to your parents."

"It did. Abigail and I lived there, too, until I built the house."

"Four people in one room—that's awfully cramped quarters."

Lawrence barked out a laugh. "Yet, somehow, we managed to conceive Rachel."

Jacob chuckled. But as the words sank in, his chest ached with a deep sense of loss. The only child he and his wife ever conceived had died with her. He managed to keep his feelings from showing on his face. "Have you found a buyer yet?"

Lawrence shook his head. "A couple of inquiries, but no firm offer." He leveled a mildly assessing look. "Have you ever considered moving west?"

"I've thought about it," Jacob replied, flicking a piece of chaff off his trousers.

An unspoken '*And...?*' hung in the air.

"And I'm still thinking about it."

Jacob pulled a pristine globe of crimson from the basket and held it up. "Would *you* care for an apple?" At Emerson's smirking denial, he set the fruit aside and stood. "Then let's get back to work. Your fields aren't getting any smaller, and the days aren't getting any longer."

Rachel tromped over the hill beyond the barn and angled down the slope that led to the hogs. Her shoulders ached from the strain of carrying twin buckets loaded with apple refuse. She always rued the long walk on her way to the pen, then promptly switched to being grateful as soon as the stench invaded her nose. She swallowed to keep from losing her supper.

In the waning light of evening, Rachel eyed the pen from a distance, the way her pa had always taught her. The fence appeared to be intact and its occupants safely contained. Holding her breath, she leaned over the rail and dumped the scraps in haphazard piles along the dirt, giving rise to a raucous eruption of snorts and squeals. Rachel frowned at the uncivilized creatures and gathered the empty buckets.

"Don't fall in."

She spun around.

Earl sneered at her from atop his horse. "Your pa's pigheaded, just like his swine. He's sendin' his lovely little girl to do his dirty work when he could be sendin' me instead."

She straightened and put on an indifferent face, but she eased away from the sty. "What do you want, Earl?"

His mocking smile faded, and anger flinted his eyes. "I want work. I want to earn money so I can *eat*."

And so you can drink. Rachel marshalled her patience. Between Earl's inferior raising and his blameless loss of good sense, he had a right to be bitter. "My father told you he'd hire you and Edgar to help with the hogs."

Earl nudged his mount closer and glared down at her. "Your pa's an ass, and so is that stingy bastard he hired." He tapped his index finger several times on the side of his misshapen hat. "I've been askin' around. That Jacob fella's no drifter. He owns his own farm, but he ain't farmin' it." Earl's flat nose wrinkled with his angry scowl. "They coulda put three men to work for the season—each. Instead, they're huddled up and keepin' it all to themselves."

"Perhaps I should tell my pa how you feel," Rachel said, her ears burning, her temper rising, and her Christian sympathy reaching its end. "I'll be sure to put it to him as coarsely as you put it to me."

Earl swung out of the saddle and stomped toward her. "Don't you dare. Don't you *dare* ruin this for Edgar and me." His putrid breath warmed her face, and the odor of liquor turned her stomach.

Rachel took a step back, but he didn't let up. The gleam in his eyes turned feral.

He's drunk. Get away. Get away now.

She threw the buckets at him, hard, and stumbled backward.

A few more steps and she could turn and burst into a run. A root snagged her right heel, so Rachel shifted her weight and stepped with the other boot. Her toe met air. Her foot plunged into a hole. Pain exploded in her ankle as she fell.

Jacob tightened the cinch of his saddle. Deep pink tinged the cloud-raked sky, and his horse's bay coat had turned chocolate in the waning daylight.

The Shire tossed his head in response to porcine squealing in the distance.

"Easy, boy." Jacob patted his mount. He cringed when another burst of squeals assaulted his ears. "I'll tell you a truth, Goliath: I'm glad you're not a hog."

Jacob began the perfunctory chore of checking the state of his tack and his animal. The leather was in excellent condition, though the same could not be said of his steed. The usually docile draft was as twitchy as a felon in a room of executioners.

A commotion erupted from the pen so loud that birds took flight from the trees and the entire coop of chickens flapped and fretted.

Jacob calmed Goliath and tied him to the paddock rail, then withdrew his revolver from his saddle bag. Whatever had stirred the hogs into mayhem couldn't be small.

He trotted past the barn and down the hill, muscles coiled and senses sharp. The odors of pine and hay gave way to the pungent smell of mud and muck and swine. Squinting into the dappled shadows, he eased around the copse of trees that lay between him and the sty.

Jacob's eyes widened.

Rachel lay on the ground, staring up at a man crouched over her. Not just crouched—poised to attack!

Jacob lifted his colt and stepped clear of the trees. He longed to kill the bastard where he stood, but he didn't have a clear shot.

C'mon, you son of a bitch. Move.

Hooves pounded the ground to his right. Edgar Grimes rode into the clearing. "Earl!" he yelled as he lost his hat to the swat of a low hanging branch. "What the hell are you doing!" He swung down off his horse and stalked toward his brother. "Damn it, Earl. Have you completely lost your mind!"

Earl straightened and took a swaying step back. "I–"

"You're drunk," Edgar spat in disgust. He looked down at Rachel cowering on the ground and ran both hands through his hair. "My God. What did you do to her?"

"Nothin' She made me mad, and I yelled at her. That's all. I didn't hit her ner nothin'. She tripped."

Edgar leaned over Rachel and extended his hand. "Are you all right?"

Jacob took a step closer. He cocked his revolver and watched Edgar's spine stiffen at the ominous sound. "Back away from her—both of you."

Edgar raised his arms and turned around. Earl merely scowled.

"I said back away."

The look on Edgar's face was one of true confliction. His tired eyes betrayed every emotion from anger to fear to shame. "We don't want any trouble."

"Tell that to your brother," Jacob taunted with a growl. "Get on your horses—now. Leave and don't come back. If I see either of you here again, I'll shoot you where you stand."

Earl puffed up to argue, but Edgar shoved him. "Just get on your horse."

Jacob kept the colt trained on them until they were out of sight. He stashed his weapon in his coat pocket and hurried over to Rachel. Strands of hair had come loose from her bun. Her face was pale as death, and her clothes were rumpled and streaked with mud.

"Did he hurt you?"

She shook her head. "I fell."

Jacob reached for her, but, just as she'd done in the garden, she scooted away. She drew her legs under her and pushed herself from the ground with her arms. It took her a couple of wobbly tries, but she managed to stand, albeit balancing on one leg.

"What's wrong with your foot?"

"I turned my ankle when I fell."

Rachel's reluctance versus her obvious unsteadiness put him at odds. "You don't look well. Let me carry you."

"I'm fine. I can walk."

Stubborn woman. He grudgingly winged an escorting arm.

Instead of looping her arm in his and giving him her weight, she placed her hand on his forearm very lightly, as if he were a hive of angry bees.

He frowned but went along.

Rachel hobbled alongside him, grimacing each time she put weight on her injured limb. Eventually, she stifled a whimper. Or tried.

Jacob stopped. He couldn't do this—couldn't let her endure pain for the sake of propriety. For all he knew, the ankle was broken and she was making the injury worse.

He turned toward her, and she nearly fell backward in her haste to get away.

His hand shot out and grabbed her wrist. "Stop."

Rachel's eyes rounded at the sharp dictate.

Jacob ignored the way she trembled and stared at him like a frightened animal, though it gouged him deep. He edged closer again and carefully scooped her into his arms.

Her body went completely rigid.

"Miss Emerson," he said gently, "I realize this puts us in an overly familiar position, but you are injured. I will not stand by and let you suffer when I have the means to spare you pain. Now relax and trust me to take you safely home."

She softened at that, but only slightly. She was still a marble statue in his arms. A beautiful, petite, rose-scented statue.

Jacob stalked in the direction of the house, his insides burning like rotgut and twisting as if he were a calf with the scours. He wanted to track Earl down and beat him—hell, kill him. Anyone who'd threaten a lady didn't deserve to live. He drew a furious breath as red blurred the edges of his vision.

Roses. The scent registered again and cooled some of his ire.

He detected a small squirm and looked down. Rachel stared up at him with pale skin and huge eyes.

Holy hell. He was crushing her. If he tightened his hold any more, she'd have cracked ribs and a snapped thigh bone to go with her likely broken ankle.

Jacob managed a small smile and eased his grip.

The fire in his stomach flared again, but its fury had nothing to do with the men he'd chased off Emerson land. It had everything to do with the frightened woman cradled in his arms.

His first impression of Rachel hadn't been wrong. Someone had hurt her. Badly.

Lawrence's voice cut through the chill evening air. "Rachel... *Rachel.*"

Jacob topped the rise at the edge of the yard and tensed at the sight of her pa coming toward them.

Lawrence's expression was thunderous. His fists were clenched so tightly, it looked as if the man would tear him limb from limb the moment he got in within grabbing distance.

Jacob's steps faltered. But then he drew a breath and pressed forward, having no choice but to trust the gentleman's restraint. "She's hurt."

Emerson's gaze shifted to his daughter. Dread muted his eyes. "It's her ankle."

Those eyes shot back to him, their harsh intensity renewed, but the bulk of the fury gone.

Jacob leaned in and lowered his voice. "It was Earl. He was drunk. He frightened her and she stumbled. Edgar came after him, but I chased them away."

Lawrence gave a curt nod and went ahead of them. He marched up the steps and threw open the door. "Abigail," he bellowed. "I need you."

Emerson's missus rushed into the foyer just as Jacob stooped and shouldered in. Her hand flew to her mouth, and her eyes widened with fright.

"It's all right," Lawrence said to her. "Rachel fell and injured her ankle."

Glancing hastily around, she turned and beckoned them to follow. "Bring her in here."

Jacob carefully eased his precious cargo down the hall and through the doorway of the kitchen. Emerson's missus placed a chair near the work table in the center of the room, and Lawrence stood guard as he lowered Rachel into it.

Her pa squatted at her feet and began unlacing her boots. "Thank you, Jacob," he said, glancing up. "We'll take it from here."

Jacob snapped his errant manners back into place and bid the Emersons goodnight. They wouldn't disrobe their daughter's legs to care for her as long as he was present. His gut-twisting, bone-aching concern was of no matter. His part in this was over.

Rachel watched him as he left, her cautious green eyes fixed on his, unblinking. He wasn't sure, but it seemed a large amount of her fear had been replaced with relief... and, maybe, a fraction of it with gratitude.

Adults usually looked like children from her upstairs window. Not Jacob. He was bigger than anything else in the yard.

Rachel sat propped up in her bed and watched him move his things into the log cabin. Last night, when he'd carried her, it felt as though her body had been wedged between chunks of solid stone. She'd been frozen by fright at the time. But later, when he set her down and walked away, she'd regretted not reaching out to touch him. His massive chest was so firm, she wondered if her finger would make an impression. Probably not.

A worse regret was how she'd treated him. Paralyzing terror had rendered her helpless, and her panicked mind had lumped Jacob in with the threat. It wasn't until her pa came into view that sane thought gained a foothold over mindless instinct. The odors of clean air and pine had settled her stomach, and the betrayal of an old friend had been eased by the kindness of someone new.

The bear-man had rescued her, and she hadn't even said thank you.

Chapter Six

Jacob kept his eyes on the small piece of wood and the knife in his hands, but the woman in the fringe of his vision had his attention. Her brown skirt rippled as she walked, and her hair gleamed a deep chestnut in the slanted rays of the evening sun. Her body was reed thin and her chest flat, a childlike figure at first glance. But Rachel was no child. His mind had long since registered that whether he wanted it to or not.

Jacob hid his surprise when she approached his porch, carrying the stack of folded clothes her mother usually brought. Rachel hadn't come near the cabin since he'd moved in. And not because she was injured. Three weeks had passed since she'd hurt her ankle, yet she'd only been abed for one.

He stood when she stopped a few feet away. "Good evening, Miss Emerson."

"Good evening, Mr. Evans. I brought your clothes." She glanced down at the stack of impeccably ironed garments she held, then stood there, looking at him expectantly.

Decorum notwithstanding, she wouldn't go inside his bachelor's quarters, even if he remained very visibly and very properly outside. Rachel was cautious. She never cornered herself, never trapped herself between him and an exit. His mind had long since registered that, too.

He gestured at the small table between his chair and its mate. "You can put them there."

Her floral scent filled the air as she climbed the steps and set the items down. At least she didn't balk at coming within arm's reach of him anymore. That was progress.

Say something so she doesn't go away. "The stew was good. Did you make it?"

"Yes." She gave a quick upward glance—a perturbed gesture, to be sure—but not quite a full roll of the eyes. "Ma is still assigning me chores I can do sitting down with my foot up, and insisting I do them that way."

"Good for your ma." He waited for another bodily display of pique but got a nervous smile instead.

"I never thanked you for helping me when I fell."

He shrugged. "You were hurt."

"Still, I should thank you."

"You're welcome."

Her gaze settled and lingered on the items he held in his hands with curiosity, but she didn't say a word. Her polite restraint was adorable.

To answer her unspoken question, Jacob turned his hand so she could get a better look. Surely she'd seen someone whittle before. "I'm passing the time and enjoying the fair weather." And he'd be standing until she either left or sat down. He indicated the other chair. "Will you join me?"

Rachel hesitated a full five seconds, but she accepted his offer.

More progress.

Jacob resumed his seat once she was settled and angled the chunk of maple in his hand. He set the blade of his folding knife against it and sheared off a thin strip.

"Is that a lamb?"

"It will be."

She tilted her head this way and that, watching him. "The art of carving has always fascinated me... how someone can take a simple piece of wood and turn it into something intricate and beautiful. I'd probably cut off something vital if I tried to do it."

"Like your thumb?" he teased.

Rachel blushed. "That wasn't what I meant, but, yes. I'd probably cut that off, too."

Her embarrassment faded. She leaned in again, watching him trim away tiny bits. She no doubt held back another question—one that other's before her hadn't been shy about asking: How could someone with such big hands manipulate something so small?

"My grandfather taught me how to carve." He glanced up at her. "Believe it or not, I wasn't always this large. I was scrawny when I was a boy. But then I grew four inches in a single summer, and five more by the next. I went from being the runt to being the proverbial bull amidst the china. I knew my own strength, but I couldn't control it. My grandfather decided he'd best find a way to help me tame myself before I demolished everything we owned.

"He started with simple chores... common things, then he taught me this. I nearly gave up at one point, but he encouraged me to stick with it. Eventually, I developed enough control and dexterity to not snap spindly little legs in two. And look." He grinned and splayed both hands. "I still have my thumbs."

Rachel's smile was warmer this time, amused not timid. "What about your brothers? Are they big like you?"

"I don't have any. Only sisters." Jacob gambled on Lawrence's discretion. "You?"

Rachel stared at her fine-boned hands clasped primly in her lap. "I have one brother. Seth."

"Older?"

"Younger, by two years. He just turned eighteen."

"So you're the eldest."

She looked up and nodded.

"I assumed there were more of you, married off and such."

"Ma and pa wed later than most."

"They're not that old." Jacob stopped himself before commenting further on her small family and let the implication suffice. He was already treading on indelicate ice.

"Ma caught a fever when Seth was born. She recovered, but..." *—it left her barren.* "No more blessed events."

"No."

Though he felt regret for Abigail and Lawrence, he also envied them.

Jacob focused on the wooly, wooden coat he was painstakingly shaping and chose his words with the same care. He wanted to watch Rachel's face, but she'd say more if he didn't. "You seem sad when you speak of your brother."

"I miss him."

"Does he live far?" During the long stretch of silence after his question, Jacob kept his eyes on his work and willed Rachel to tell him the truth.

"I don't know," she finally said. "He didn't tell us where he was going when he left."

Jacob stopped carving and looked at her. Rachel's wary, hopeless expression told him to stop pushing.

"Well," he said, serving up dubious hope with a tactful smile, "that's boys for you—they have to go off on their adventures. Once they've had their chance to explore, and they discover the world is not as grand and exciting as they thought it was, they come back home."

The half-hearted curve of her lips said she saw right through his feeble reassurance. He didn't have all the facts, and she wasn't ready to give them to him.

"What about your sisters?" she asked.

"All but one still live in New Hampshire. The other lives in Vermont."

"Are you the oldest?"

Jacob shook his head. "Middle, I'm afraid. Two older, three younger."

"You must miss them."

"I do."

Rachel fiddled with one of the folds of her skirt. "Can I ask you something personal?"

"I suppose it's only fair."

"How did your wife die?"

Her question landed like a fist to the gut. Jacob hadn't cried since that horrid day, and he wasn't about to now, but the emotion was still so intense, he had to look away. "She died giving birth. Our son died, too."

"How awful. I'm so sorry." It was one of the most genuine condolences he'd received, and that made it chafe all the more.

He pasted on pleasantness—something he'd mastered over those wretched twenty-four months—and ignored the pity in her eyes. "Did you do my laundry?"

She blinked. "Yes."

"Let me guess. You put starch in my work shirts in retaliation for me eating your apples."

A smile crept across her lips. "I did no such thing."

Jacob moved to resume his carving, but too much of the daylight had faded. He pocketed the items and gazed up at the sky. "*While barred clouds bloom the soft-dying day, and touch the stubble-plains with rosy hue.*"

"Byron?"

"Keats."

"You're a poet, too?"

"The town I grew up in had no school, so my grandmother

taught all six of us. I managed to avoid sewing and embroidery lessons, but Grandmama insisted I memorize lines of verse."

"Good for your Grandmama."

He smirked at her rejoinder.

Rachel took in the rising moon and the gathering dusk. "I should go. I enjoyed talking with you, Mr. Evans."

He stood when she rose and watched her lithe, feminine form sway as she descended the steps. "Miss Emerson?"

She turned back, a mixture of patience and uncertainty glittering in her mossy eyes.

"I'm six years your senior, but I'm not an uncle, and I'm certainly not ancient enough to be your grandfather. I think it's time you started calling me Jacob."

Without a word, she continued toward the house, leaving him to wonder if he'd offended her. A few steps later, she turned a demure smile in his direction. "Goodnight, Jacob."

Jacob split open a shuck, snapped off the cob, and threw the ear of corn into the slow-moving wagon behind him. Number three thousand eighty-two, if his count was right. Three thousand eighty-two for the day. Twenty-three thousand, four hundred seventy-six for the week.

He winced when he grabbed the next one. The leather of his shucking tool protected his right palm, but the gloves that covered his hands had worn thin. He pushed himself to keep going. This was the last row of the last field. The job was almost done.

The steady thud of ears hitting the bangboard followed him and Lawrence to the end of the row. Jacob straightened up and rolled his shoulders. *Thank the Almighty.*

Luke, Amos Everhart's middle son, dismounted the wagon and pocketed the coins Lawrence paid him for driving. "Goodbye, Mr.

Emerson... Mr. Evans." He tore off for the stables as soon as he'd said his farewells.

Lawrence smirked. "I'll wager twice what I paid him that he visits the store before he goes home." With a groan common to the middle-aged, he hoisted himself onto the seat. "Let's go. I don't want to be in the corn crib after dark."

Jacob resisted the urge to smile as he mounted the other side, sounding nearly as old. Emerson was as dauntless as they came, but the man did *not* like snakes.

Lawrence flicked the reins, and the conveyance creaked into motion. They rode a ways, the jostle of the bench jarring their bones and shaking the kinks from their aching muscles. "Wood Creek's harvest festival is next Saturday," Lawrence eventually said with a glance in Jacob's direction.

"Ah, yes. Our town has one, too—the annual sacrament of gossiping, flirting, and fierce female competition under the guise of thanksgiving and good Christian fellowship."

Lawrence's chest rumbled with a contained laugh. "That'd be the one." He squinted at the slanted afternoon light, a smile still playing at the corner of his lips. "You're welcome to come, you know?"

"And be a target for all those matchmaking mammas?" *And apparently one matchmaking boss.* Jacob gave an exaggerated shudder. "Thank you, but no."

"Suit yourself." Lawrence lined the wagon up with the entrance to the crib and urged the horses forward. "I found a buyer for the house," he said more softly and more seriously.

"You'll be leaving this spring then. Do the women know?"

"Not yet. I plan to tell them tomorrow after services." Lawrence halted his team in the center of the crib and shot Jacob a keen stare. "Come with us."

"Me?"

"Why not?"

That was a better question than Jacob cared to admit. He couldn't run a farm without a wife, and he was unwilling to remarry. He'd planned to sell his homestead and move into town. He could find work, earn enough to pay room and board, but he'd sorely miss working the land.

"If you go with us," Lawrence added after a mildly assessing pause. "I'll help you work out the details, and I'll make it worth your while."

"I'd have to find a buyer, too. And I didn't plant this year."

Lawrence shrugged. "Worthy concerns, but none that can't be overcome." He clapped Jacob on the shoulder with a couple of friendly swats. "Think on it. You don't have to make a decision tonight."

As soon as the horses had been stabled, the men climbed into the bed of the wagon and shoveled ears as fast as they could, racing the dusk. Corn crunched and cobs flew. Shifting mounds soon gave way to solid footing.

An amber ball of light danced down the hill, visible through the open crib door. As it neared, so did shadowy, skirted forms and the silken, treble notes of feminine voices.

Jacob paused at the sight of Rachel deep in genial conversation with her mother. He would miss all three Emersons when they went west, but he would miss her most of all. He let himself suffer the twinge, then shook it off. "The ladies have come to light our way."

"So they have." Lawrence took the shovel from him and set both aside. "The rest can wait till morning." He took a couple of steps, then stopped and bent down. Lawrence straightened again, holding a red ear of corn. "Did you pick this?"

Jacob stared mutely at the item in question—an item coveted by every male of the species from the time they were old enough to attend a shucking. The finder of a red ear got to kiss the girl of his choice.

"It had to be you," Lawrence said, handing it over.

"Oh, no." Jacob held up his hands and backed away. "Mine or not, I don't want it. You'd murder me no matter which lady I chose."

Lawrence grinned. "You're right." He jumped down from the wagon and bounded across the yard, whooping and waving the cob like a victory flag.

The women came to a heel-digging stop and stared at him as if he'd lost his mind.

Jacob chuckled at Abigail's startled squeal when Lawrence grabbed her, swung her around, and planted an indecent kiss square on her gaping mouth.

Rachel's ma had cried the first day, gone about her work in silent sufferance the second, then accepted her husband's plans by the third. On the fourth, Abigail Emerson had turned into a veritable human whirlwind of lists and needs and musts.

Rachel was still numb.

"I must write to Hester, my friend out west, and ask her advice," her ma said from her place at the dry sink, where she was busily kneading dough. "Oh" –she wagged a sticky, floured finger in the air– "and we must buy plenty of yardage next time we're in town. We'll need to sew some practical garments over the winter."

"Yes, Ma." Rachel finished greasing the bread pans and went back to the pumpkin she was preparing to boil. Losing herself in the mindless task was a solace. She could handle being elbow deep in slimy squash guts. Being miles deep into savage Indian country was something she couldn't yet contemplate.

"Save those seeds, Rachel. Save every seed you possibly can. Your father and his–" An exasperated female groan spewed out. "It's already November. How are we going to get everything packed and ready by spring!"

Rachel rinsed pumpkin seeds while her mother muttered

verses from the fifth chapter of Ephesians and followed those with a flawless recitation of the thirty-first chapter of Proverbs. She spread the seeds out to dry, then started peeling the pumpkin and chopping it into pieces.

Her ma molded a portion of the dough and laid it in the first pan. "I'm glad you offered to make the pie. Yours always turn out better than mine." She paused before going back for more dough, her lips finally curving into a smile for the first time since Sunday. "You should make one for the festival. You'd garner the highest bid in the dessert box auction."

And have to sit and share it with whichever man won the bid.

"Maybe."

You're such a coward, Rachel chided herself. She hadn't planned on going to the festival at all, even though her parents would be disappointed by her choice. They'd all stayed home three years ago, just days after she'd been assaulted. Then the next year, when she was only marginally better, she'd begged off and her parents had understandingly gone without her.

The festival wasn't the only thing she avoided. Ladies luncheons, trips to the store, even Sunday services—she begged off nearly everything she could.

Rachel had become a master at shirking social contact and the probing looks that came with it. Each foray into the presence of people not privy to her secret required that she school everything about herself. Every word. Every deed. Every facial expression. Each and every interaction put her reputation at risk.

She'd been raped and she grieved for her brother—both were true—but, to explain away the changes everyone saw in her, they'd offered only the latter. Her parents had said whatever truth she projected was the truth the town would believe. But still, she wondered.

Grief eased with time, and marginal excuses eventually wore thin.

Her ma's hand brushed across hers. "I know it won't be easy for you, but consider it, at least."

The pressure her mother had dished out with good intentions engulfed her like a suffocating cloud. Rachel put the pumpkin on to boil, then took up her basket and escaped to the garden. Her lungs welcomed the clean, chilled air. With the familiar creak of the gate, the knots in her shoulders began to ease.

"Good morning," Jacob said from a shady corner.

Rachel yelped and jumped back three feet. She pressed a palm to her chest in a futile effort to calm the pounding heart beneath it.

The blasted man chuckled. He stabbed the ground with the blade of his shovel and leaned on its handle. "I'm sorry I startled you, Miss Emerson."

"What are you doing in my garden?"

"Your pa asked me to turn under the fading plants."

Her gaze shot to ground and scanned the rows. He'd already buried half of them! "You should have warned me. I needed to save the seeds."

Jacob left the shovel impaled upright and stepped into the light. "Never fear, Miss Emerson. I saved them for you."

She looked in the direction he indicated and blew out a very relieved breath. Shriveled peppers, dry bean pods, and various other vectors of seeds lay in neat piles on squares of brown paper. Her gaze reluctantly worked its way back to his.

"Oh." He held up a finger, then patted the pockets of his coat with both hands. He reached into his left one and withdrew a stack of small, sturdy envelopes. "I brought you these to store them in. You can write the names of the vegetables on the outside."

Now she felt like a ninny. "Thank you, Jacob."

He smiled and tipped his hat. "You're welcome, *Miss Emerson*."

She narrowed her eyes at the mischievous twinkle in his. What was he about? "Why do you keep addressing me like that?"

"Like what?"

He knew very well *like what*. "You keep calling me Miss Emerson. And quite unnecessarily, I might add."

He lifted his shoulders and let them fall.

"Why don't you use my name?"

"That is your name."

Fool. "Not that. My given name."

"I can't."

Holy Mother Mary and Joseph—where was a kitten box when a person needed one? "Why not?"

"You haven't given me permission to do so."

He finally cracked a smile when she groaned and stomped her foot in exasperation. "My name is Rachel. Call. Me. *Rachel.*"

She spun on her heel and stormed over to gather the rest of her seeds. If only her parents could hear her now. Too quiet? Hmph. Not around the infuriating *Mr. Evans*. In his presence—whether she wanted to or not—she became exceedingly verbose.

Rachel removed the pods and seed heads from the rest of the plants, then she knelt in front of the piles on the papers and began stacking them in her basket.

Jacob's shovel sliced through dirt right behind her, and Rachel's pulse leapt. She glanced over her shoulder. She'd turned her back on him. She never turned her back on him or any full-grown male, save her pa.

Dratted man. If he hadn't goaded her into such a perturbed state–

Rachel sighed. It made a good excuse, but it wasn't the only reason she'd let her guard down. Just as Mr. Weeks had done, Jacob had earned her trust.

He kept scooping and flipping wedges of earth, and she kept layering seeds in her basket. She barely tensed when he got between her and the only gate. Just a brief, instinctive reaction until her rational mind took control again.

Jacob set aside the tool and sat with his back to the fence

a couple of feet away. He lifted his hat long enough to blot his forehead with his sleeve, then he tilted his canteen and took a deep drink.

Out the corner of her vision, Rachel watched a single drop of water roll down the side of his jaw. It continued down the long cord of his neck and disappeared into the vee of his shirt collar.

She jerked her eyes away. Jacob stirred wanton feelings in her. Potent, inconvenient feelings.

"Your pa mentioned a town festival," he said after a second long drink and a longer silence.

"The annual harvest festival," she replied, barely breaking her gaze from her work.

"You don't sound very enthusiastic."

Rachel tilted her head to the side and lifted a shoulder. "It's all right, but I doubt I'll go."

"Your parents— Well, your ma at least, seemed to be looking forward to the outing."

"She is."

"And you'd make her miss it? That doesn't seem like you."

Rachel carefully laid the last layer of seeds into her basket and sat back on her heels. "She won't miss it. Pa will take her like he did last year."

Jacob shook his head. "Not without you. He won't leave you here alone after what happened with Earl."

"But—" She'd started to say, 'But you'll be here.' Only he wouldn't. Her parents wouldn't leave the two of them alone on the farm together, even staying in separated houses. Trust aside, the gossips would have a field day.

"Rachel, your family is moving west. This is the last social event your parents will have the opportunity to attend in Wood Creek, ever. Your ma is gracious. She'll pretend she doesn't mind staying home, but she'll be disappointed. You should go, for them and for you."

She bowed her head like a scolded child. Jacob was oddly soft spoken for a man of his size, but, no matter how gently he uttered his words, his deep baritone always held an edge of authority. And he was right, damn him. He was right.

He drew up his far leg and placed the sole of his boot flat on the ground. "I'll make you a deal. I'll go if you go."

She looked at him and blinked.

One corner of his mouth quirked up, and his eyes twinkled again. "It'll be fun. We can hide amongst the wallflowers and gossip about the poor swains who have no fashion sense."

"Very well," she said as grudgingly as she could with a smile creeping across her face. "I'll go."

Chapter Seven

The closer they got to town, the harder Rachel fought the urge to jump off the buckboard and run for home. Occasional trips there were manageable—it was easy to disappear among bolts of fabric in the general store or to hide in church with her head bowed in prayer—but tonight, she would be expected to interact with the entire town, to make conversation without the crutch of rote rituals. Her pie would be the least thing on display.

By sheer force of will, Rachel slowed her pulse to match the steady cadence of the horses' hooves. She clenched and splayed her hands repeatedly, trying in vain to get some feeling back into her fingers and to convince herself that she could do this. Dressed in a pale-blue taffeta gown and a cobalt velvet jacket, she was the image of innocent, affluent perfection. She just had to keep her face and her conduct from giving her secret away.

Her parents occupied the rest of the bench to her left, and Jacob rode Goliath alongside the wagon, to her right. He sat tall in the saddle of his massive mount, wearing a brown frock coat and trousers. From time to time, he'd glance down at her, causing other parts of her to tingle.

Rachel closed her eyes and shut it all out. She was fast reaching her limit of dread and inconvenient feelings.

In the absence of sight, her mind parsed another source of worry. Her and Jacob's conversation in the garden had left her as unsure of her place in the Emerson household as she was anxious about attending the festival.

Once she'd recovered from her attack enough to get through the average day, she'd done her best to share in the work and not be a burden. Although they'd never stated it out loud, her parents seemed to know she would never marry. They seemed to accept the fact that she'd always be with them. Was it possible they wished differently?

Rachel opened her eyes and chanced a tentative look at her ma and pa, who were sporting their own finery and engaged in affectionate chatter like a couple newly affianced. They didn't *seem* to mind her presence in their home. Were they simply too gracious to say otherwise?

Jacob dropped back as her pa steered the team around the curve that led to the meeting house. The cold evening air suddenly thinned, and Rachel's palms turned clammy inside her gloves. Wagons, buggies, and horses lined the road, crowding out her breath and marking the path to her own personal hell. Her heart fluttered and the edges of her vision shimmered like waves of heat on a summer day.

"Miss Emerson."

Rachel jerked her head to the right. Jacob had already dispensed with Goliath and was holding out his hand, looking up at her expectantly.

She grasped it and stood. When she made no further move, he gently placed her hand on his shoulder and left it there. He extended his arms and grasped her about the waist. Surprisingly, the feel of his large hands was more welcome than alarming. He waited until she'd braced both hands on his shoulders, then lifted her and set her lightly on the ground.

Jacob's handling of her had been entirely proper, and he'd released her as soon as she'd steadied herself, but a fleeting glimpse of fleshly regard in his eyes had stolen her wits faster than the sight of the meeting house had stolen her breath. At least that's what she *thought* she saw. She was never completely sure what lurked in men's expressions anymore.

Her ma appeared at her side with the box containing the pie. Abigail practically glowed in the rose and cream brocade she wore, and Rachel felt a moment of peace—of relief that Jacob had convinced her to go. She also felt a gust of trepidation. What if she embarrassed them?

Rachel took the pie and waited while her ma retrieved her own dessert and the basket of food for the buffet. Her palms went clammy again.

Jacob moved closer and offered her his arm. He smelled of horse and leather, but also of cedar and spice. "The ruts are deep," he said when she looked at his arm instead of taking it. "I wouldn't want you to hurt your ankle again."

Shifting the box to one hand—and secretly hoping she'd drop it—Rachel wrapped the other around his thick forearm.

As the four of them walked toward the gaping doors of the building, her parents on her left and Jacob on her right, Rachel kept feeling the weight of their glances. They flanked her and moved cautiously, as if they feared she'd bolt or faint.

Jacob leaned down near her ear. "Don't forget our plan," he whispered. "Wallflowers and spying on clueless swain."

Rachel smiled and mentally shook her head at his foolishness. She was glad for it though. Jacob's teasing—when it wasn't stoking her ire like a bellows—had the effect of squelching dread and fear in an instant.

If only it could last.

Rachel released Jacob's arm as they approached the entrance. Heads turned, brows lifted, and jovial chatter all but ceased. She'd been spotted.

The truth you project is the truth people will believe.

Holding her dessert with both hands to still the tremble, Rachel formed a genial expression, complete with a maidenly hint of pink in her cheeks and a touch of sadness for the absence of her brother.

Good manners finally befell the group, and proper greetings rang out. Rachel maintained her façade and acknowledged each one, hoping no one would ask any difficult questions.

Once the four of them had gained the stairs and passed through the door, she and her mother split off from the men. Voices quieted and bodies moved back to make way. A bubble of curious silence followed her all the way to the buffet tables on the far side of the room.

Abigail strode up to the buffet and set her basket in one of the few empty spaces. Friendly greetings ensued, and the basket was relieved of its contents amidst a cloud of lively female chatter.

Rachel stood a few steps behind her ma and quietly endured the skeptical glances passing over her.

"Hello, Rachel." Mary Lambert appeared on her right. She was barely thirty, but her kind smile—her *genuine*, kind smile—and her round, motherly face made her seem older... wiser, at least.

Mary's brown eyes warmed as the curve of her lips made their edges crinkle. "I'm so glad you came. How are you?"

"I'm well, thank you." The question had been as genuine and unassuming as the smile of the woman who'd asked it, but the answer was a lie. Although not quite as much of one as it would have been a minute ago. Mary's presence was comforting. She was the kind of person you'd want taking care of you if you were ill, and the one you'd want to laugh with and visit with over tea once you were well.

Mary spied Rachel's pie all done up in ruffles and bows that complemented her outfit. "Oh, what a lovely box! That'll bring a nice bid." She held out her hands. "I'll put your dessert with the others."

Rachel had the immediate urge to clutch the box tighter and refuse to let go—more so, to drop it and stomp it—but she reluctantly handed it over with a muttered gratitude. She was enough of a spectacle already.

Prodded by Mary's reception, or out of deference to her mother, the cluster of women enveloped Rachel and peppered her with greetings.

She kept a smile pasted in place and made her best effort to be genial. It was difficult, though, to make conversation while whispers and giggles wafted from hen-like clutches along the fringe. Three years ago, she wouldn't have paid it any mind. Now, the sounds of gossip made her tense.

The crowded conditions didn't help either. Rachel had to brace herself and not jerk when someone brushed up against her. With rare exception, she didn't like to be touched. Well, *she* did, but her body didn't. And it chose to revolt at the most odd and inconvenient times.

Except for the memories and the nightmares, that was the worst legacy of her attack—the aversion to human touch a part of her still longed for.

Between cinched waists and shawled shoulders, glimpses of paradise flickered in and out of view. A row of empty chairs lined the wall. The tension in Rachel's shoulders abated some. Now that she had a place of peaceful solitude as a goal, working her way through the social maze became easier, even pleasant. A few more feet, a few more alms to politesse, and she'd be there.

Eudora Waters gaped at her. "I didn't expect to see *you*, Rachel. What a nice surprise!"

Rachel blushed at the backhanded compliment, although it wasn't backhanded coming from Eudora. The teen was about as subtle as a thunderstorm, but she didn't have a maligning bone in her tall, gangly body. She simply lacked tact. Or rather the guile that came with arrogance and ulterior motives, of which she also lacked.

Eudora craned her already long neck and waved at someone behind Rachel. The motion made the wilted ribbons hanging from her hair swing like floppy hound dog ears. "Row..." She frowned and waved more vigorously. "*Rowena.*"

Rachel cringed at the bellowed beckoning, and at the prospect of Rowena. Verses about Pharisees came to mind, followed by those calling for brotherly love and forbearance. Rachel forced a smile.

Eudora's dress turned from warm bronze to mud-puddle brown when Rowena swept up beside her in lavish flounces of emerald taffeta. Rowena's shiny brunette crown barely reached Eudora's shoulder, and she was at least two inches shorter than all the other females in the room, yet she managed to look down her nose at each and every one.

With eyes the same color as her dress, Rowena raked Rachel, scorching her on the way down and slicing her on the way up. Cordial evisceration was Rowena's specialty.

Rachel served the first volley. "Hello, Rowena." The sooner her public gutting got underway, the sooner it would be over.

Rowena's gaze glittered and sharpened like a lion sighting its prey. "So... The rumors are true."

The line was bait, dangled by somebody fishing. But the innuendo—and the way it caused a hush to settle over everyone within earshot—sent a tingle through Rachel's nerves. *Don't bite.* "Your gown is lovely. Is it new?"

"Yes it is. It arrived from New York this very week." Rowena stopped preening long enough to scrutinize Rachel again. "Yours is nice, too. Isn't that the dress you bought to wear to the festival three years ago?"

Hiding the impact of the jab was nearly impossible. Not because it was rude, but because it flooded Rachel's mind with violent memories. Three years ago, she'd been near death, and the dress had almost been her shroud.

Rachel pressed her hand to the bodice and smoothed it over seams that had been altered several sizes down. "This is the first chance I've had to wear it."

"Oh, that's right. You missed the festival that year. And last year, too. A headache, wasn't it?"

Someone nearby gasped. "Rowena Butterfield Richardson!"

When was a scold not a scold?

When both the scolder and the scolded dissolved into laughter.

Rachel excused herself. She'd had her fill of teasing and pitying glances. She'd no sooner turned her back when a lively debate over the coming auction started up as if she hadn't even been there.

Needing solitude more than ever, she escaped the throng and headed for the wall. A young woman sat bent over a basket at the end of the row, but the chairs were otherwise unoccupied.

Rachel turned to sit just as the woman lifted her head.

"Rachel?"

"Charity?"

"I didn't expect to see you here." The soft statement held no contempt, but it pricked Rachel more deeply than all the others combined. Charity Sims, a younger version of Mary Lambert with blue eyes and a narrow face, was her best friend. Or had been. Whether or not their relationship was a casualty of her attack remained to be seen.

"I didn't expect to see you either," Rachel managed as she moved closer and lowered herself into a chair. A tiny babe with fair skin and dark hair like his mother's dozed at their feet. "I thought you'd still be lying-in."

A longsuffering expression claimed Charity's face. "I would be if Saul had his way. I wore him down by promising I'd rest. As a result, I'm relegated to sit by the wall." She shrugged. "At least it's a different wall."

Poor Charity. She'd lost her first baby, then endured months of confinement due to a difficult pregnancy with the second. By the time Rachel had recovered enough to venture to church and to town, Charity had been virtually homebound.

"He's beautiful."

"Thank you." Her friend brightened with maternal pride. "He's a good baby."

Several moments of silence ticked by while Rachel mustered her courage. "I never apologized for missing your wedding."

Charity's smile dimmed. "It's all right. I know you wouldn't send regrets without good reason." Her countenance was free of anger and full of understanding.

Rachel wanted so badly to tell Charity the truth, to confide in just one person outside her immediate family. But something held her back. Maybe it was that she sensed her friend already knew something horrific had happened.

Reverend White's deep voice echoed from across the room. A herd of boot scuffs nearly drowned out the call to order for luncheon.

Rachel rose. "Shall I fix you a plate?"

"Please. And come eat with me—if you don't have a better prospect, that is. I've missed you."

"I will. I've missed you, too."

Rachel took her place in line, plagued by a sudden stinging behind her eyes. She'd wasted months—years—hiding away from everyone, including her very best friend. Now she was moving west, and Charity was burdened with marriage and motherhood. Quite likely, this was the last time they'd see each other.

The Reverend blessed the food, and everyone began making their way down the buffet line amidst a simmering rumble of voices. Rachel noticed her parents looking at her from a spot along the snaking line, their worry barely concealed. She managed a smile for them.

Finally, she reached the food. It was difficult balancing and loading two plates, but the crush of people was becoming more and more difficult to endure. She didn't want to make the trip twice.

"Hungry, are we?" a deep voice said.

Rachel glanced back. Jacob stood behind her, plate in hand. Or rather, he towered over her. "One of these is for a friend."

His gaze narrowed. Was he puzzled or jealous?

"Charity Sims," Rachel explained. "She's barely out of her confinement, and her husband has bid her sit for the entire gathering."

"Ah." His brows lifted and smoothed. "I'd be happy to serve your plates along with mine," he said, taking the serving spoon from her hand. "Just tell me what you'd like."

Rachel knew a moment of uncertainty, but—after weighing the risk of rumors his attentions might bring against the prospect of dropping the food and having to start over—she let him help her.

"Not so much," she cautioned when Jacob kept serving portions she could never hope to stomach.

"Your friend needs nourishment. And so do you." He glanced up, as if to gauge her reaction to his bold statement.

She didn't disappoint. Her lips had immediately pressed into a flat, annoyed line.

He had the nerve to smirk, the jackal.

When they reached the end of the last table, Jacob leaned down. "You've spurned me for another," he whispered, "but that's all right. Having observed the sad state of the male complement here, I'm confident you and Mrs. Sims shall have much to gossip about.

"You, however," he added just as softly, "are not worthy of gossip at all. You look lovely this evening."

Lovely? Perish the saints, she was breathtaking!

When Rachel had descended the stairs, all done up in blue with her hair swept into a looser style than usual, he'd had to pick his jaw up off the floor. He'd also had to distract himself with thoughts of mucking stalls and tallying farm figures to keep his lower half from becoming a raging embarrassment.

Rachel's transformation had been as unexpected as his body's reaction to it. The fairer sex had not so much as turned his head in over two years.

Jacob watched her retreat as long as he dared, then he turned to find a place to eat his lonely meal.

"I'm not sure whether to thank you for helping my daughter or interrogate you as to what you said that made her blush."

Lawrence's pointed stare could cleave granite, and Jacob found immense relief in its barely perceptible waver. He could escape paternal wrath if he gave the right answer.

"I complimented her on her appearance."

"I believe you. I also believe there's more you aren't telling me."

Damned parental intuition. Jacob's gaze faltered, and his midsection clenched in defense of a possible punch. "There may have been some good-natured teasing imparted along with the compliment."

Lawrence's eyes narrowed, then they twinkled as a smile formed. "Nettled her, did you? You *are* quite adept at provoking her."

"You've noticed?"

"How could I not? You goad her into a fit of pique on a regular basis. I'm hard pressed not to laugh, most of the time."

Jacob shook his head. "I'm surprised you haven't beaten me senseless." Or turned Rachel loose and let her do it. He bit back a grin at that thought.

Lawrence sighed. "Perhaps I should, but she's better for it." He half-smiled, the corners of it weighted by guilt or some other heavy emotion. "Rachel is better for knowing you, Jacob, and for that, I thank you."

"I'm better for knowing her, too."

Lawrence's smile grew stronger. "Shall we join the men before our food gets cold?"

"You're not eating with your missus?"

Lawrence barked out a laugh. "Not if I value my life. The women are fierce when it comes to their fellowship at these gatherings. They'll show us males some interest later, when it's time to dance and bid on boxes."

Jacob followed Lawrence to the other side of the room, where they joined a cluster of men gathered around a second bowl of punch. The group's attire ranged from pricey and fashionable to outdated and worn. The image was a visual exposition on settlement manners as well. The farther one went west, the more the strict etiquette of the East was eschewed in favor of freedom and practicality.

"Mr. Ledbetter." Jacob greeted the farrier, glad for a familiar face. Simon's carrot-colored hair and boyish freckles were the perfect garnish for his genial nature.

Simon grinned. "How's that mammoth beast of yours—Tiny, was it?"

"Goliath. And he's as surefooted as ever, thanks to you."

Amos Everhart appeared on his left, his weathered eyes twinkling with mischief and merriment. "*Mammoth* is right. 'Course a horse should fit its rider." He reached up and landed a friendly swat on Jacob's shoulder. "Anything less than an eighteen-hand draft wouldn't do."

Jacob smiled and went along with the ribbing. He was well used to it by now.

Lawrence refilled his cup and took a sip. "So, Luke," he said to Amos's son, who stood quietly next to his father, "will you be bidding this year?"

Luke stuffed his hands in his pockets and flushed as only a stripling could. "No."

Several men chuckled.

"Why not?" Simon asked. "It's only dessert, and there's nary an ugly lady in the bunch."

Laughter rumbled again. The lad's ears flamed.

"As if you care, Ledbetter," someone behind Jacob called out. "You're disqualified by matrimony—the result of a winning dessert wager, as I recall."

That garnered hoots of laughter.

Simon saluted the heckler with his punch. "As are you."

"As are most of us," Lawrence said. He lifted his cup. "To comely wives and familiar desserts."

Jacob joined in the hear, hear's. He also wondered if there was something stronger in the men's punch.

Wood Creek newcomer, Toby McDaniel, spoke up. "Who's the favorite this year?"

"Same as every year," Simon replied. "Rowena Richardson."

Toby frowned. "Her cooking's that good?"

"Her dowry's that good."

"Her character's not," Amos grumbled. "Someone should sneak a lizard into her box."

More than one man choked on his punch as muffled laughter spread through the group.

Lawrence pressed his smile into a twitching line and cut his eyes to the youth. "You did not hear that, Luke."

"No sir."

Hopefully, no male relation of Rowena had either.

One of the men standing in the fringe of a nearby circle kept looking Jacob's way. At first, he feared someone of consequence had overheard Amos's insult, but the man's attire indicated that was unlikely. He dressed like an Easterner, but his hems were too short, his fabrics inferior, and his garments just shy of mismatched.

Jacob leaned over and whispered his observations to Lawrence.

"That's Jasper Cobb," he murmured back. "He's lived here a couple of years. He's a typesetter... Works for the printer in Keller and stays at Norma Schaffer's boarding house." Lawrence shrugged. "He's a passable fellow, if a little odd."

Thomas Massey, another of Lawrence's neighbors, tucked his thumbs into his pockets and rocked on the balls of his feet. "Speaking of poor character, I'm surprised Old Man Grimes isn't here, cadging sips from flasks and pillaging the feast."

His comment was met with grimaces and grunts of acknowledgement.

Simon glanced around, then leaned in. "Word is, the bank took his house."

Jacob shared a look with Lawrence amid more grunts and a few shaking heads, but both kept quiet.

"Maybe this will prompt the lot of them to move on and find work," Simon continued. "His boys, anyway."

"Maybe so," several agreed.

The subject was dropped and the mood shifted again. Good-natured banter continued, and Jacob let himself enjoy it as the food and the punch disappeared.

Reverend White called the room to attention and—after spending nearly as much time as a Sunday sermon stirring sympathy for Wood Creek's widows and orphans—announced the start of the auction.

One by one, the married men dropped coins into the reverend's jar and paired off with their respective, box-holding wives. Their dessert-sampling days were over, yet Jacob could muster no pity for them. Commitment to a spouse was not the burden some claimed it was. At least it hadn't been for him.

White held up the first single ladies' dessert. "This lovely box belongs to Caroline Phelps and contains her famous lemon custard. Who'll give us an opening bid?"

"Twenty-five cents," one of the young men called out.

"Fifty," another one said.

The bidding continued to the peak of one dollar. The winner proudly collected his box and a blushing Miss Phelps.

White reached for another box.

Jacob scanned the room until he found Rachel awaiting her turn. Though she masked it well, he could tell she was uncomfortable. He caught her eye and offered a smile.

The auction continued, the bidders eager and the winning bids growing with every round. Rowena's box went for the most—three dollars—and Jacob felt a twinge of disappointment when it held no stowaway reptile.

He had seen the way people looked at Rachel when she arrived. A couple of the women had smiled at her with happiness and genuine compassion, but the others either stared down their noses or sneered as if a year's worth of fresh fodder for gossip had been set before them on a silver platter. Rowena especially.

"And this beautiful box," Reverend White said, holding up the very last one, "contains Rachel Emerson's delectable pumpkin pie. Can I have an opening bid?"

The six remaining men stood silent.

"Come now. I know you gentlemen have a few Coronets in your pockets, and Miss Emerson's cooking is worth more than that."

Nothing. Not a single bid.

Rachel's bearing went from uncomfortable to humiliated to resigned.

Jasper Cobb stepped forward. "Ten cents."

"We have ten. Anyone else…?"

One of the young men glanced around and fidgeted a bit. "Twelve."

Cretin. His bid was so reluctant, Jacob wondered if the preacher even heard it.

"Fifteen," Cobb countered.

You've got to be kidding me.

Jacob's ire rose. Every other woman had had at least five men bidding on her dessert. Rachel barely had one. "One dollar."

Heads turned—including Rachel's and her father's.

Shit. What have I done?

Cobb frowned at him. He lifted his nose a notch, making his weak chin disappear and causing light to glint off the oiled blond hair he'd slicked down flat. "One dollar and five."

Only five? *Jackass.* He couldn't stop now. "A dollar fifty."

Rachel was gaping and Lawrence was glaring. Well, only half-glaring. A part of him was grateful.

Cobb scooped the change from his pocket and glanced down at his hand. He looked up. "Two dollars."

Rachel looked at Cobb and then at him. Among the myriad emotions paling her face and swirling in her eyes, he saw silent entreaty.

"Three dollars."

"Three and ten."

Jacob squared his shoulders and used the most assertive voice he had. "Five dollars."

The air in the room was consumed by one collective gasp.

Silence lingered, and Jacob reveled in it.

He'd bid to save Rachel from embarrassment, and then he'd kept bidding to save her from sharing her pie with a man who made her uncomfortable. But the reason he'd bid a mint was to show the entire, godawful town what Rachel Emerson was worth and all those brainless, heartless fools what a treasure of a woman they had shunned.

Reverend White tugged at his collar and cleared his throat. "I believe we have a winning bid."

Damned right you do.

Jacob allowed a little smugness to creep into his smile as he strode forward to collect Rachel and her box. He even offered her a modest bow before winging his arm.

Wood Creek could stand some eastern civility.

Jacob led Rachel to a section of empty chairs along the wall on the least-crowded side of the room. He'd have preferred to take her outside, away from conspicuous scrutiny, but dining alone would smudge her reputation.

Once he'd seen her comfortably seated, he took the chair two seats over and placed the pie between them. Rachel seemed to relax a little, but her back stayed straight and her hands were clasped a bit too tightly in her lap.

He opened the box and peered in, trying not to drool.

"Here, let me," she said, reaching for a small knife secreted next to the pie. She placed a generous slice on one of two small napkins tucked opposite the knife and handed it to him.

Jacob did drool then, but he waited for the lady.

"Aren't you going to eat it?" she asked.

"I'm waiting for you."

Some color finally infused her cheeks. "Oh, thank you, but I..." She glanced around, apparently realizing what it would look like if she refused. "Maybe a little."

She served herself a sliver.

Jacob wanted to frown at her, but he smiled and lifted his pie instead. He closed his eyes in ecstasy and prayed pumpkin-tinted saliva wouldn't drip down his chin as he took the first luscious bite.

He chewed slowly and rumbled his approval with an undignified groan. When he opened his eyes again, she was still primly holding her pie and staring at him.

He dabbed his lips with the corner of the napkin. "Forgive my manners. You make excellent pie."

Rachel lowered her sliver to her lap. "Thank you for bidding on my pie. You spent far too much."

"No, I didn't."

She fingered the pale gray broach that rested at the base of her throat with slender fingers. "I'm not ungrateful, but I know you did this as a favor—to me. I have some egg money saved. I'll pay you back when—"

"I know you mean well, but your offer insults me."

Her eyes rounded, and then her gaze and her hand dropped to

her lap. "I apologize."

"Look at me, Miss Emerson." He'd rather have placed his finger under her chin and gently tipped her face up until their eyes met, but they were in public.

Slowly, she lifted her head.

"I bid on your box of my own free will. I could have stood silent, and I could have offered a lesser amount, but you are well worth five dollars." He grinned. "Your pie is worth ten."

Color suffused her cheeks again as a smile nudged its way onto her face.

"Eat, Miss Emerson, or I'll swipe that shard of dessert you consider a serving."

With consistent display of impeccable manners and boring mediocrity, the novelty of their spectacle wore off, and the vipers of Wood Creek turned their attention elsewhere.

A few men with fiddles and banjos gathered on small stage and began to tune their instruments. *Now I just have to get her through the dance. Her and myself.*

Jacob had no sooner closed up the remains of the pie—he'd made a pig of himself and eaten half of it—when an impish, dark-haired girl skipped over and stood before them. She wasn't even in braids.

"I'm Emily."

"Hello, Emily," he replied. "I'm Jacob."

A crease appeared between her brows. "Is that your Mister-name or your Christian name? I'm not 'posed to call adults by their Christian names."

Jacob suppressed a smile and matched her seriousness. "In that case, you should call me Mr. Evans."

Contentment returned to her little round face. "I'm not 'posed to ask for dances either, but mamma said it would be okay this one time."

"Oh?"

She looked over her shoulder at a group of women clearing food from the buffet, then turned back to him with big brown eyes. "Would you dance with me?"

He'd hoped not to dance at all.

Rachel leaned closer as if to whisper a confidence. "She's Mary Lambert's daughter."

A friend, then.

Jacob put his feelings aside and smiled. "I'd be honored."

He rose and held out his hand.

Emily curtsied. She took his hand, then reached for Rachel's. "You, too, Miss Emerson. I'm 'posed to dance with you, too."

Jacob and Rachel exchanged another glance. They'd been set up. And Rachel didn't look any happier about the matchmaking than he.

Resisting the urge to sigh, Jacob extended his free hand to her and willed her to accept their fate. It was only a contra dance, after all; and if they didn't go along, subversive schemes would pelt them all afternoon. "Might I have this dance?"

Rachel agreed, albeit reluctantly.

Rather than subject her to the large group forming in the center of the room, he kept the three of them off to one side. Dancing with an odd lot was tricky at first, but they managed to make it work—and got away with it, thanks to the child in their ranks.

In fact, the thought of how the three of them must look made Jacob smile. He actually felt a twinge of regret when the music came to an end.

He caught his breath and bowed deeply to the imp. "It has been a pleasure, Miss Lambert."

Emily's mouth formed a perfect O at the use of her—what had she called it?—her 'Miss-name,' but she recovered and made a polite egress.

Jacob faced Rachel. His bow to her was a nominal gesture, but his sentiment was no less sincere. "I quite enjoyed myself, Miss

Emerson. Thank you for the dance."

"I'm sorry you got coerced."

"I'm not." He offered her his arm. "Would you join me for some punch?"

For once, she didn't look conflicted. "Yes, I'd love some."

He escorted her to the main bowl and procured two generously filled cups. He and Rachel slaked their thirst, then refilled their cups and watched the crowd dance their way through several tunes while they sipped more leisurely.

Jacob looked over at Rachel when the music paused. "Are you glad you came?"

She tilted her head in thought for a moment. "I am."

One of the fiddlers announced a waltz, and Jacob wrestled with conflicting emotions—avoid painful memories or endure them for the sake of the ones he was making for Rachel. The lady's enjoyment won. "Will you dance with me?"

Rachel moistened her lips and took in the couples pairing off. She glanced at the chairs where her parents had been, as if seeking approval, but they were empty. "I don't know."

He considered giving her an out, but then he caught a glimpse of longing. As much as it unnerved her, she wanted to dance. "You've reached majority, and I am a familiar to you. I doubt your father would object, but if he does, I'll take responsibility."

She hesitated, but only a moment. "All right."

Jacob grasped her gloved hand and lifted it properly between them as he led her out. When he faced her, uncertainty had returned to her dainty features, but determination lurked there, too. He set his free hand on her back just above her narrow waist. Her muscles tensed with the contact, then they softened some, and the silk-covered hand that hovered just above his shoulder finally came to rest.

He started off gently, being sure to keep a proper distance between them. It took a few steps for their movements to synchronize and smooth, but they did. Not long after, Rachel's frame became more pliable. Her bearing turned more pleasant, too.

Jacob wondered if his sadness showed. No matter how much time passed, the waltz would always stir strong memories.

He decided to tell her. Usually he avoided pain and buried his feelings, but sometimes it hurt less to simply say what was on his mind. "My late wife, Sarah, loved waltzes. She was reserved... truly, she was introverted. But when it came to dancing, she wasn't shy. She'd ambush me at odd times, humming in triple meter." He shook his head with fond recollection. "Many a task lay forgotten as we sashayed about the field."

Rachel smiled. It was a sweet smile that softened her whole face and conveyed every sentiment from sympathy to joy to kind commiseration. "I can see why. You're an exceptional dancer— something I would never have guessed."

He smirked. "Figured I'd lumber around and crush your toes?"

"No! Well, maybe." She blushed. "It's just that you're so..."

"Big. I know."

"It's more than that. You look entirely built for labor, like a mason or a– a *lumberjack*. And that's in total conflict with the person you are today. You wear a suit much better than a man of your stature should. But I don't believe that's entirely a function of your garments. You have impeccable manners, and you move with preternatural grace. You're an enigma."

Now Jacob was grinning. That had to be the longest string of words he'd ever heard her utter. "Not preternatural," he corrected, "merely practiced."

He pulled her a little closer on a turn. Rachel was so absorbed in conversation, she didn't notice. The stiffness in her spine was gone. "Before my grandmother married my grandfather," he went on, "she taught at a finishing school. As you can imagine, ballroom etiquette was part of my mother's education, and later, my sisters' as well.

"When grandmama required a male counterpart for one of her sessions, I was summoned and expected to participate. Whereas my sisters each got *one* practical lesson per topic, I got *five*." He winked. "I assure you, no lumberjack has ever known so much polish."

The music ended, and Rachel's beautiful smile began to fade.

"Shall we dance one more?" he asked at the call of a second waltz.

She brightened. "I'd like that."

He embraced her again, and they whirled about the room as if they hadn't a care. For the moment, they didn't.

When the music faded away, Rachel tugged him down by his shoulder and went up on her toes. "Thank you, Jacob," she whispered near his ear.

He filled his lungs with her warm, rose petal scent and noted the way the velvet of her jacket moved against his palm with each breath of her fading exertion. "You're welcome."

Rachel suddenly went rigid in his arms.

Jacob lifted his head.

Jasper Cobb was standing nearby, glaring at him. He looked expectantly at Rachel. "Pardon me, Miss Emerson. The band is about to play the last waltz. I was hoping you'd partner with me."

Jacob took in Rachel's wan complexion and the rapid flutter in the hollow of her throat.

Woodenly, she faced Cobb. "Thank you for asking, but—"

"Please, Miss Emerson. It's just one dance."

"I, uh..."

"Mr. Cobb," Jacob intervened, putting on a mask of graciousness when he'd rather growl and wring the barbarian's neck, "what Miss Emerson is trying to say is that she isn't feeling well. In fact, that's what we were discussing when you walked up."

Cobb narrowed his eyes at Jacob. "Are you sure you won't dance one more?" he asked Rachel.

Jacob didn't give her a chance to answer; the question should have never been asked. "Mr. Cobb, from what I've heard," he lied again, "you are one of the most well-mannered men in Wood Creek. You can plainly see that Miss Emerson is shaky and pale. I'm sure—being such a gentleman—you would never impose a dance on a lady who is under the weather."

Cobb opened his mouth, then closed it. He looked back and forth between the two of them, inclined his head to Rachel, and walked away.

Chapter Eight

Rachel raked the tongs of her fork through her sweet potatoes, drawing looping swirls that reminded her of the patterns she and Jacob had made as he swept her around the room the afternoon before. She would never be courted, never know the affections of a mate, but at least she'd gotten to dance again.

"You haven't played with your food since you were a child."

Her gaze locked with her father's as her hand slipped silently to her lap. "I'm sorry."

He was staring at her with an equivocal expression, but not one that was the least bit happy or kind. He'd been unusually quiet all morning.

"Are you upset with me for dancing with Jacob?"

"You're calling him Jacob now?"

Rachel clenched her hands together in her lap to keep the tension from spreading to her face. "He asked me to."

The accusing pinch of her pa's brow deepened, then smoothed. "No, I'm not upset with you for dancing." He laid his napkin on the table and rose. "Come to my office when you've finished eating."

Trepidation chilled a path up her spine and squelched her meager appetite. At the quiet click of the office door, she looked to her ma. The wary expression she saw distressed her more.

"I don't know what this is about," her mother said softly. "I asked him what was bothering him when we returned from church, but he wouldn't tell me."

Rachel nodded. She considered her plate, which was still half full. If she took one more bite, her stomach would revolt. She lingered a moment, then excused herself from the table.

Pausing outside the door, Rachel drew a fortifying breath and replayed all the events of previous evening. Other than dancing two waltzes with her father's employee—for which he'd said he held no ill will—she couldn't name a single thing she'd done that was worthy of rebuke.

She raised her arm and knocked.

"Come in."

Scents of leather and ink filled her nose when she pushed open the door.

As a child, she'd hidden under her father's desk and played peek-a-boo with his smiling face. Later on, after she'd begun attending school, she often brought in her slate and pretended she was filling out ledgers with him. Her pa had handed down lectures and punishments in this room, but mostly it had been a place of familiarity and love.

He pushed his chair back and stood.

Rachel closed the door behind her and turned to face her fate.

"Jacob asked for your hand."

Her eyes widened. "He asked to court me?"

"No. He asked to *marry* you." Her father raked a skeptical gaze up and down her person. "Is there something I should know?"

Rachel's knees wobbled and her thoughts spun. "I... I'm not sure what you mean."

"He danced two waltzes with you, and his bid for your box was arguably exorbitant. It definitely went beyond mere fun and generosity. What's going on between the two of you?"

"Nothing. We're just..."

"Just *what*?"

She swallowed at his tone. "Friends."

"A man doesn't ask to hastily wed a *friend*. Has Jacob been courting you without my consent?"

"No."

"Then why the rush? Have the two of you anticipated your vows?"

"I–"

"Are you carrying his child?"

She gasped. "*No*."

Bile burned the back of Rachel's throat. She tried to hide how deeply her father's last question had wounded her, but her eyes grew wet despite her efforts. "Is that what you think of me?" Maybe he did. Maybe, deep down, he blamed her for what happened.

Bitter anger steeled her voice and stilled her trembling lip. "I'm ruined, but I'm not loose. You know me better than that."

Her father paled. A look of sick regret dulled his eyes. "You're right." He looked away, as if scanning the room for answers, for dignity—both his and her own. "Jacob's request was so unexpected and so urgent, I thought..." His gaze met hers again. "I should never have doubted you, Rachel. Forgive me."

Rachel blinked away the tears and dipped her head in acknowledgment. Her pa could be hurtful in his zeal, but when he admitted fault, his remorse was sincere.

He gestured in the direction of the chair next to her. "Please, sit."

She did as he asked and clasped her hands in her lap.

Quietly, he took his seat, his spine as straight and his expression as pragmatic as hers. Their mirrored posture calmed her as much as the return of soft speech and civility.

Though their genders were at odds, the two of them shared many mannerisms, as well as a logical, practical mindset. Their symmetry perplexed her mother and sometimes caused Rachel to doubt her own femininity, but at times like this, she was glad for it. Subtlety and stratagem were overrated. No matter how difficult the topic, a discussion with her father would be free of artifice and ambiguity.

He drew a breath slightly deeper than the ones before. "Jacob approached me after the festival. He asked permission to marry you and sought my blessing."

Rachel clutched her hands tighter to keep from pressing a palm to her roiling stomach. "What did you tell him?"

"I told him I'd think about it. I wanted to speak with you first."

"Thank you," she whispered.

His gaze sharpened, but something about it also softened. "I manage this family, and I do so unapologetically, but I would not betroth you without your consent. I'm sorry if you feared otherwise."

"I wasn't sure. The subject has never come up."

Her father's brows rose briefly, and then he sat back in his chair. "No, it has not."

She knew he hadn't acknowledged that fact to be cruel, but it hurt nonetheless.

"You've always been stoic and sensible, Rachel. I've not had to coddle you the way other fathers must their girl children, and you've seemed to appreciate it, in fact. I hope you'll continue to suffer my frankness, for I don't know any other way to be with you. And I don't believe that avoiding truth for the sake of courtesy is in your best interest. Not with this."

Rachel nodded. He was right. Everything he'd cited was true.

"You're already twenty. That alone is reason not to refuse an offer of marriage, at least not casually, not without just cause. You're also no longer... pure."

Her stomach leapt to her throat. "You told Jacob this?"

"I did not. I've told no one of your attack, save the late

Mr. Weeks, and that was only because he'd already parsed it out. I confirmed it so I could implore him to hold the knowledge in confidence.

"I've done everything within my power to protect your reputation, but you were a sociable young lady who suddenly withdrew amidst the scandal of Seth's disappearance. I'm sure some people view your behavior as suspect. And even the mere *possibility* is enough to send most men courting elsewhere."

It was a painful truth to hear, even if she didn't aspire to wed.

The shame searing its way through Rachel's insides must've shown on her face. She'd never seen her father look so empathetic.

"There's something else to consider," he said, his tone softer and somewhat pensive. "We'll soon be moving west. If you and Jacob were wed, he would be duty-bound to take care of you if I... if something were to separate us along the way."

He'd started to say *if I died*. Her pa was not entirely incapable of coddling.

He cleared his throat. "Once we're in California, we'll live among people we know little about."

"Which means they'll know little about us."

"That's true. And while that might bring more suitors, I won't be in a position to advise you about them—not the way I am here." He leaned forward on his elbows and turned out his hands. "I've worked side by side with Jacob for months, and I've made inquiries as to his character. By all accounts, he is an honorable man and was a good husband to his late wife."

Rachel's lungs deflated. Bit by bit, her fortress of opposition was crumbling with every well-aimed volley of sound reasoning.

Her father sat back. "I won't force you to wed, but if you are not completely averse to the idea, you should accept Jacob's suit."

"You plan to give him your blessing, then."

"I do. Unless you want me to decline in your place."

"No. That won't be necessary."

PRECIOUS ATONEMENT

His brows arched. "You'll say yes?"

"I'll think about what you've said."

"Very well. I'll give him permission to approach you. Whether or not you accept is up to you."

Rachel nodded and rose, hoping her legs would carry her from the room and praying that her rattled fortitude would get her through the conversation she'd be forced to have with Jacob.

The mere possibility of rape was enough to send most men courting elsewhere—that was true. The absolute assurance of it would deter all the rest.

***

Breakfast was tense, and more so was lunch. As large as Jacob was, he sat stiff and shrinking in his chair, like a nervous youth.

His anxiety apparently arose from hopeful anticipation.

Rachel wished she could claim the same.

After a nearly unbearable supper, Jacob excused himself and left for the cabin as always.

Rachel wanted to go to him and put them both out of their misery, but he'd only been granted permission to ask. He hadn't yet proposed.

How long would it take him to work up the nerve?

His request had been swift and sudden. Impulsive. Maybe his awkwardness wasn't what it seemed. Maybe, after thinking things over, Jacob had changed his mind.

Rachel plunged the rag into the dishwater and scrubbed the pots with agitated strokes. She'd give him a week. If he hadn't approached her by then, manners be damned—she'd confront him and get it over with.

The echo of feminine footsteps filled the room as her mother came up behind her. "Jacob's waiting in the parlor. He's asking for you."

Suddenly, a week wasn't such a long time.

Rachel dried her hands and tried to ignore the hopeful look in her mother's eyes as she brushed passed her and left the kitchen. She tucked the strands of hair that had come loose from her bun behind her ears and stepped into the room.

Jacob looked different. His hair was damp and combed back neatly. He'd changed shirts. Worst of all, he looked hopeful, like her ma. "May I speak with you?"

"Yes."

He indicated that she precede him to the settee, but she didn't accept his offer to sit. Wherever they held this conversation, painful memories would linger for a lifetime. "Would it be all right if we went for a walk?"

He looked completely nonplussed. "Yes... of course."

Once they'd donned their coats and descended the porch, Rachel took Jacob's arm and let him think he was leading. With subtle hints and tugs, she steered him past the cabin to the old oak tree—the only place fitting. It was where her father told her of her favorite foal's passing... where she'd gone, time and again, to mourn the loss of her brother and her innocence. It was the place all her dreams went to die.

Jacob looked up at the oak's sprawling branches that were gray-black in the waning light of a winter sky. "You're not cold?"

"No." Her skin was icy, but the chill came from the inside.

He seemed to gather his resolve once more. "I met with your father last night."

"He mentioned it."

"What did he say?"

"He interrogated me about the nature of our affiliation."

"What? Why?"

"We danced two waltzes together, after you placed the highest bid in Wood Creek history for my dessert box. My father thought..." Rachel's face warmed.

Jacob's eyes rounded, and his skin turned a pasty hue. "I apologize. I never meant to cause any difficulty between you and your father. I'll speak with him about it."

"That's not necessary. I explained it to his satisfaction."

"Are you certain? I don't mind talking to him if you think it would help."

"There's no need." No need indeed. The incident was of no moment, compared to what she was about to reveal.

He regained his composure—a third time, poor man—and smoothed the front of his coat. "Did he mention anything else?"

How much she should say? *Just get it over.* "He said you asked for my hand."

Jacob blinked a few times. "I did."

Rachel bolstered herself and waited. She wished she could muster a smile for this kind, honorable man, but it took all her strength just to stand there and not be sick.

"I know my suit is unexpected," Jacob continued, "but I'd hoped..." His massive shoulders drooped. "If you don't want to marry me, Rachel, just say so."

"I– It's not that." She closed her eyes in dread and frustration. "There's something I need to tell you."

"I'm listening."

Rachel studied the crease between Jacob's brows before settling her attention on his deep blue eyes. She lingered for one, brief self-indulgent moment. He'd never look at her this way again. "Three years ago, my father hired two men to help us harvest. When the job was done, he told them they could stay in the cabin an extra night. The next morning, they didn't come to breakfast. Pa assumed they left to get an early start. We all did.

"Seth hadn't shown up either, so Ma sent me to go call him in." Rachel's chest tightened. She shifted slightly and focused on the top button of Jacob's coat. She wanted to look him in the eye—he deserved that much—but she simply couldn't. "The paddock was empty, so I checked the barn. Seth wasn't there, but the men were. One of them grabbed me and covered my mouth while the other closed the door."

She glanced at Jacob's face. Gone was any affection. His jaw was tight, and he stared at her with flint-like eyes.

Rachel focused on the button again and forced herself to finish. "The man warned me not to scream. He dragged me toward an empty stall. I didn't know if he was going to hurt me or kill me, but... Then Seth came in. It distracted the man, so I tried to run. He jerked me back and struck me. Seth started to come to my aid, but the other man put a knife to his throat and held him still.

"The man who'd grabbed me had a knife, too. He... He shoved me to the ground, and then he raped me while the other man forced my brother to watch."

Rachel closed her eyes. She wanted to look up at Jacob, to see his reaction, but the vicious memories kept crashing into her like waves. She had to wait for the living nightmare she'd roused to subside.

Once she was able, she raised her gaze slowly.

Jacob wasn't looking at her anymore. His jaw was still tense, but the lines around his eyes made them look bleak. "This is why your brother left," he finally said.

"Yes."

"And the men?"

"No one has seen them since." That eased his bearing some, but he still wouldn't look at her.

"Have your injuries left you unable to have marital relations?"

She knew he was speaking of physical scars. "No."

"When he..." Jacob's lips pinched as if his tongue had turned bitter. "Did you conceive?"

"No."

He made eye contact with her, grudging though it was. "Has the ordeal left you barren?"

Rachel drew a measured breath. "That I don't know. The doctor said it was possible, but he couldn't be certain."

He looked away again and gave a barely discernable nod.

Jacob stood mute for several minutes, then stiffly offered his arm. "It's getting dark. I'll see you home."

Not another word was said.

Rachel went straight to her room. She couldn't face her parents right now.

She busied herself with her mending and listened to the echoes of an angry man chopping wood long past the hour when loss of light made it unsafe. After that, she lay in her bed and listened to her aching heart throb in the ominous silence.

Chapter Nine

Rachel managed to dress and slip out of the house without encountering either of her parents. She'd heard them the night before, when they'd paused and whispered to each other outside her bedroom door, but—thankfully—they'd passed on by without disturbing her.

Clutching her coat collar closed against the bitter, pre-dawn air, she hurried to the hen house, her boots crunching through leaves and frost. Despite the biting weather, Rachel lingered in the coop, drawing out the task of distributing feed and gathering the scanty offering of winter eggs. She loathed facing Jacob. And her parents with their disappointed looks.

Her boots dragged like a plow through hardpan as she walked back toward the house. Ten feet past the chopping block, her legs stopped moving completely.

The door to the barn was ajar, spilling a wedge of lamplight onto the dirt. Jacob stood just outside, holding two steaming pails of milk and staring blankly into the space.

Rachel hung her head and continued toward the house.

His heavy footsteps came up behind her as she neared the porch. "Rachel, may I have a word with you before you go inside?"

PRECIOUS ATONEMENT

She readied herself for Jacob's disdain and turned around.

His eyes were dull and shadowed with dark circles. He looked more tired than angry. "I'm sorry about the way I left things last night. I needed time to think."

"It's all right. You don't owe me an explanation." She turned to go. There was no sense dragging this out and making it anymore uncomfortable than it already was.

"Wait. I wasn't done."

Rachel faced him reluctantly. He must want to formally withdraw his proposal, to scold her for letting him make a fool of himself. She should have never danced with him—never led him on.

"I apologize for my rude behavior last night."

Rachel shrugged. "You were angry."

"Yes, I was. But I should have been more considerate of you, of how difficult it was for you to tell me what happened."

Jacob set the pails on the edge of the porch. "I know you value your solitude. To some extent, I value mine. But remaining alone benefits neither of us. I could find work in town, but I don't want to. Working the land, it makes me feel productive and alive. It's all I've ever wanted to do.

"Your father invited me to go west with him, and I want to—badly—but I don't want to be someone's employee the rest of my life. I want my own land. I can run a farm, but not without a helpmeet to manage my home, and you…"

She was mildly frowning at him now. What an odd jilting.

He cleared his throat. "What I mean to say is: a day will come when your father can no longer provide for you and ensure your safety. It's unfortunate, but it's true. You'll need a protector, eventually. You and I suit well enough. I enjoy your company, and you tolerate mine." His hands twitched at his sides, then lifted to enfold the one of hers not holding the basket of eggs. "I know this isn't the passionate proposal on bended knee that young ladies dream of, but it is offered in truth. I'll take care of you, Rachel, with everything that I have, until I draw my last breath. Will you marry me?"

His eyes beheld hers with candid expectancy as his last words wove through her mind and bored their way into her chest. *Will you marry me?* Rachel's throat tightened. This wasn't a jilting. This wasn't a jilting at all.

The air around her thinned. She'd been so sure Jacob would withdraw his suit when he learned the truth, she hadn't considered any other scenario.

Dear God, what would she say? She couldn't ask for time to think; she'd already had the better part of a day. She obviously had her mother's approval. And her father was all but pushing her into his arms.

The only person's motives in question were Jacob's.

Rachel drew herself up with the starch only a social leper possessed. "Are you certain you want to marry a ruined woman?"

He clearly wasn't expecting that, but it had to be asked.

Men had power over all females by virtue of their gender, but a husband's dominion was absolute. He had both the latitude and the privacy to mete out punishment for any perceived wrong. Nuptial vows always carried a measure of risk, but more so for her. Some men married fallen women on purpose—men who took pleasure in degrading them and beating them on a regular basis.

Jacob's hands tightened on hers, and anger flickered in his eyes. "I don't see you that way." He looked away, then focused on her again, his grip and his expression having eased. "I have thought this through at length. I need a wife. I could choose any one of several available ladies in Millhousen or Wood Creek, but you are the lady I want."

The world took on an unmistakable stillness, and time slowed down, the way it always did when the outcome of something monumental loomed. She'd felt this way right before she uttered the letters of the winning word in the spelling match... during the breathless, elongated moment when Mr. Weeks teetered before tumbling from the roof... the swift eternity when she'd seen victory in her rapist's eyes.

Destiny was largely immune to her actions and choices. But sometimes...

"So. Will you marry me?"

Rachel considered all that she risked by saying yes. Then she numbered every single thing she stood to lose if she said no.

Jacob's throat bobbed with a swallow. His expression held no malice or barely restrained triumph, only patience and honest entreaty.

Her heart fluttered. She swallowed and forced the word out. "Yes."

He smiled and kissed the back of her hand. "Thank you, Rachel. I promise you won't regret it."

Jacob picked up the pails of milk and followed her into the house. "Good morning, Mrs. Emerson," he said as he set them in the kitchen.

"Good morning," her ma replied, giving them both an assessing look.

"I'm off to help Lawrence," Jacob said, unnecessarily. "See you both at breakfast."

"He's in a cheerful mood," her ma remarked as the front door closed.

Rachel tiptoed around the subtle lure that had been tossed out, rinsed her hands, and started making the biscuits as reality landed on her with a smack and stung as it sank in—she was betrothed. And the engagement wouldn't be secret for long.

"Ma?"

"Hm?" Links of sausage sizzled as they met the bottom of a hot pan.

Rachel turned the biscuit dough out onto a floured board as

the scents of pepper and sage filled the air. "What's your opinion of Jacob?" She started rolling the dough while she waited on the answer.

"I think he's an honest, respectable man."

She rolled the dough some more, hoping her courage wouldn't desert her. "Do you think he would be a good husband?"

"I do."

"He, um. He asked me to marry him."

"I know. Your father finally told me yesterday." The sound of crackling grease occupied a modest pause. "What did you say?"

Rachel's whole body tingled with fear and anticipation. "I said yes."

Her mother smiled at her over her shoulder. "I'm glad."

"I thought you would be shocked, or at least surprised."

"I am a little surprised that you accepted, but not that he asked." Abigail prodded the links in her pan, then looked back over her shoulder again. "I knew Jacob would offer for you. It was just a matter of time."

Rachel's lips parted and she stared in disbelief.

Her mother shoved the skillet to a cooler spot on the stove and came over to where she stood. "He champions you, Rachel. And not only in regards to your standing and your safety. He does it with little things." A warm smile rounded her cheeks. "He has since that first morning, when he sat across the table from you.

"I don't know what it was about you that impressed him, but he took one look at you and took up your cause. His eyes glinted with such a vivid call to honor, it brought to mind the knights of old. Jacob was instantly yours, pledged to slay your dragons and lay them limp and conquered at your feet."

"Why didn't you say anything?"

Her mother's smile lingered, but it dimmed some. "Would you have believed me if I had? ...and would it have mattered?"

Rachel sighed. "No, probably not."

"Jacob needed to prove himself—to you and to me. It's a man's nature to protect, but that's only one portion of honor."

Her mother hugged her and kissed her cheek. "Congratulations." She hurried back to the sausage.

Chapter Ten

Jacob opened the Emersons' barn and thanked every saint, martyr, and prophet he could name that this was the last time he'd have to set foot in the place. His two weeks of torture were finally over. He'd be taking his chickens and cow home as soon as the milking was done.

He seated himself next to his gentle Durham and tried not to look at the patch of ground to his left. How Lawrence, Abigail—or, God help her, Rachel—could even stand to walk inside, much less stay to finish a task, escaped him.

Reckless wastefulness be damned. He'd have torched the place and burned the structure to the ground.

Jacob forced himself to give both bovines a good and thorough milking, then he tied his cow to his wagon and delivered the pails to the kitchen.

He paused at the sight of Rachel removing toast from the oven. Did anyone truly know how brave she was?

When she'd told him of her attack, he'd been so filled with rage, he'd had to spirit her back to the house so as not to lose his composure and do violence in her presence. For the first time in his life, he'd hungered to kill.

He still craved revenge to the point of distraction, but more than that, he wanted to wrap Rachel in his protection so no one could ever hurt her again.

"Are you sure you won't stay for breakfast?" Abigail asked.

"I wish I could, but I can't. My neighbor's wife, Nettie Bishop, and the Widow Clark are arriving at my house this morning to ready it for Rachel's arrival. These women have graciously seen to my mending and sustenance for most of the last two years," he said with a half-smile, "and they have threatened me that my garments will suffer and my invitations to meals will cease if I am but one minute late."

Abigail's face glowed with merriment. "In that case, I'll pack you something posthaste."

Jacob turned to Rachel, who looked on him with the same pleasant, reserved expression she'd worn ever since she consented to be his wife. "Will you see me off?"

She followed him out of the house and waited patiently while he tucked the food under the seat of his buckboard and hitched up Goliath.

"I'm going to miss you," he said honestly. He'd grown accustomed to being alone, but he couldn't deny that Rachel had become part of his daily routine, an enjoyable part.

"I'll miss you, too." Her reply seemed no less true, but there was a reticence to it that gave him pause.

"Are you sure of your choice? You could still cry off if you wish." He prayed she wouldn't, but the gentleman in him was compelled to give her the out.

Rachel's gaze roamed over his face and returned to his eyes. "Are you having second thoughts?"

"No. I was asking if you are."

"I'm not."

"Good." He cradled her hand in his and brought her knuckles to his lips. "Until Friday, then."

One week. One long, worry-filled, insufferable week.

Jacob heaved a great sigh and hoisted himself onto his wagon. It was time to get his bride.

He'd endured not one but *three* days of hen-like fussing from the neighbor women—regarding the state of his house, the state of his clothes, and the state of his pantry stock or the lack thereof. He appreciated the ladies' concern and their hard work on his behalf, but he repeatedly gave thanks that his demure, diminutive Rachel was not the nagging sort. At least not vocally. She wouldn't carp. She'd just turn a scorching glare on him from time to time.

He grinned. That he could take.

Jacob flicked the reins and filled his lungs with cold, clean morning air. Punishing winter storms would come soon, but for now, a light dusting of snow covered the landscape and made it glisten.

He slipped his hand inside his coats and patted the pocket of his new silk vest, an ivory adornment sewn and gifted by the Widow Clark, to assure himself he hadn't forgotten. Although his and Rachel's wedding plans had been rushed, he'd made the time to get her a ring.

The extravagance wasn't part of his original plan, but the state of his future had changed once he'd spoken to Lawrence regarding the details of the nuptials. Jacob would still need to finance his trip west, but there would be no need to purchase a farm. If he shared in the work of establishing the Emerson estate, Lawrence would deed him half the land.

At first, stepping into the role of heir had felt presumptuous and awkward. Then the truth of the matter sank in. Seth hadn't returned in three long years, which meant he probably wouldn't. He had either drowned himself in liquor and guilt or met a violent end while seeking revenge.

Today is supposed to be a happy day.

Jacob cleared his mind of dark thoughts and counted his blessings. His soon-to-be in-laws were one, and their sweet daughter was most certainly another. Marrying Rachel would allow him to realize his dream. And in return, he'd give her his name and his protection.

"I thought this gathering was to be small," Jacob grumbled to Goliath, who kept plodding steadily along, merely flicking an ear. Wagons and buggies filled the Emerson's yard.

Jacob hadn't forbade a large wedding. He'd have wed Rachel in a packed-to-standing church if she had asked him. A modest ceremony at home had been her plan.

A band of male neighbors—a mixture of his and hers—began shouting and waving as he neared the house. He touched the brim of his hat and put on a smile.

"We were beginning to think you wouldn't show," Simon Ledbetter called out. "Bets were about to be made."

"You obviously haven't seen the bride," Jacob shot back. "I'd be a fool to leave a beauty like that standing at the altar."

"Hear, hear," Amos Everhart said, saluting with a flask.

Jacob shook his head. Amos was already imbibing and it wasn't yet noon. But even the men who were sober seemed genial and supportive.

A few well-meaning citizens of Wood Creek had pulled him aside in the days before and whispered their suspicions about his bride-to-be. Jacob, just as earnestly, assured them they were wrong. It was a lie, but a justifiable one. Few people made a moral distinction between fornication and rape. He did.

Rachel had been ambushed and attacked—she hadn't fallen by choice.

"I'll stable your steed," Simon said when he dismounted. "Can't have the groom smelling like horse—the bride might leave *you* at the altar."

Jacob joined in the laughter. He'd managed to hitch Goliath without soiling his clothes, but he chose not to argue the point. "You fellows can tease and cosset me all you like, as long as you don't follow me home when the wedding is done." He winced at the chorus of boos. "I'm serious. Anyone who sets foot on my land after dark risks meeting his maker."

The men grumbled, but they seemed to accept his decree. They had better. The last thing Rachel needed was a shivaree.

"Stop harassing my future son-in-law." Lawrence descended the porch steps with a broad smile and gave Jacob's hand a hearty shake. "Abigail and Rachel are still secreted up stairs," he said as Jacob followed him into the house. "Reverend Dawson arrived shortly ago. I showed him to the parlor."

"Good." Jacob had worried the Emersons would prefer their own town's clergy, but they'd agreed to use the preacher from Millhousen. It was a wise concession. Dawson didn't grow suspicious when Jacob asked him to substitute the giving of the ring for the seal of a kiss, and—though such things were not unheard of—Rachel's guests would be far less likely to question the variation from someone unfamiliar.

The female counterpart of the welcoming committee gathered in the foyer to greet him. By the time he made his way to the parlor, joined Dawson, and went over some final details, it was time for the ceremony.

The room, well heated by the fire and smelling of pine from all the ribbon-laden boughs and wreaths, warmed more as the guests filed in and took their places. Children settled. Joyful murmurs faded to quiet.

Elbows straight but loose, Jacob clasped his hands in front of his hips and waited.

Rachel descended the stairs, and time slowed. She looked even lovelier than she had the day of the festival. The pale green silk of her dress complemented her coloring better than blue, and the soft winter light coming through the windows lit her skin and made it glow with the translucence of fine china.

Jacob suffered a twinge of poignancy. He would never risk his heart again, but, if he'd met her first, he could have loved Rachel. As it was, loyalty and admiration would have to do. Destiny had placed them together—two damaged people who could meet each other's needs.

Lawrence gave his daughter away with dignified pride and went to stand with her mother.

Reverend Dawson addressed the crowd, led Jacob and Rachel through affirming their vows, and then prompted Jacob to seal their union with the ring.

He withdrew the slim, gold band from his pocket and held it ready to be slipped on Rachel's finger. Lamplight glinted off the carvings that encircled the band—a twining of vines and roses. He'd chosen that because roses would always remind him of her.

She stared at it, and then up at him. He enjoyed the way gratitude and surprise seemed to settle her nerves... or at least distract her from them for a time.

"With this ring, I thee wed," Jacob said as he pushed it gently on.

Dawson cleared his throat. "What, therefore, God hath joined together, let not man put asunder. In so much as Jacob and Rachel have consented together in holy wedlock, and have witnessed the same before God and this company, having given and pledged their troth, I now pronounce them husband and wife."

Jacob wrapped Rachel's hand around his arm and turned them to face the crowd. Lawrence was still standing straight and proud, and Abigail was silently but happily crying.

Within moments, they were enfolded by a cluster of well-wishers. Jacob kept Rachel close, and she tolerated it well enough.

Fellowship and festivities continued for most of the afternoon.

Everyone shared the cake of fruit and raisins, and Rachel enjoyed a treasured visit with her friend Charity. Finally the time came for them to say goodbye.

Jacob stowed the last of the gifts, trunks, and bags into the back of his wagon. "Is that everything?"

Rachel nodded, notably quieter and more ill at ease than she'd been before.

"It must be difficult for you to leave all you've known."

"It is," she agreed, though both of them knew there was more to it than that.

"Don't worry. We'll visit. And we'll be spending every day with your parents when we go west."

She nodded again, the movement nudging the hood of the green velvet cape she wore.

They said their farewells. Then Jacob lifted her onto the seat and drove away amid cheers and stinging pelts of rice.

Rachel sat stiff and silent all the way home.

He handed her down once he'd parked the wagon in the yard. "It's smaller than the home you grew up in," he remarked as her gaze scanned his house, "but I think you'll find it livable. Besides, it just has to get us through winter."

She wore a tight smile. "I like it."

Jacob adjusted his tie. "There's a chamber pot inside, but…" He gestured in the direction of the outhouse.

Rachel mumbled her thanks and headed for the necessary.

While she was occupied, he busied himself stabling Goliath and unloaded their things. She joined him as he brought in the last of the parcels.

"I still have to stoke up the fire. I'll be glad to heat some water, if you'd like a bath."

"No, thank you. I already had one."

"So have I." Jacob helped her off with her cape. "You're welcome to go upstairs and settle in if you like."

"All right."

"Here, let me show you the way." He reached for her valise, but she clutched it tighter.

"I can find it, just tell me which room."

"My–" He corrected himself. "*Our* room is upstairs. First door on your right." He watched her back as she hurried to the stairs and slowed her steps as she climbed up. "Make yourself at home. I'll only be a short while."

Fingers grasping the sill, Rachel touched her forehead to the cool window pane and stared down at the yard, just as Jacob disappeared into the barn. He wouldn't be long, maybe fifteen minutes at most, and then he'd come to her. Her heart flailed in her chest, and what little she'd eaten for supper leapt from her stomach and raced toward her throat.

She swallowed hard and wrung her trembling hands together as she turned and stared at the bedroom door. Jacob was a gentle man, as kind and tender in spirit and deed as he was mountainous in stature. But she'd married him in front of God and witnesses. That gave him certain rights. If he insisted on claiming her body, she couldn't turn him down. And he would insist, wouldn't he? This was their wedding night.

The creak of the side door being closed downstairs yanked her from her frantic musings. She needed to get out of her clothes and into her gown before he made it up the stairs, or she'd be forced to change in front of him. It was a silly reasoning, really. He'd eventually see her unclothed. But if she could put that moment off a while longer, everything would be okay. It would. She just needed time.

Rachel fumbled with the fasteners of her dress as Jacob's boots scuffed the floorboards downstairs. The location of the sound changed below her, and she could picture him walking from place to place, blowing out the lamps and making sure everything was secure and ready for night. She laid her underthings aside as he paused at the base of the stairs and hurriedly worked the cotton nightgown over her head as he climbed the steps at a calm, steady pace.

She was anything but calm or steady. She gulped air, yet she couldn't seem to draw a deep enough breath. Her limbs tingled and bright spots speckled her vision.

A soft knock came from the other side of the door, and she whirled around so fast, she nearly lost her footing.

"Rachel...? May I come in?"

She glanced down to make sure she was properly covered. Arms stiff at her sides, she fingered the gathers of her gown and fixed her gaze on the door. "Yes."

The latch clicked and the door eased open. Jacob's shoulders filled the doorway as he stepped in. The corners of his mouth turned up a few moments later, but something about his smile seemed disappointed.

Maybe I shouldn't have changed. Maybe—

He walked toward her with unhurried steps. When he got within arm's reach, she fought the urge to back away. *Stay calm. Stay calm.* He lifted his hand toward her face and she flinched. A tiny crease appeared between his brows and he lowered his arm to his side.

His gaze trailed down her gowned form, but not in a lewd way. Gingerly, he touched her elbow and slid his fingers down her sleeve. It wasn't until he tried to lift her wrist that she realized she had curled her fingers around the fabric, trapping the fine lawn in tightly clinched fists. He eased the fingers of her left hand loose, then engulfed it in his. His skin was so hot, it burned.

She watched Jacob rub her slender fingers with his large thick ones, kneading them so gently, it seemed impossible for a hand that size. He could snap them like fresh string beans if he took the notion.

Rachel looked closer. His flesh wasn't hot, hers was cold. Her nails were blue and her fingertips had blanched completely white.

Jacob bent forward, planting the lightest of kisses on her palm. "Goodnight."

He released her hand and turned as if to leave.

"Wh– where are you going?"

"To sleep in the spare room"

"Why?"

He turned fully back to her then, kind resignation muting his sapphire eyes. "You can barely stand to be in the same room with me. I won't force you to share a bed."

She watched him walk to the door, unable to say a word, unable to decide which emotion pouring through her was stronger—relief or regret.

Rachel's heart beat so fast, it thrummed a constant quiver in her chest. "Wait," she called as his broad body filled the frame.

He paused and looked back at her over his shoulder.

"Don't go." Her nerves settled a bit. "I don't want you to go."

His eyes narrowed briefly, then his brow smoothed. "Very well. If that's your choice."

"It is."

Her anxiety rose again as he turned around, stealing what little serenity she'd gained.

Jacob walked to the other side of the bed and sat, causing frame to creak and the mattress to sag deeply. With practiced ease, he removed his boots and began to disrobe. He stood long enough to lower his trousers and lay his clothes across the back of a nearby chair, and then he climbed into bed, wearing only his drawers. After pulling the covers up to mid chest, he rested his arms casually atop the quilt.

Rachel stood frozen, trying with all her might to force her feet to move. She'd already disappointed him once. If she could manage to lie next to him, maybe she could salvage what was left of their first night together.

Jacob looked over at her, his face calm.

Swallowing, she crossed the room and climbed in. With a small and probably unconvincing smile, she turned her back to him and pulled the covers tightly over her shoulder and under her chin.

He blew out the lamp.

Her composure finally broke. She'd thought she could do this—that her will could override her fear—but she'd hurt Jacob's feelings and ruined their wedding night. She held her sobs inside as tears spilled from her lids and trickled sideways down her face.

"Roll over."

She shook her head. She was ashamed enough as it was.

"Turn and face me, Rachel. I'm not a harsh man, but I'm your husband and I expect to be obeyed. The bed is shaking. You're either cold or you're crying. Regardless, you will accept comfort from me."

Reluctantly, she did as he asked, catching a glimpse of her reflection in the dressing table mirror as she turned. Moonlight glimmered along the tracks her tears had made, turning them silver. She quickly swiped them away.

Jacob held out his arm in invitation. "Come. Put your head on my shoulder. I only wish to hold you close to my side. Nothing more."

Rachel moved closer and eased herself into the crook of his arm. She stiffened when his forearm wrapped around her waist, but swallowed the urge to panic and reminded herself where she was and, more importantly, whom she was with. Warmth radiated from her husband's skin, and her rigid posture began to ease.

"Would it be all right if I kissed the top of your head?"

"Yes." At least she hoped so. After the way her traitorous body had spoiled things, she wasn't sure of her reactions anymore.

Muscles bunched under her cheek as Jacob pressed his lips to her hair. She and Jacob both released a long breath as he relaxed against the pillow.

"This is how it will be between us," he said, snugging his hold as if to punctuate his words. "This is your safe place. Whenever you wish, you can come to me like this, and I will comfort you. I won't take your approach to mean anything more.

"Do you understand what I'm saying to you?" he asked when she didn't respond.

She nodded. His kindness pricked her heart, and tears threatened again. "I'm sorry I behaved the way I did." She looked up at him tentatively. "I'm not afraid of you."

"I know you're not."

"I thought I could..." Her lip trembled. "I ruined our special night."

"No, you didn't." He brushed a fresh tear from her cheek. "I'm honored that you agreed to marry me, and I'm pleased that you trust me enough to share my bed, even if only for sleep."

Jacob tugged the quilts up around them with his free hand. A short while later, his breathing grew slow, deep and even.

One day, he would want more than sleep.

Rachel closed her eyes and let blackness claim her weary mind.

Jacob awoke to the smell of coffee and an empty bed. It was still full dark. Had the rooster even crowed? He lit the lamp and quickly pulled on some work clothes. Normally his breath formed puffs of white on winter mornings, but the house was already beginning to warm.

He paused to brush his fingers over the nightgown Rachel had folded neatly and left on the seat of her dressing chair and felt a pang of guilt for being so stern with her the night before. He'd never been one to take pleasure in imposing his will on others, and he didn't make light of Rachel's past, but the fearful way she'd acted had wounded his pride.

Still, he had let things lie. The two of them would soon face harsh conditions and innumerable dangers on the trail—threats that might require unquestioning compliance with his instructions. Her swift obedience might mean the difference between life and death. Or worse.

A small amount of fear could be a good thing.

He paused when he reached the bottom stair and swallowed hard at the strong emotion the sight of Rachel in the kitchen evoked. The sentiment was not among the ones he'd expected.

She turned around, and Jacob quickly took control of his face. "You didn't have to get up so early. I would have built up the fire and put the coffee on to boil."

"I don't mind." The bright reply had been given with a genuine smile, and she appeared ready for a day of work. She'd traded her green gown for a simple dress of dark-brown wool, covered by a lighter brown, embroidered cotton apron.

"Did you sleep well?" He had. He'd slept so soundly, he hadn't a clue about her night... save the gray hollows he was just now seeing beneath her eyes.

"Well enough." She smoothed her hands down the front of her clothes—a nervous motion, it seemed. And for some reason, that only irritated him more. "What would you like for breakfast?"

"Something simple." He was hungry, but it took time for a woman to adjust to a different kitchen. Sarah's kitchen. "I've got chores." He ignored the way Rachel's face fell at his clipped tone and started toward the door. For her sake and his, he needed to get out of there.

Jacob welcomed the bracing winter air stinging his face. Maybe it would help him get his blasted emotions under control. He'd sought Rachel and convinced her to marry him. She didn't deserve the dung he was dishing out.

PRECIOUS ATONEMENT

Work calmed him as it always did, and he returned to the kitchen with a generous pail of milk and a kinder attitude. It had occurred to him, once he'd stopped brooding long enough to think of someone other than himself, that Rachel likely felt like a failure after the night before. She was only trying to please him.

She eyed him with a fair amount of tentativeness, and he couldn't blame her.

He sat at the head of the table and waited while she brought the coffee and food. Four trips later, the table held every breakfast item known to man.

She reached for her chair, then gasped. "The marmalade." She spun on her heel.

"*Rachel.*" Jacob winced. He hadn't meant to use such a firm tone.

Her steps halted, and she turned around.

"Do you have everything you need for your meal?" he asked more politely.

She glanced at the table. "Yes."

He smiled, though it felt stiff. "So do I."

Once she was seated—and it had been a cautious motion, with tight lips and wary eyes that never let him out of her peripheral vision—he placed his napkin in his lap. "Some men like their wives flitting about and waiting on them like royalty, barely caring if they eat or sit. I'm not one of them. I prefer the company of my spouse and a bit of conversation." Jacob took a sip of his coffee and watched Rachel do the same with hers. "I have some fence repairs I need to do. What are your plans for today?"

She stared at him like a frightened rabbit, unblinking. "I'd like to spend some time organizing the cupboard and familiarizing myself with the house."

Her comment exhumed some of his resentment, but he shoved it back down. "That sounds good."

"I thought I'd make a pie, too."

"That sounds even better."

Her gaze lingered on him a moment, then she nudged one of the platters in his direction.

"If this is what you fix when I ask for *something simple*," Jacob muttered as he forked a slab of ham onto his plate, "I'd hate to see what you'd cook if I asked for a feast." The smile that followed came easily. It wasn't stiff at all.

Rachel stood at the window and watched Jacob ride Goliath out into the pasture, still trying to fathom what she'd done to make him so cross. He'd been firm with her about refusing his comfort the night before, but they'd resolved that.

Maybe he was simply testy upon rising. Until today, she'd never encountered him before morning chores.

Rachel reordered the items in the cupboard to suit her, and then she began making her way through Jacob's modest house. The downstairs was mostly one large room that consisted of the kitchen and dining area on one side, and a sturdy fireside chair and sofa on the other. The only walled off rooms on the lower floor were a closet nearby the stove for tub bathing and space that appeared to be an office.

Rachel started to go in, then decided against it. She turned and took the stairs instead.

The rooms above—two bedrooms, including theirs—were much more feminine. Soft hues of pink and green coated the walls, and frilly, embroidered curtains hung over the windows.

Rachel ran her hand over the quilt on Jacob's bed, now illuminated by mid-morning light. The patches were carefully pieced, and the stitches were small and neat and even. She moved to the window and fingered the edge of the curtain. An intricate border of daisies, bluebells and humming birds extended several inches up and ran the entire length of the hem. Sarah's presence was everywhere.

I'll never be able to fill her shoes.

Jacob had packed food and was working through lunch, so Rachel returned to the kitchen and peeled the apples for the pie. Had Sarah made hers with nutmeg and molasses?

Rachel put some soup on to cook after she'd put the pie in to bake, and then she sat on a chair and stared about the place. Jacob's neighbors had done such a thorough job of stocking and cleaning that, for today at least, there wasn't much to do.

She built up the fireplace fire to warm the house for her husband's return, and then she wandered over to the sideboard next to the dining table. She'd glimpsed some linens when she'd searched for the items she'd needed to set the table. Now she withdrew a few and looked them over more closely. The hems were perfect, and the decorative needlework was just as accomplished as on the items upstairs.

Rachel brought one of the napkins to her nose and wondered at the faint scent of jasmine. Was that how Jacob's first wife had smelled, or was it merely the odor of something she'd added to her laundry.

Boots clomped on the porch, and the door swung open.

Rachel lowered the napkin and drew a tight breath at the disapproval in Jacob's eyes. "You're home early." She felt foolish, but she didn't know what else to say.

He marshalled his expression some. "The repairs didn't take as long as I thought."

"Your wi– Sarah was very talented."

"Yes, she was."

Rachel tucked the napkin away and shut the drawer. "I'm sorry if I touched something I shouldn't have."

His shoulders lost some of their starch, and so did his face. "You didn't. This is your home now. Sarah would want you to have her things."

Rachel wasn't indifferent to his grief, but she was at a loss for what to make his shifting moods.

Jacob was like a lake on a spring morning, calm but deep, at least in places. Sometimes when she looked at him, she still felt a chill. A mild, unnerving shiver that warned of danger. As if beneath his placid surface lurked a deadly current or bottomless abyss. But other times, a dark desperation weighted his posture and carved harsh lines in his face, suggesting that Jacob was the one struggling not to be sucked under.

They dined on soup and pie, mostly in silence. Then Jacob excused himself and disappeared into his office.

Several minutes later, he returned and approached her in the kitchen. He withdrew a folded piece of paper from his pocket and stared down at it, rubbing it with his thumbs as if he couldn't make up his mind.

He finally looked up at her with and expression so humble, it pricked her heart. "This is an old family recipe of Sarah's," he said, handing it to her. "It's a favorite of mine."

Rachel unfolded the paper and began to read. It was a recipe for Scottish meat pie, but one with an odd assortment of ingredients.

"I was wondering if you'd make it for me."

She looked up at him. "I'll be happy to try. But, even with instructions, no two cooks make a dish exactly the same."

"I haven't tasted it in over two years. I'll be grateful, however it turns out."

He excused himself for evening chores as she tucked the recipe safely away.

And from then on, that was how she and Jacob went about their days— considerate but quiet, living like friends and sharing a house with the ghost of a woman he still grieved. Committed, but without any acts of affection or mention of love.

Rachel lay in bed and stared at a pale moon framed by ruffles and hummingbirds.

Jacob had said something about young ladies dreaming of romantic, bended-knee proposals. That was true.

She had dreamt of that and so much more.

Chapter Eleven

If she was going to spend the rest of her life in a loveless marriage, she would at least assure herself that she hadn't married into poverty. That was the justification Rachel used as she laid aside her dusting cloth and opened the ledger on Jacob's desk.

Figures printed in a bold, slashing hand edged each page. She smoothed her finger over them, then mentally tallied one of the columns. It was accurate to the cent.

And Sarah couldn't have done it. The entries were much too recent.

Rachel flipped through several of the pages and sobered at what she found. Jacob's home was small and his tastes were relatively simple, but that was not because he couldn't afford better. He was as competent at managing money as he was at dancing.

"May I help you?"

Her gaze flew to the doorway. Jacob stood just inside, staring at her with an intense expression... not angry, but not amused either.

He walked closer, and she realized why she hadn't heard him. On days when snowmelt muddied the paths, he removed his boots at the door.

Rachel closed the ledger and slid it back into place.

"This is my office."

Had he emphasized the word *my*, or was that just her imagination?

"I'd prefer that you respect my privacy here," he continued in the same calm tone, "but if you're curious about something, you have only to ask."

"I'm sorry. I..." *I thought you were too dull-witted to do your own math.* She was the stupid one.

Rachel picked up her cloth and headed for the door.

Jacob closed his eyes and sighed when Rachel ducked out of the room like a meek, scolded child. Where was the stubborn woman he'd met in the garden that day, the one who hadn't thought twice about challenging him?

He wasn't angry with her. She was an excellent wife. She cooked for him and cared for him—she even cosseted him on occasion—but the light had gone out of her eyes. In a matter of weeks, Rachel had changed from a woman content to a woman resigned.

Once the sun had dried the paths, he sought her out. "Are you almost done?"

She looked up from pressing one of his shirts. "No, but I can put this aside if you need something."

"Thank you. I do." He waited for her to dispense with the iron. "Come," he said, holding his hand out to her. "Take a walk with me."

She frowned mildly when he led her to the door, put on his coat, and fastened her into hers, but she went along without question.

The old Rachel would have scolded him for interrupting her work.

"Watch your step," he cautioned as he guided her around a lingering puddle. He wrapped her hand around his forearm and covered it with his own. Though the sun was out, the air was bracing, and he spent a few moments breathing it in while he chose his words.

She strode beside him patiently, taking in the muted winter surroundings.

Jacob paused when they reached a spot along the fence that gave them a view of both the pastures and the fields. "I'm not entirely pleased with the way things are going between us, Rachel." Her face fell, and he hurried to correct the misunderstanding. "That is to say, I am very pleased with *you*, but not so much with myself."

"Why not? You're a good husband."

"Am I?"

"Your expectations are reasonable, and you provide well for us."

"Then why are you unhappy?"

She fidgeted a bit and wouldn't meet his gaze. "Marriage is an adjustment."

"Yes, it is. Do you miss your parents?"

"Some."

He suspected it was more than just *some*. "I spoke with your father yesterday, when I took Goliath to be shod. Weather permitting, we'll be visiting them at Christmas."

The smile that brightened her face was one he hadn't seen since he'd waltzed with her at the festival. "Would it be alright if I make them a gift?"

"Of course. I'll take you to town with me tomorrow, and you can buy what you need." He glanced at the sky. "We should stock the pantry while the weather holds, anyhow."

They strolled a while more, him telling her of the plans he had for their farm out west, and then they stopped again. This time the view included the hillside where Sarah and the baby were buried.

Jacob started to walk away, but decided to confront the source of his pain and what he suspected was the source of Rachel's discontent.

She leaned closer to him when they reached the headstones.

"I miss them," he said honestly.

Rachel hugged his bicep. "It must be awful for you."

"Even after two years, thinking about them hurts, and memories sneak up on me at times. I suppose that's why I've been so temperamental." He glanced down when she didn't respond. Rachel didn't look angry or vindicated, merely sympathetic. "I noticed the winter roses. Was it you who put flowers on the graves?"

"Yes." She inclined her head and looked up at him through her lashes. "Are you angry with me?"

"No. Why would I be?"

"You might consider my actions intrusive."

"I don't feel that way. You can visit them if you like, but why did you?"

"You love them, and they deserve to be remembered."

Jacob blinked at a sudden sting of emotion, then he smiled at her and took her by the hand. They ambled on in companionable silence until they came to the pond and gazed out over the cold, calm water.

Rachel stared down at their clasped hands with an expression that held puzzlement and something else he couldn't identify.

"Don't worry. It's still there."

"What is?"

"Your hand." His was so large, it all but hid hers from view.

The corner of Rachel's mouth lifted the way it often did when he teased her. "That's not what I was thinking."

"What were you pondering, then?" It had occurred to him right as he asked it, she *was* pondering something.

Rachel still hadn't looked up. She stayed quiet so long, he thought she wasn't going to answer.

"I was thinking," she finally said, "about how nice it feels when you kiss my hand and wondering if it would feel the same—" She touched her lips with the fingers of her free hand. "–here."

Her comment drew him up short. Of all the things she might

have said, he hadn't fathomed that. "Would you like to know instead of wonder?"

She nodded as her fingers fell away.

Jacob urged her closer. "Look at me, Rachel."

She did, and he spent several moments studying her face and her eyes. Uncertainty mingled with trust and curiosity, but longing was there, too.

Jacob brushed her bottom lip with his thumb. He gently grasped her chin and touched his lips to hers. When she sighed instead of stiffening or backing away, he grazed her lips a few times in a lazy nibble.

He restrained his kiss so as not to frighten her, but there was no restraining his body's reaction. He'd been forced to bend at the waist to reach her, which had put space between their lower bodies. He was suddenly glad for their disparity in height.

Rachel sighed again and leaned into his chest. She smelled of roses and tasted of soft, sweet woman.

Jacob nibbled some more, this time not so lazily. Rachel didn't open her mouth, and he didn't seek entry. He contented himself with what was given and enjoyed a simple pleasure denied him far too long.

A few moments later, she withdrew, and he let her. Her slender fingers returned to her lips. This time her expression was indecisive, almost troubled.

"Well?" he prompted. "How was it? And take care in your answer. If the look on your face is any indication of my skills, my fragile male pride is in terrible jeopardy."

She lowered her hand. "It was... nice. More than nice. It was better than I ever dreamed it would be."

"You say that as if it's a bad thing."

Rachel grimaced. "I didn't think I would like it so much."

The shame that flitted over her features made everything clear. Genteel women weren't supposed to lust. En masse, they shunned bodily stirrings in the name of purity.

A fallen genteel woman did so one hundred times more.

"You're supposed to like it," Jacob said a little too firmly. He tipped up her face with his index finger. "You're a married woman, Rachel Evans. You are free to filch as many kisses from your husband as you can—and like it."

She blushed then, but it was a bashful blush, not one borne of shame.

They made their way back to the house, stoked the fire, and ate a simple lunch.

Jacob joined Rachel in the kitchen as she dried a plate and stacked it with the others she had washed. "You're quiet, sweet."

"I'm all right. I enjoyed our walk," she added with a smile.

Rachel turned back to the dishes and winced. Her hand gripped the edge of the dry sink and squeezed so tightly, her knuckles blanched.

"What's wrong?"

"Nothing."

"Women don't fist oak for no reason."

Her gaze slid downward and she blushed. "I'm indisposed."

Indisposed... "Ah." Jacob hugged her to him and ran his hand soothingly up and down the length of her back. He drew away enough to see her face. "Are you suffering much?"

Her thin auburn brows knitted together.

He pulled away a little more and covered her lower abdomen with his hand. "Are you hurting?"

Rachel's eyes widened and her lips parted slightly.

Jacob quirked one corner of his mouth. "Not only was I married before, I grew up with five sisters. I know more about women's ablutions and ailments than a man should."

The bashful warmth tinging her cheeks bloomed into a fiery glow.

"I'll fix you a toddy if you'd like."

"I'm fine."

His impugning frown said, 'No, you're not.' He took her hand in his and tugged her along behind him. "Come."

Jacob led her to the sofa that faced the fire. He urged her to sit, then lifted her feet and slid a footstool underneath. Next thing she knew, Rachel was holding a hot toddy in her hand and an even hotter, flannel-wrapped brick to her cramping abdomen. The steam from her cup flushed her cheeks as much as her husband's matter-of-fact attending of such a personal condition.

He lowered himself and sat beside her, apparently aware of her embarrassment and completely unfazed by it. "There is more to marriage than bedding and breeding. Husbands and wives are supposed to take care of each other." He gestured at the stone. "Even with things such as this."

Rachel tasted her drink. The vapors rising up with the steam invigorated her nose, and the liquid itself burned a trail down her throat. Her breath sputtered just shy of a full cough. "What is this?"

"Cider, sugar, and spices mixed with a little brandy."

"A little?"

He shrugged. "More than a little."

"My husband is turning me into a drunkard," she admonished without heat.

His lips twitched and his eyes twinkled. "Your husband is pampering you so you won't poison his food for being an insensitive lout."

Rachel smiled and took another sip. As flames danced and wood crackled, her mood took a melancholic turn. She tilted back her head and looked up at him. "Why did you marry me?"

A crease appeared between Jacob's brows. "Did you not hear my proposal?" His frown grew to include the edges of his mouth. "I certainly blathered on long enough."

"I heard it. But those were only reasons to marry. Why me?"

The vertical line in his brow remained as he studied her. Then it smoothed. He grasped her free hand in his and stroked his thumb over the backs of her knuckles. "Your presence comforts me, Rachel. I know you think yourself inadequate as a wife, but the truth is you are perfect for me. You make me happy. And that is more than many men can say of their spouse."

He released her hand and propped his large booted feet next to hers.

Rachel finished the rest of her drink. As it snaked its way through her body, warming and weighting her limbs, her head listed in the direction of Jacob's shoulder. She gave in and gave him her weight.

He extracted the empty cup from her hands and set it aside.

"I should be doing... something," she said, her speech lingering a bit on the s's.

He squirmed lower to better accommodate her short size. "There's no chore so pressing it can't wait a day, and our friends have seen to it that we won't starve before spring. Rest, wife."

Rachel did as he said and let her eyes drift shut.

As a cozy, tot-induced sleep tugged her under, a sad truth pulsed its way through her heart. She was Jacob's bride, but she wasn't his wife. Not really.

Chapter Twelve

Jacob stood naked from the waist up, eyeing the stack of fabric on the table next to him. "There's a weight limit applied to the wagons, you know."

Rachel took the pencil from between her teeth and jotted down a number—the length of his would-be sleeve, apparently. "Clothes don't weight that much."

"Ha. 'Twasn't you who toted that pile of yardage in from the buckboard."

She cut her eyes at him sideways, making him glad to see that some of her spunk had returned. "We will need practical garments for the trail. You could do with some new shirts, besides."

"What's wrong with the ones I have?"

"They've shrunk from so many washings, and they're threadbare in places." She reached behind him to draw the tape around his torso, and he lifted his arms to accommodate her. "Will you be home for lunch?"

"No. Clarence Bishop needs my help building a shed, and he's as meticulous as a monk. We'll be at it all day."

"He owns the farm to the west?"

"Yes. Clarence and Nettie. You met them at the wedding. Nettie will feed me. She misses it, I think. Mark my words—she'll insist I stay for supper."

Rachel jotted down another number, then measured his neck.

He resisted the urge to make gurgly strangling sounds just to goad her.

As the noose slipped from his skin, she stayed very still and stared at the mound of muscle above his left nipple. Her breath stirred tufts of hair and other parts of him, too. He was about to step back from the intoxicating sensation when, without warning, she aimed her index finger straight out and poked his chest.

"What was that for?"

She snapped to with rounded eyes, like a child caught doing mischief. "Nothing."

If he lived to be a thousand, he would still not completely comprehend the human female.

Jacob turned around so she could measure his back. "I enjoy your hands on me," –and, may his maker smite him, that was the truth– "but I prefer a softer caress."

"Jacob Theodore Evans, you are shameless. Put your shirt back on."

There had been a smile in that scold—he'd heard it.

Jacob turned back around and grinned.

Rachel gasped and stilled her scissors on the brink of disaster. She'd nearly ruined a piece she was cutting out for Jacob's new shirt. How was she supposed to keep her mind on the garment when all she could think about was the man who would wear it? Every time she tried to concentrate, her thoughts drifted to how enticing Jacob's bare chest was, and how wonderful his lips had felt when they'd brushed against hers.

Something landed with a plop on the end of the table. She

jerked and nearly ruined the piece again. *Foolhardy cat.*

Rachel frowned. "You are about to get yourself thrown out, Oliver."

The adolescent calico—one of the barn cats Jacob had rescued and later adopted—studied the tempting spread of cotton, then turned his attention to licking his paw. A few moments later, he launched himself from the table to the sideboard, where he stretched out and watched her through half-closed moss green eyes.

"Some mouser you are. I let you indoors to guard the pantry, and all you do is lie about like a sluggard."

"Cow is approaching her dry off, you know," Rachel went on at his apparent unconcern. "Perhaps the lack of milk will do your hunting ambition some good." Perhaps Jacob would expedite the process and stop spoiling the feline with snacks at milking time.

She folded the shirt parts she'd cut and set them aside.

Oliver flicked his tail lazily and continued squinting at her.

"I'm not sure what to make of this marriage, Oliver," she remarked, snipping along the edge of the last piece. She wasn't sure what to make of her sanity either, discussing such things with a cat. "My husband looks on me with fondness and shows me some affection, but—" *he still hasn't consummated our vows.* Even in the presence of a cat, she wouldn't speak that last part aloud. "According to his proposal, he married me out of convenience, but my mother disagrees. She thinks he's smitten. Charity does, too. But if that's true, then why doesn't he treat me like a real wife?"

Oliver sprang to his feet, his gaze locked on the far corner of the kitchen, his shoulders stock-still, and his haunches shifting restlessly. With powerful feline precision, he launched himself and was gone.

"I'm glad Jacob esteems me," Rachel murmured to an empty room, "but I want him to love me."

She pinned the first seams together, then moved to the fireside chair to do her stitching. A folded paper tied with a length of cornflower blue satin ribbon rested next to her sewing roll. It hadn't been there that morning.

She picked it up. Something narrow and firm was wrapped inside.

Rachel tugged the bow loose and opened the paper carefully. Nestled in the inner fold was a pair of carved wooden hair pins with a cluster of roses and rosebuds decorating the curved ends.

Familiar penmanship covered the interior of the paper they were wrapped in—the same bold hand she'd seen in Jacob's ledger. She lifted the note to her nose. His unique scent permeated the fibers, reminding her of a forest on a clear spring day.

Dearest Rachel,

You probably think it odd that I would write to you when I am only away for the day. Perhaps it is, but it isn't foolish. Your happiness is important to me.

I wed you in haste because I wanted you settled and safe in my home before the worst of winter, but I fear that haste is to blame for our rather awkward beginning. It can't have been easy for you to move into a house filled with my late wife's things, yet you've handled it gracefully, while I have not, and for that I apologize.

I want to make things right. We never properly courted, but I hope to do that now, even though we are already wed.

Do you think that is silly? Are you laughing at me, Rachel?

No. No, she was not.

We married for practical reasons, as people often do, but I am not without affection for you. You are beautiful to me, and I miss you when we are apart. I hope you will accept these hairpins I made for you and think of this each time you wear them.

Yours faithfully,
Jacob

Rachel sniffed the note again and clutched it to her chest. Smiling, she bounded up the stairs to her room. She tucked the paper into one of the dressing table drawers, then made use of the mirror to apply the hairpins. Not only had Jacob done a wonderful job carving them, he'd chosen wood of a color that complemented her hair.

Taking the stairs nearly as fast as she had going up, she hurried to down to his office to use his pen and paper. He wouldn't be home for hours, but she wanted plenty of time to choose her words, and time to choose the best place to leave the letter containing her reply.

Dearest Jacob,
I did not laugh at your letter, not at all. On the contrary, your kind words brightened my morning. Thank you for the beautiful hairpins. I shall treasure them always.
My heart is full of so many things I want to say to you. I–

Rachel's hand halted. Did she love him?

Yes, she did. Perhaps not ardently, like a spouse of many years, but her feelings for Jacob had grown beyond simple affinity and girlish infatuation. Her true dilemma was whether she should tell him.

She rolled the pen between her fingers and pondered the choice.

Not yet. She loved Jacob, but that was beside the point. He hadn't made the same declaration. Doing it first carried too great a risk. What if he didn't feel the same way? She was ruined, after all. He might *never* feel the same way.

I…

I harbor a deep fondness for you, and your happiness is important to me also. Would you think less of me if I told you that, when we're apart, I conjure handsome images of you to the point of distraction? I hope that is not wrong of a wife. If it is, I shall be plagued by temptation the rest of my days.

I am so thankful we met. Your friendship and your chivalrous treatment of me have touched me profoundly. I do not deserve a husband such as you, and I am grateful that, through your mercy, you have seen fit to give me your name.

We may have wed in haste, but I did not make my vows carelessly. I am wholly devoted to you, Jacob, to your home, to your happiness, and to your future.

Truthfully and with much affection,
Rachel

She barely finished the shirt in time without sacrificing the quality of her stitches. Heart fluttering with anticipation, Rachel watched from the washroom as Jacob came through the door, his hat and coat dusted with snow.

He glanced around. "Rachel?" She'd only opened the door a crack.

A pang of guilt prickled, but she didn't respond. She wanted to see his reaction, his candid reaction.

Jacob removed his outerwear, then walked up to the table and fingered the note she'd propped up against his folded shirt. He opened it, and her heart thrummed faster. She could tell which lines he was reading by the expressions on his face.

First he looked a bit relieved, then contented and pleased. Seconds later, a mild flush rose in his cheeks. Her remark about his looks had apparently embarrassed him—but in a good way. Had he known she was present, he'd have preened and strutted around like a rooster.

Jacob's face grew contemplative, with a fine line creasing his masculine brow. His countenance eventually smoothed. He carefully folded the note and tucked it into his pocket.

With a quirk of his lips, he lifted the shirt and inspected it, front and back, then held it to his torso. Seemingly satisfied it would fit, he put it back.

As soon as the door to his office closed, Rachel hurried into the kitchen.

Jacob returned a few minutes later. "There you are."

"You're home." She smiled, probably a little too brightly.

"Where were you when I arrived?"

"The necessary."

"So was I."

Oh, what a tangled web... "Well, after the cellar. We must've just missed each other."

He grunted an acknowledgement. She loved when he did that. It rumbled through his chest and made him sound like a bear.

Jacob grasped both her hands. He lifted them to his lips and kissed her knuckles. "Thank you for the shirt."

"You're welcome. Do you like it?"

"Very much. You sew better than the Widow Clark. And don't tell her I said that."

Rachel giggled. "Are you hungry?"

"No. Nettie insisted I stay for supper, just as I told you she would. She scolded me thoroughly for not bringing you to visit."

"I wish I could have gone. There's just so much to do before spring."

His chest rumbled again. "Make me some coffee while I see to chores."

Night was upon them by the time he returned, and the weather had worsened. They would be housebound for the next few days.

Jacob washed with the water Rachel had heated and left in the basin for him. His back was to her, but he could feel her watching him in the dim light.

"You never wear a nightshirt," she remarked when he joined

her in bed.

"According to your letter, you like the sight of me." Too bad he'd already blown out the lamp. He'd have liked to see her blush.

"Won't you get cold?"

"Not with you next to me."

Frigid, wailing wind swirled around the house and seeped through the cracks. He tugged the quilts higher.

Rachel scooted closer and settled herself the length of his side with her cheek on his biceps. She'd only approached him this way twice in all the days they'd been married, and one of those times had been at his insistence. He wished he knew whether the reason tonight was the note he'd left or the falling temperature.

Jacob dislodged her long enough to wrap his arm around her shoulders, then adjusted the quilts again.

She breathed out a soft sigh and rested her delicate hand on his chest. The flannel of her thick winter gown touching his skin was nearly as soft, and—blizzard be damned—he wanted to peel it off her body and see her without it.

Jacob sighed and shooed the thought away. "The sheriff rode over while I was at Clarence's."

Her head shifted on his shoulder, and she looked up at him. There was just enough moonlight to see the reflection of her eyes and the tip of her narrow nose.

"He said a few citizens of Millhousen had complained of thefts. There've been similar reports in surrounding towns."

"What about Wood Creek."

"There, too, though not in the last few days. Briscoe said to tell you that your parents are all right. Your pa's farm wasn't involved."

That apparently settled her nerves some, but she snuggled closer anyhow. "He'll stop him, right?"

Judging by how much was being taken, it was *them*, not *him*, but Jacob didn't correct her assumption. "Briscoe will try, but he may not be able to. Thieves like that are difficult to catch. Often, they're just drifters who steal and move on."

"What do we do?"

"We're safe for now, thanks to the weather; but when it clears, Clarence and I are going to form small groups with a few of our neighbors and take turns keeping watch. We may not catch him either, but at least we'll scare him off... encourage him to go do his thievin' elsewhere."

Jacob could tell by the way Rachel ducked her head and snuggled even closer, she didn't want him to go.

"I found a buyer," he said to change the subject.

"You did?"

"Mmhm— Clarence's eldest son. He's been working for the railroad, but he wants to settle down and farm. Clarence didn't admit it, but I think he misses him." Jacob grinned. "If I renege, he'll probably kick me off my land to have his boy nearby."

"This is really happening, isn't it," Rachel whispered.

"Yes, it is. Are you having second thoughts about moving west?"

"No."

She stayed quiet, her fingers absently stroking his chest.

Jacob closed his eyes and yielded a bit of his discipline. He was playing with fire, but Rachel's touch left a tingle in its wake, a sensual tenderness that he sorely missed. When the warmth moved downward from his heart to regions less honorable, he covered her hand with his and stilled it.

He turned so he was facing her. "I was pleased by your letter. Your devotion means a great deal to me." The snow was subsiding, giving way to pearly moonlight that illuminated her smile. "You're wrong about one thing, though."

"What?"

"I didn't wed you out of mercy. I think more highly of you than that. Much more highly." He grazed his thumb along her jaw and planted a kiss on her forehead. When he pulled away, she was staring at him.

Her eyes focused on his mouth, and she stretched up until her lips met his. The simple contact touched him deeply. Any intimacy initiated by a woman was a treasure, but from this woman, it was a gift.

Jacob waited to see if Rachel would pull away. She didn't, so he tilted his head and returned the caress. When they'd kissed before, he'd noticed what kinds of contact she liked. He commenced to gently nibbling, and she leaned into him more.

Her hands splayed over his chest, heating his skin and igniting his loins.

Kissing was as far as he would go, but his body had other ideas. Rachel's reluctant, innocent gestures tempted him, and he burned for her. He deserved to burn, but he had to get control of himself.

Jacob slid his hand down her back and held her firm as he flexed his hips to counter some of the pressure. The hardness of her thigh against his groin brought as much agony as it did relief. Holy saints, this marriage would be the death of him.

Rachel's sighs changed to grunts of exertion. She thrashed like a trapped animal and tried to shove herself away.

He released her instantly. "What's wrong?" he rasped as she propelled herself to the other side of the bed. "Did I hurt you?"

She shook her head, her braid disheveled and her chest heaving. Then panic turned to tears.

Jacob gathered his wits. "It's all right," he said as much to himself as to her. "Everything will be all right." He sat up and held his arm out to her. She shook her head again, but he didn't withdraw. "I won't force you, but if you can bear my touch, please, let me hold you."

Rachel stared at him with wary eyes. She moved closer and went haltingly into his embrace as if she didn't trust him. Or perhaps she didn't trust herself. He knew enough of victims to know that—that sometimes their own bodies were their worst enemy of all.

Jacob held Rachel carefully and let her cry. Every sob gouged a piece from his heart, but he endured it because the catharsis was good for her.

"I'm sorry," she snuffled against his chest.

"You have nothing to be sorry for. I should have been gentler with you. I'm sorry I upset you."

He smoothed the loose hairs back from her face. "Kissing you does things to me, Rachel. My body responds to you, as it should. It's something I can't always control. But that doesn't mean I can't control my actions toward you. I won't ever force myself on you, even though, as your husband, I could."

She nodded and dried her eyes.

He reclined against the pillows and nestled her into the crook of his arm. "You can trust that promise. I don't wrestle affections from unwilling females. Where's the prize in that? Some men would call me soft, but I don't comprehend the appeal."

She lay quietly, as she had before, but this time she didn't stroke his chest. She didn't move at all, save to breathe. Rachel wasn't asleep, though. There was too much tension in her limbs.

Jacob relaxed and stared at the ceiling. He'd wait until she dozed off, then he'd slip out of bed and go add another log to the fire.

Rachel's next breath fluttered, and he sensed dampness where her cheek touched his skin. Before he could debate whether he should acknowledge the return of emotion, she whispered something unintelligible.

"Did you say something?"

"You shouldn't have married me." The wealth of sorrow in those five simple words wounded him worse than a million of her tears.

"Why do you say that?"

"You deserve a proper wife. I don't know if I can ever be that for you."

Jacob tugged the quilts up around them, then hugged her and

kissed her crown. "I told you, I chose the lady I wanted. I am still happy with my choice."

Jacob stared out the window of his office at the thick blanket of white that glistened in the moonlight. The quiet stillness of winter was lovely, and it was deceiving. At first, its beauty brings relaxation and pleasant thoughts. But then, as night settles over the land, the air grows bitterly cold and the lack of sound quickly turns depressing.

He picked up the letter he'd written and returned to the warmth of the freshly stoked fire. Rachel finally slept, but he could not.

My precious Rachel,
I harbor a deep fondness for you, too. I also harbor feelings less pure.
I married you because we seemed a good match. I did not misrepresent my feelings on that. Truly, I did not. Your attack has, understandably, left you averse to intimacy with men, and I have vowed to never again sire a child. A marriage of convenience suited us both. You would have the benefit of my protection and chaste affection, and I would have the helpmeet I need. You would never be subjected again to carnal acts, and I would never lose you to childbed. It was perfect, or so I thought.
The problem is that I have grown to care for you much more than I ever dreamed I would. And I burn for you. A little desire is good. I deserve a certain level of torture for what I did to my late wife. But this is my sentence, not yours. If I lose control, you become the punished one. In fact, I fear that you already have, and that is something I never intended.
You have married a murderer, Rachel. A murderer and a selfish, dishonorable man.

Jacob curled his lip in disgust. He crumpled up the letter and lobbed it into the flames. Then he watched as fire consumed his

deepest secrets and aberrant thoughts.
    Some truths weren't meant to be shared.

Chapter Thirteen

Something heavy lay across her waist. The weight of it was suffocating. Her back was braced by a body long and hard, and hot moist breath coated her ear. He had her pinned!

Rachel struggled, but she couldn't get free. "No!" she screamed, ramming an elbow into the ribcage behind her. "Get off me!" She rammed her attacker again and kicked his shins with her heels.

"Huh…?" He lifted up and caught her arm in his huge fist. "It's me. Rachel, it's me."

She jerked her elbow free and scurried away from him, her heart pounding so hard, she feared it would burst.

Jacob. It was Jacob.

He reached for her, but she pulled away.

"Don't!" Even in her frightened, disoriented state, Rachel knew better. If he touched her—if anyone touched her right now—the contact would send her into an uncontrollable panic. "Please," she managed to rasp out in a softer voice, "I'll be all right. Just don't touch me."

Jacob stared at her, distraught as she'd ever seen him, but he raked a hand through his hair and nodded.

Rachel sat there, cowering and shaking. She hated that he

was seeing her like this, and she hated that it made them both feel helpless.

"I need water," she said, though it was barely a truth. "Will you go downstairs and get me a cup of water?"

"Of course."

He quickly complied, and she relaxed a little. She could collect herself better in private, and the errand gave him something to do.

When Jacob returned, he started toward her but stopped short.

Rachel offered a meager smile and held out her hand. She'd calmed enough to take the cup from him.

He handed it to her gingerly and took a step back. "Should I sleep in the other room?"

Rachel considered the violet tint of the semi-darkness. It had to be near dawn. She doubted either of them would sleep again tonight, but she wouldn't send him away. "No. I'm better now." She took a sip of the water to reinforce her words.

Jacob rubbed his palms on the legs of his drawers, then circled the bed and climbed in on his side. Guilt-ridden eyes cut to her from under thick, dark lashes. "I must have rolled over in my sleep. I'm sorry."

"It wasn't that. I had a dream."

"About your attack."

She nodded.

"Do you have them often?"

Not like this. "I still have them sometimes. This one was worse than most."

"You can tell me about it if–"

"That won't help." It never helped. Reliving her nightmares was the worst thing she could do. Rachel took a deep breath and forced her thoughts to something else.

Most of the sweat that coated her skin and saturated the neck of her gown had evaporated into the cold air, but now she had a bone-deep chill. She eased herself under the covers, facing Jacob.

Jacob did the same, leaving a wide space between them. He lay perfectly still, with his arms drawn close and his shoulders folded in. He'd never looked so powerless.

"Talk to me, Jacob."

"What about?"

"About anything. The sound of your voice is soothing to me."

He stared at her for a long moment, his eyes glittering with pearly moonlight. "*She walks in beauty, like the night... Of cloudless climes and starry skies, and all that is best of dark and bright...*"

Rachel closed her eyes as her husband's words wrapped around her like soft wool. She'd never faced the terror of fighting a physical body when waking from one of her nightmares, but she'd also never had someone to comfort her afterward the way Jacob could.

He went quiet when she slid her hand across the sheet and linked her fingers with his, and then he kept reciting verse after verse until she drifted into a peaceful sleep.

Rachel beamed at him. "Merry Christmas." She served his coffee with a kiss to his cheek.

"Merry Christmas to you."

She bustled around the kitchen, gathering breakfast, then took her seat and pointed to a platter filled with odd, round objects covered in crumbs. "These are Scotch eggs. Grandmother Burgess, used to make them every year on Christmas morning, and it became a tradition. I thought they would go well with the ginger cake you requested."

Jacob sniffed the air. Ginger... spices... the slight sulfur of eggs... and sausage, perhaps? "Smells good."

Rachel sipped her coffee and looked over the rim at him. "Will we be able to make the trip?"

The childlike hopefulness in her expression was touching.

She would stoically endure, no matter the answer—that was his Rachel—but she would be crushed if he said no. "I won't know for sure until sunrise, but the weather has cleared enough that the roads should be passable."

Her mouth pinched as if he'd asked her to wait a month to open her gifts, but joy sparkled in her eyes.

Daylight revealed clear skies and tolerable travel conditions.

Rachel hurried up the stairs to change, and Jacob followed shortly behind to do the same. A bashful look flitted across her features when he walked in on her in little more than her chemise and her stays, but she didn't rush to cover up. Bit by bit, they were making progress.

She pointed to the dress she'd laid on the bed, the same pale green one she'd worn at their wedding. "I added some lace. What do you think?"

"I think you'd look good in rags." He winked and she smirked.

Jacob shed his shirt and turned to freshen up at the basin.

Rachel approached him when he turned back around. "Thank you for planning this trip. It's the best gift you could've given me." She took his face in her hands, went up on her toes, and kissed him on the mouth; and he let her, though he didn't join in. Ever since she'd woken frightened from her dream, he'd been sparing with physical contact. All things considered, that was better for both of them.

Rachel slid her arms around his waist and rested her head on his chest.

Partially clothed as they were, he knew he was tempting fate, but he lifted his arms and returned the embrace.

She lingered a while, then looked up at him. Her gaze strayed to his mouth again, followed by her lips. This time, he drew her closer and played an active part, right down to the blasted encouragement of his loins.

Rachel went still. She didn't pull away, but he knew she wanted to.

"It frightens you when my body stirs against yours."

A bit of tension left her spine. "Yes."

"Hm. Then we shall remedy that."

Jacob stepped back so that there was a few inches of space between them. He had no intention of consummating their vows, ever, but he wanted to be able to kiss his wife and hold her close without inducing anxiety.

"The male member is nothing to be feared," he said. "Harm can only come in the way a man uses it, and I have already made promises to you regarding that." He guided her hand to the front of his falls and released her wrist. "Touch me, Rachel. This is a God-given part of me, just as any other."

Rachel hesitated. Then, cautiously, she grazed his arousal with her fingers.

Jacob's eyes fluttered closed. He held perfectly still and did his best to regulate his breathing as she grew bolder and shaped him with her hand. He could do nothing about the way his cock twitched and increased further, so he didn't even try.

Thankfully, and regrettably, Rachel took her hand away. "Are you in pain?"

He was in agony, but only because he refused to act on his body's urges. He looked down at her and hoped lust hadn't obliterated all charity in his expression. "No, it does not hurt."

Jacob gathered his wits and kissed her forehead. "I do believe I made you forget about your parents, Mrs. Evans. I'll help you with your buttons if you'll help me with my necktie."

Jacob leaned closer to Rachel as he guided the buckboard up the path leading to the Emersons' home, so he could be heard. Her ears were buried under a wool scarf and the hood of her cloak. "Your parents will be curious about how we're getting along. Perhaps an affectionate gesture or two in their presence wouldn't go amiss. We're newly wed, after all. We're allowed to skin the knee of decorum." Amid the privacy of home and close relations, Lawrence lopped off its entire leg on occasion. "I promise I won't shame you. Are you willing?"

"I am." She sounded agreeable and somewhat relieved.

Jacob drew them to a stop when they reached the yard and engaged the brake. Boots crunched snow from the direction of the barn, and the curtains in the kitchen window moved. "Look at me," he said. When Rachel turned her face up to his, he cupped it with his hands and planted a chaste kiss on her lips. He pressed a second one to her forehead and smiled at her. "We'll let them think they caught us unaware."

"They're watching?"

"Your mother is peeking out the window, and your father is walking up behind us. Didn't you hear his steps falter just now?"

She shook her head, making her cheeks brush his palms.

Jacob winked at her. "Let's go have Christmas."

As soon as he'd handed Rachel down, Abigail emerged from the house, all smiles, and hurried out to greet them.

Jacob lifted his hat. "Merry Christmas, Mrs. Emerson."

"Merry Christmas to you." She turned to Rachel, her hands clasped tightly at her waist, as if she had to do so to keep from throwing her arms around her daughter. "Merry Christmas."

Rachel initiated what he knew to be a rare hug and held the embrace a good long time. "Merry Christmas, Ma."

Moisture gathered along Abigail's lashes. "I've missed you."

"I've missed you, too."

Lawrence joined the group as the ladies parted. He shook Jacob's hand and clapped him on the shoulder. "Good to see you. The trip was uneventful, I hope."

"It was."

"Rachel, you look well." His eyes skimmed over her just as her mother's had.

"Merry Christmas, Pa." She had a hug for him, too, as well as a kiss for his cheek, and Jacob pretended not to notice the mistiness in Lawrence's eyes.

Lawrence cleared his throat when Rachel released him. "Let's get this wagon unloaded so we can set Goliath before his feed and the two of you before the hearth."

The women filled their arms with parcels and went, happily chattering, into the house while the men gathered what remained.

Jacob stomped the snow from his boots and stepped inside the foyer. The house smelled of cloves and cinnamon and pine. He and Lawrence placed their cargo on a console table in the parlor, and then he went back to unhitch Goliath.

The barn was still an unwelcome place, but the sight of it didn't rip his insides to pieces the way it had before. Jacob dried and groomed his mount and settled him into the stall Lawrence had prepared for him.

He had no sooner joined Lawrence by the parlor fire when Abigail swept into the room, swathed in festive crimson and gold. She'd always looked on him with favor, but today her eyes twinkled and her smile seemed twice as bright.

She handed him one of two steaming cups of coffee on her tray. "I'm glad the weather eased so you and Rachel could come."

"So am I."

Abigail served her husband with equal care and took her leave.

Lawrence watched her go until she'd pulled the double doors completely closed, his eyes glued to her like a besotted youth.

Jacob's lips quirked up. "It appears someone is madly in love with his wife."

Thankfully, Lawrence turned as red as Abigail's dress instead of hurling the nearest heavy object. "I admit it; I'm a goner. And you're a bastard for noticing."

Jacob lifted his cup. "To lovesick fools and the bastards who suffer them."

Lawrence chuckled and gave a half-hearted salute. He took a sip, then cradled his cup in his hands. "I meant what I said to Rachel. She looks better. She's put on weight."

"I insisted on it." –starting the day after their wedding, in fact. He urged her to go back for seconds at every meal and hand-fed her snacks while she was elbow deep in chores. "She'll need the extra pounds to survive the trip."

"Things must be going well for you two. Rachel seems happy."

"It has taken some effort on both our parts, but we're finding our way with each other."

Lawrence settled deeper into his chair and sipped at his coffee.

"I care for Rachel very much," Jacob added. "Her wellbeing and her happiness are important to me."

"I know." A subtle smile played at the corners of Lawrence's lips. "I wouldn't have let you marry her otherwise."

They sipped the strong, aromatic brew in silence for a time, watching flames dance amidst glowing wood, and Jacob's thoughts took a doleful turn.

He envied the Emersons so much, it hurt to look at them sometimes, but he could never let himself fall for another woman the way he had Sarah. It no doubt saddened Lawrence and Abigail that their fertile years had been cut short, but it was also a boon. How freeing it must be to copulate at will without the risk of pregnancy or the fear of losing one's wife to birth. If only a man could be gelded like a horse...

Jacob set his cup aside. "Millhousen has been quiet. What about Wood Creek? Have there been any more thefts?"

"No. None. I spoke to Briscoe yesterday. Not a single crime has been reported in the entire county. He thinks the thieves have moved on."

"That's good. My neighbors and I will keep watch for a while, though, in case they're still holed up from the bout of bad weather."

Lawrence's eyes took on a menacing glint. "I'll be doing the same, and I told the sheriff as much."

Jacob mentioned the pending sale of his farm, and the mood lightened. He and Lawrence dove deep into conversation regarding preparations for the trip until a knock sounded.

One of the doors eased open and Rachel's head poked in. "We'll serve the meal as soon as you're ready."

Lawrence looked at Jacob. "Shall we continue this conversation later?"

"Fine by me."

"To the dining room, then."

They stood by and watched the women fill the table to bursting, then they seated their wives and took their own places.

Rachel glowed with joyful contentment, the likes of which Jacob had only seen when they'd danced, and not to this degree. She joined them in conversation all the way through the meal. His eyes strayed to his beautiful wife so often, he was still working on his second helping of roast goose and dressing when everyone else was done and ready for fruitcake and pie.

Once they'd stuffed themselves on sweets, Lawrence excused himself from the table and invited everyone to gather by the fire and exchange gifts, so Jacob paid a visit to the necessary while the women cleared the table.

Abigail stopped him on his way to the parlor, her eyes brimming with tears. "I haven't seen Rachel truly happy in a long time. Thank you, Jacob."

Before he could respond, she dabbed her eyes and ducked into the kitchen.

Jacob stood in her wake, frozen by emotion just as strong.

Some days, marriage to Rachel felt like an act of incredible selfishness. On others—days like this—it felt like atonement. Precious atonement.

"We're almost done," Rachel said as she entered the hall moments later. "Ma went to get the cider."

Jacob glanced around. He bent down and nibbled at her lips.

She tensed at first, then leaned into him and sighed, allowing their mouths to casually mingle. She tasted of cloves and felt like heaven.

Jacob groaned and pulled himself away.

"Are they watching?"

"No. I just wanted to kiss you. Husbands are allowed to filch kisses, too."

Rachel shot him a look of bashful annoyance, but she left for the kitchen with a broad smile on her face.

Jacob smoothed his shirt and entered the parlor, hoping a smile was the only manifestation he wore.

The women served hot cider that was rich with spices and spiked with peach brandy. Rachel's childlike excitement returned, and Jacob doubted it had anything to do with the effects of the alcohol—she could barely wait to finish hers so she could start handing out her gifts.

He watched with satisfaction and a bit of curiosity. He'd taken her shopping and bought the materials, but he hadn't seen what she'd made from them.

Lawrence set the brown paper wrapping aside and examined a gray knitted scarf. "This is very nice, Rachel."

"Look," Abigail said, holding up hers. "What a beautiful shade of green."

Rachel perched on the chair next to Jacob's and handed him an identical parcel.

He untied it and lifted out a soft wool scarf patterned with three shades of brown. It was a practical gift, but a welcome one. The weather would still be cold when they left for Independence. "I like this very much. Thank you."

"I made this for you, too." She handed him a smaller package this time.

Jacob opened it and found a set of embroidered handkerchiefs. A thin strip of cutwork framed their edges, and the borders were decorated with sheaves of wheat.

Rachel leaned close and looked up at him through her lashes. "They're not as nice as Sarah's, but I tried."

He lifted her hand and kissed the back of it. "They're perfect."

Jacob and Lawrence opened their gifts from Abigail—journals for recording their experiences and a pair of sturdy trousers for each that would stand up to the rigors of the trail.

She rose amid their expressions of gratitude and motioned for Rachel to follow. "Would you excuse us for moment?"

She led her daughter to the far side of the room, and the two of them turned their backs to the men. Though Rachel was shorter, she had the same lithe carriage and graceful curves as her mother.

Jacob drew his eyes away. He tried to respect the intimate exchange, but when Rachel held up an item to examine it, he caught a glimpse of gathered white flannel.

"It will keep you warm at night," he heard Abigail say. "And the gathers allow plenty of room... for later."

For pregnancy.

Guilt spread like an ache through Jacob's chest. Seth was gone. And now, thanks to him and his selfish scheme, Rachel wouldn't be giving them grandchildren either.

Rachel thanked her ma and accepted the gown, but the look on her face when she returned said she was as conflicted as he. It also suggested that she'd make the best of things. At least he and Rachel were of the same mind, albeit for different reasons. After sufficient time had passed, they could intimate that she was barren, and no one would be the wiser.

The four of them sipped cider by the fire and chatted until they'd exhausted at least ten topics of conversation, and Jacob gave up wallowing in miserable fate. There was simply too much to be happy about.

"I miss them already," Rachel said as they pulled away. She was dabbing at tears. He imagined Abigail was, too.

"We'll visit again." Jacob transferred the reins to one hand and put his arm around her narrow shoulders. They were out-of-doors, but there was no one around to see. "What do you think? Did we make a good impression?"

"Pa seemed satisfied, and Ma... Ma smiled the entire time." Her voice faltered on the last few words, and she started blotting her eyes again.

He wondered if she was thinking about the gown.

Jacob drove along silently and gave Rachel time to gain control of her emotions. "Your parents are quite fond of each other," he said as they made the turn that put them on the last leg of the journey home. "How did they meet?"

"Pa never told you the story?"

"No."

"They met when my father's family moved to Ohio. Papa Burgess—my mother's pa—was notorious for turning away suitors. If one of them so much as looked my mother's way without first gaining his consent, he'd shun them on principle. He'd also turn them away if they weren't well enough born. But Pa was determined, and he was willing to be a little devious. So was Ma.

"With some help, they arranged things so Papa Burgess *chose* Pa. To my grandfather and everyone else, my parents' betrothal appeared to be as sensible and advantageous a match as any other; but in truth, it was a love match."

"Really?" That they'd been in love from the start was no surprise, but the rest of the story had him intrigued.

Rachel nodded. "My mother's aunt was a romantic at heart. She knew my mother fancied my father. When her husband discovered the same was true in reverse, they set about making sure the two of them ended up together. It took a few months of dropping hints about what a coveted catch my father was, but—"

"Hints that may have been exaggerated—no disrespect to your father or his lineage."

"You're smarter than you look, Mr. Evans."

"Wench."

Rachel giggled and snuggled closer. "My mother claims she nearly died from waiting and feigning indifference, but in the end, her father fell for it."

Jacob hugged her tight and kissed the top of her head. "I'm glad he did. Otherwise I wouldn't have you."

The buckboard rolled up the long, curved drive toward home. The air was still and peaceful, and the late afternoon sun cast blue-gray shadows across the pristine snow that blanketed everything but the pond. It was the perfect end to a very enjoyable day.

Well, almost. "One of the chickens got loose... Make that two."

"I'll help you catch them."

Jacob set the brake and surveyed the property. Nothing else seemed amiss. "All right. We'll herd them back in, then you can feed them while I milk Cow and see to Goliath."

They fanned out from the wagon and edged toward the pair of wayward fowl in a crouch. Step by careful step, they closed in.

Rachel caught Jacob's eye and gestured her intention to swing around and block them from running past the coop. He nodded his approval. A few steps later, her eyes rounded and her hand clamped over her mouth.

"Rachel?" Jacob hurried to her side.

She was backing away from tainted snow littered with severed chicken heads and splashes of blood.

"Come. Now!" He grabbed her arm and dragged her with him, back to wagon. Jacob snatched his revolver from under the seat of the buckboard, and then he pulled Rachel to relative safety near a stand of leafless trees by the road. "Cover your ears." He stepped out a few paces and fired two shots in the air.

Minutes later, a single report sounded from one of the surrounding farms, then another.

Jacob went back to Rachel. He kept his gun at the ready, but he wrapped his other arm around her shaking body and held her to his side. "Help is on the way. Clarence is coming, and probably Elias. The second shot came from his direction."

"Was it a wolf?"

"No. The cuts are too clean."

"I don't understand. Why would someone kill the chickens?"

"It was thieves. But they're probably gone now. They take what they want and they leave."

"They?"

"The sheriff thinks it's a group of two, maybe three."

Hooves thundered up the slope to their right. Clarence topped the rise, and Elias was coming up fast on his tail.

Jacob waved. "Clarence. Over here." He waited till both men arrived and told them what he'd seen.

Clarence gave a sharp nod and slid his shotgun from its scabbard. "You stay here with your missus. We'll check things out and report back. C'mon Eli."

Once the men had made a wide circle around the house and the barn on horseback, they tied their mounts a safe distance away and began investigating the structures.

Rachel grabbed handfuls of Jacob's coat and clung to him.

"You're safe. I promise, you're safe. I'll kill before I let somebody hurt you."

The waiting was exasperating. So was leaving the dangerous tasks for his neighbors.

"What did you find?" he asked when they returned.

Clarence tipped his hat to Rachel and rested the butt of his shotgun on the toe of his boot. "Best we can tell," he said, scratching his grizzled beard, "they only got your chickens and your eggs. They came up from the back... 't'was why you didn't see the tracks."

"Did they take anything from the barn?"

"They may have walked inside, but nothing's amiss. Your cow is antsy for her milkin', but she's fine."

"And the house?"

"The cellar appeared to be untouched. The house, too. The floors in there are pristine. Not a single boot mark. Well, except for ours. My apologies, Mrs. Evans."

Elias stepped forward, his lean tall frame bent with the same humble curve as his youthful eyes. "Same here, ma'am. Sorry for marking up your floors." He looked to Jacob. "We checked the loft, the washroom—anyplace a man could possibly hide. There's nobody here."

Jacob shook both men's hands. "Thank you for your help."

"Yes, thank you," Rachel added. She had recovered some, but she was still visibly shaken.

"Any time," Elias said.

Clarence shouldered his gun, and the four of them started walking toward the men's horses. "I'll stop by on my way to town tomorrow. If the sheriff hasn't gotten wind of this and made it out here by then, I'll clue him in. Need some eggs?"

"We can manage without."

"What about your wagon? You need help unloading?"

Jacob looked down at Rachel; she shook her head. "No, thank you. We'll do it."

"Suit yourself. Good night, Mrs. Evans."

"Good night."

***

Jacob followed Rachel upstairs. Mud and straw soiled the hem of her lovely dress. He should have sent her indoors and done the chores himself when he saw they weren't going to have enough daylight to change, but she refused to leave his side.

He dipped his fingers into the wash bowl. "The water is frigid. Would you like me to fetch some that's warm?"

"No. This will do."

He turned his back and began removing his own grimy things. The sound of Rachel slipping out of her clothes was a potent temptation. He envied earlier days when she would only change if he was absent from the room.

Water dripped from a squeezed cloth, then Rachel sharply inhaled.

"I'm having second thoughts about my bath," Jacob joked. He slowed his pace so she could finish washing and don her gown before he turned around. It was their nightly pretense, something he did as much for himself as for her. Keeping his baser urges in check was difficult enough without the image of Rachel's naked body branded on his mind.

The dressing table stool creaked—his cue she was done.

Jacob took his turn at the basin in just his drawers while Rachel sat a few feet from him, brushing and braiding her hair. Most nights, he stripped down to nothing and bathed unashamed, even though she could see him from where she sat. Exposing her to his nakedness had helped her grow accustomed to him. In fact, she seemed to enjoy it. He'd caught her admiring his attributes on more than one occasion.

Not tonight, though. Rachel was quiet and withdrawn. As soon as they'd turned the covers back and climbed into bed, she molded herself to his side.

Jacob held her close and kissed the top of her head.

"Do you think they'll come back?"

"No. They had the entire place to themselves, and all they took was four chickens and some eggs. It was just a group of stranded, hungry men looking for a meal. Now that the weather has cleared, they'll move on."

Rachel relaxed as if she believed his prediction.

Jacob would believe it after several weeks passed without another theft.

The next few days proved uneventful, and Rachel went back to being her busy, independent self. Except she wasn't happy. When a crease of worry wasn't dividing her brow, a mask of sadness overlay her pretty features.

Jacob had been preoccupied as well, but with carnal cravings twisting his thoughts. He had actually caught himself questioning his vow to abstain. He desired Rachel so intensely, he was grasping at anything that might allow him to slake his lust without getting her with child, even though every preventive device and scheme he knew could not be trusted.

Spilling his seed inside her would never be an option. But there were many roads to pleasure, other intimate acts that could benefit them both. Maybe that was what they both needed. It would make her feel like a useful wife, and it would douse the fire that consumed him night and day.

Jacob set his work shirt back down and looked over at Rachel

Her fingers were deftly unfastening the buttons at the top of her gown in pursuit of her morning ablutions.

This time, he didn't turn away. He went to her and drew her into his arms. "Have I told you recently how beautiful you are?"

She smiled a small smile.

"Are you still worried about the thieves?"

"No."

"Then what is it that's upsetting you? Ever since Christmas, you haven't been yourself."

She rested her head against his chest, and he stroked her silky hair. "People will expect us to have children. My parents will expect it. What do we tell them?"

"We have plenty of time before we have to account for ourselves. Common courtesy will protect us even then."

"What if I never get over my fears?"

"Don't browbeat yourself. You have already conquered an entire battalion of them. You've danced with me. You've kissed me. You've even touched me intimately, albeit through my clothes. You have more courage than you think you do."

Jacob nuzzled the spot just beneath her ear. He nibbled a trail down the side of her neck and took over where she'd left off with the buttons. He wouldn't go too far—he couldn't. But he would take her far enough to give her back her smile.

"Jacob—"

"Relax."

Rachel clutched her gown closed and jerked away.

Jacob released her and clenched his jaw. He'd vowed he wouldn't force himself on her. Didn't she trust him?

All the sympathy he felt could not quell the spike of resentment her rejection had rent. His frustration was borne of his own lust—that he could not deny. But it was also borne of his ever-increasing affection for his wife.

"Keep one thing in mind," he bit out. "You were attacked. You were not loved. There is a difference."

Rachel's eyes began to glisten.

"I..." He raked his hand through his hair. How could he explain his outburst without exposing his twisted, arrogant scheme and laying his heart completely bare?

Jacob picked up his shirt and left. He would not retract his words, but neither would he blame Rachel for his own self-castigation. He had willfully—purposely—wed a woman who was likely not capable of anything more than a white marriage, and he had gotten exactly what he chose.

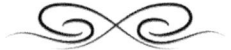

Jacob stayed gone from the house the entire day and felt justified in doing so. Rachel hadn't come down by the time he brought in the milk, so he tucked some day-old biscuits in his pocket and didn't bother returning for breakfast. It was wrong to leave things that way, but he needed time and distance to think and put things in perspective.

He knew he should tell her the truth, but he couldn't bring himself to do it. He'd just have to master his urges and keep his hands and lips to himself. In time, perhaps, his desire for her would wane.

The kitchen was empty when he brought in the evening pails. Rachel had apparently cooked, though. A covered pot sat on the back of the stove, and a pan of cornbread rested next to it.

"Rachel?"

He got no answer.

Jacob searched the house and the cellar, but he still didn't find her.

Her coat was on its hook. Where in creation was his wife?

Snatching his coat from its place next to hers, Jacob hurried out the door to search the property. Goliath was in his stall, and Rachel didn't have a mount. Wherever she'd gone, she would have had to do so on foot. And without adequate garments.

He searched the yard to no avail. Moving at a brisker pace in the dwindling light, he took the path they often walked, the one that went past the graves and the pond. Night was nearly upon them, and the air was bitterly cold. He had to find Rachel soon.

Jacob's heart was in his throat by the time he spotted her sitting on a bench near the place they'd first kissed. Her arms were wrapped around her middle, and her head was bowed. He started to run to her, but forced himself to go slow. He'd already frightened her once today.

Jacob eased closer, hoping she'd see him in the edge of her vision. When she showed no sign of awareness, he called out her name.

Rachel lifted her head.

It felt as if ice cracked and gave way beneath his feet, and—if it meant he'd drown—Jacob wished it had. Rachel's skin was pale except for her eyes and the tip of her dainty nose. Judging by wide streaks of tears and the puffy, red lids, she'd been crying a long time.

Before he could move closer to console her, she rose.

Rachel shuddered out a breath and wiped the tears from her eyes. "I'm–" Her chest fluttered, but she quickly got her breathing back under control. "I'm n– not the kind of wife you deserve. But that's okay," she added with a tremulous smile. "We never c– consummated our vows. You can have the m– marriage annulled." She swiped at her eyes again. "You can have it annulled, and you'll be f– free to choose someone else."

Jacob winced from self-loathing so strong it took the form of physical pain. "I don't want someone else."

"Yes, you do. You w– will. I'll talk to my father. I'll m– make him understand. He's a man of his word. If you help him, he'll still g– give you half the farm."

He shook his head and started walking in her direction. God help him, what had he done?

Rachel scrunched up her face and stared at his advancing chest as if it were the last place she wanted to be, but Jacob kept going and wrapped his arms around her anyway. "I'm sorry. I'm so very sorry."

She trembled as though she was crying, but she wasn't. She was shivering.

Jacob cupped his hands on either side of Rachel's face and looked into her bleak, bloodshot eyes. "I don't want someone else."

Fresh tears pooled along the edges of her lids.

"I'm sorry I hurt you, and I don't want anyone else."

Jacob removed his coat and draped it around her shoulders. He guided her back inside and stoked the fire. Her hands were white and her lips were blue. It'd be a miracle if she hadn't caught her death.

He brought Rachel a bowl of stew and ate with her by the fire, but neither one of them was very hungry.

"I'll draw you a bath," he said as he collected the dishes to carry them back to the kitchen.

"That's not necessary."

"Yes it is. I'll give you privacy, but the bath is not up for discussion. You've been sitting by the fire for half an hour, and you're still shivering."

Jacob placed everything she'd need by the tub, filled it with steaming water, and left Rachel to bathe while he waited outside the washroom with a lamp, silently and thoroughly rebuking himself.

Perhaps he *should* seek an annulment—not so *he* could remarry, but so *she* could. The stronger his feelings for Rachel became, the more he wanted for her all the joys of a conventional life. She deserved motherhood, and she deserved to experience conjugal pleasure as her creator intended. So long as she was married to him, those things would never happen. Now he was faced with chaining her to a dismal existence or shaming her publicly by renouncing their vows.

Jacob stood when she emerged in her nightclothes and tried for a pleasant expression, but his heart ached as he lit her up to their room. He'd made a terrible mess of things and doomed the future of a woman who deserved better.

Rachel stood and faced him once she'd brushed and braided her hair. She seemed fairly calm, but her hands clutched folds of her gown the way they had on their wedding night.

She moistened her lips. "I'm willing to try again. I won't push you away this time."

Sweet Rachel. "I wasn't trying to consummate our union this morning."

"You weren't?"

"No. I was simply going to kiss you and touch you in ways I thought you might like. Instead, I made a mess of things and upset you for no reason. I'm sorry, Rachel, truly. I should have explained myself better."

She shifted on the floorboards and rubbed the top of one foot with the other. He'd forgotten her feet were still bare.

"Sit on the bed. I'll get you some socks."

Jacob knelt in front of her and slipped the stockings onto her chilly feet. The outline of her feminine form beneath her worn flannel nightgown sent his thoughts darting to places they shouldn't go. Such as pushing up her skirt and pressing his lips to the shadowy vee at the juncture of her thighs—for her enjoyment, not his.

Perhaps he should. He'd never done it, but he'd heard the sordid tales men shared when liquor was abundant and women were scarce. Genteel folk considered it vulgar. And God help him if the church biddies ever got wind of it. Still, if such an act could help his wife, he'd risk his reputation. He'd risk his very soul.

"Jacob?"

"Are your feet warming?" he asked as though he hadn't been sitting there mute, like some moronic fool.

She smiled. "They are."

Jacob encircled her hips with his arms and rested his cheek on her lap. If he was going to do this, he needed to go about his task carefully, slowly, lest he make her apprehension worse.

Rachel held completely still. Jacob's eyes were closed, but he could picture her sitting there, looking down on him and wondering about his odd behavior. He knew she was about to touch him a full moment before her hands made contact with his hair. Her thighs had softened, and the angle of her body had changed so that she could lift her arms.

Her torso shifted forward even more as she stroked his scalp and curled protectively over him. The gesture was maternal, and he let himself enjoy it. It gave him time to think and gave her a sense of tender domination. She would need that to carry her through what he was about to do.

Jacob turned his face to her lap and planted a kiss on the top of her thigh. He lingered there, soft flannel grazing his lips, her fingers stilling in his hair.

She released him when he sat back on his heels.

Ignoring her puzzled expression, he grasped her calf with both hands and began a gentle massage, starting just above her ankle. Slowly, he worked his way up.

Her brow remained dipped, but she didn't stop him. She also didn't seem to notice that half the hem of her gown was now bunched and resting at the level of her knee.

Jacob pressed a chaste kiss on its cap, then turned his attention to her other calf. As his hands caressed her creamy skin and molded her muscles like dough, he eased the other side of her hem to match the first. This time he planted his kiss just below the ruffle, at the inner side of the bend. Each of his hands grasped the outermost part of a thigh, and, little by little, he massaged farther and edged closer until his forearms were buried under her skirt.

His eyes met hers a breath before understanding dawned—not of what he planned, but the fact that, whatever it was, it was not platonic or in any way paternal.

"Do you trust me?" he asked.

"Yes."

"Then trust me in this."

Jacob eased the hem of her gown higher and pressed his lips in a languid trail along the top of one thigh. He turned his attention to the other, inhaling her sweet, earthy scent and insinuating himself farther and farther between her legs. Soon, the trail he was tracing with his lips ran along the tender insides.

He nuzzled higher until his nose brushed a tuft of hair. His lips curved upward at her audibly indrawn breath.

Rachel placed a hand on his head, neither pushing him away nor pressing him closer, so Jacob eased apart her thighs with his arms and spread her folds with his thumbs. Gently, he nuzzled her again. As he deepened his kiss, she was forced to lean back and plant her other hand behind her to accommodate his advance.

His bulky shoulders braced her thighs wide. She couldn't close them if she wanted to.

Rachel's body began to fill with anxious tension. If he could just keep her relaxed a little longer...

Jacob lifted his head enough to be heard. "Count."

"What?"

"Count. Count to ten." He paused until she said, "One," and then he lowered his head.

By five, her voice had turned breathy. By eight, her words had dissolved into soft mews, and her body had yielded to him.

Jacob closed his eyes and let Rachel's responses guide him. He was keenly aware of his own body's response to this most lurid of acts, the way her musky scent snaked its way through his limbs and heated his veins like whiskey, but he ignored the rising pressure in his trousers and kept his mind on Rachel's body, her needs. Soon the tension building in her frame was the kind he'd endeavored all along.

Her legs twitched. Her hips squirmed and tried to rise.

He held her firm and kept stroking her hot velvety skin with his tongue. He drew the path of it in tighter and tighter, like a lariat being cinched around legs of a captured calf. Her mews turned to moans.

Jacob stayed put and gave her no quarter.

"J– Ja–" Rachel's body bucked against his face, and a throaty cry echoed off the walls.

He softened his touch as her body twitched and her climax faded away. Moments later, they were both breathless and panting. And that was when it struck him—she was sated, but he was not. Rachel's beguiling scent that he was gulping in with every breath had gone from arousing to igniting. No wonder the act was forbidden.

Jacob's loins burned, and his fists curled around folds of her gown tangled with rumpled sheets. He wanted her. *Needed* her. All he could think of was ripping off his clothes and driving himself into her body.

No!

Rachel—he had to keep his focus on Rachel. He couldn't molest her. And neither could he walk away from her. Not yet. He'd brought her mindless pleasure, but now the euphoria was waning. Her rational mind would take back over. And what would it say?

Rachel smoothed a hand against his hair. "Jacob?"

Her breathing had steadied. His was still ragged.

Jacob lifted his head. He straightened up on his knees, wrapped her in his arms, and held her. He filled his lungs with fresh, rose-scented air and willed himself to calm, if only long enough to assure himself he'd done her no harm.

"Are you all right?" he asked once he'd regained enough of his wits to find his voice and use it.

She nodded against his shoulder. "What did you *do?*"

"I…" How in all of heaven and hell would he explain this to an innocent? "I pleasured my wife."

She snuggled closer to him, her soft skin brushing his cheek. "My mother told me what to expect from the marriage bed, but…"

He wanted to draw her onto his lap and tell her more, but lust had returned with a vengeance. If he didn't leave her now–

As gently as he could with pure fire racing through his veins, Jacob pulled himself from her embrace and righted her clothing. He urged her to recline and promptly tucked her in. "I need to go." Bracing himself over her, he leaned down and placed a single kiss above her questioning eyes.

Her gaze raked the length of him, no doubt taking in his distress and the unmistakable bulge of his trousers. "What's wrong?"

"I–" He couldn't stay to explain. If he didn't leave soon, he would lose the control he'd so often *and wrongly* prided himself on. "I have to go. For a while."

She looked as if she would protest, her worried eyes searching his.

"Rachel, I must," he said more kindly, drawing strength from God knew where. "I made a promise to you. Walking away is the only way I know to keep it right now. Please. I'll return to you. But for now, you have to let me go."

She offered a reluctant nod of agreement.

He brushed her cheek with a shaky hand, then took his leave.

Jacob nearly tripped on the rug in his haste to get away. He stumbled from the house and ran out into the frigid night, driven by lust and grief. His groin throbbed, but his heart ached more.

He grabbed the top rail of the paddock with both hands so hard, the pine beam groaned. He clenched his eyes shut and gulped icy lungfuls of air as sharp splinters pierced his flesh. The heady scent of his wife still clung to his face. Her sensuous image was seared on his mind. Together, they surged his need to an excruciating level, but he refused to take himself in hand. A thousand years of carnal torture could never absolve him of what he'd done to Sarah.

Or Rachel. He hadn't killed her, but he'd snuffed out her future.

He was a bastard. He was a selfish bastard and a pitiful excuse for a man.

The frosty night air numbed Jacob's skin, and a trip to the graves doused the rest of his lust. He trudged back to the house, threw a couple of logs on the pile of crumbling embers, and dropped into his chair.

A bottle of whiskey existed somewhere in the depths of the sideboard. A shot or two would numb his mind and soothe his conscience. Jacob rubbed his temples and ignored the bottle's siren call. He knew better. Spirits boasted of solace, but they never led to any good.

In an act of surrender, he laid his head on the back of the chair, stopped wrestling with his demons, and let the dark oblivion of sleep pull him under.

Jacob opened his eyes and blinked. The logs had burned down some, but not all the way. He rubbed the stiffness from his neck. He'd sufficiently warmed himself; he should go up to bed.

As he sat there, gathering the strength to get out of the chair, something niggled the edge of his awareness—a sense that he wasn't alone.

He wasn't.

Rachel stood at the base of the stairs, silently watching him, with the same uncertain expression she'd worn when he left.

Jacob smiled and held out his hand to her.

She padded across the floor in her stocking feet and stopped just short of his chair.

Jacob wiggled his fingers in invitation. "Come sit with me."

Rachel started to wedge in beside him, but he guided her onto his lap. She drew her feet up under her gown and laid her head on his shoulder, the way his sisters used to do when they were girls.

Jacob shook out a wool blanket he kept nearby—the one he'd used on countless nights when it hurt too much to sleep in an empty bed. He tucked it around Rachel and cradled her in his arms. "Are you warm enough?"

"Um-hm." She snuggled deeper into the crook of his neck. Minutes later, her body turned boneless and her breathing deepened.

Jacob propped his feet up on the ottoman and surrendered to sleep again.

Jacob awoke to the scent of roses and the warm weight of his wife on his lap. The fingers of one of her hands were drawing abstract patterns on his chest.

He lifted her hand to his lips and kissed it. "Good morning."

Rachel raised her head and pressed her lips to his stubbled jaw. "Good morning." Just like his, her voice was scratchy from disuse.

"Did you rest well?" he asked as she tucked back into his shoulder.

"I did... once I was with you."

Jacob kissed her hand again. "The same is true for me. Perhaps we should sleep before the fire more often."

She stayed quiet for a time, her fingers tracing patterns and plucking at one of his buttons. "What you did last night... I don't have words to describe it, the way it made me feel."

"I wanted to show you that intimate contact between men and women can be pleasant. Did you enjoy it?"

"Yes." She picked at an imperfection in the fabric of his shirt. "But it seemed you didn't."

"I did because you did, but... It's complicated." Jacob moved his feet off the ottoman and shifted so he could see her face. "It's important to me that you be content. There are ways I can give you pleasure without imposing myself on you. That is one way."

"There are others?"

"Variations of the same thing, yes." He sounded as though he were discussing seeding options instead of lurid acts.

She pondered that for a moment. "What about you...? Are there things I can do to please you?"

"There are."

She looked hopeful. Then the light went out of her eyes. "But it's not the way things are supposed to be between a husband and wife."

"It sometimes is. It can be, if we choose it."

"Is it even proper?"

The church biddies could go hang themselves. "Marriage is honorable, and the bed undefiled."

"It's *defiled* simply because I'm in it."

"Don't." Rachel flinched, and Jacob regretted his sharp tone. "I wish you wouldn't speak that way. I don't blame you for what happened, and I don't view you as ruined."

"Then you're one of few," she muttered.

"I suppose I am."

Jacob shifted Rachel to a more comfortable place on his lap. "Many years ago, my cousin was set upon by a group of drunken men. They overpowered him and did things to him... unnatural things. His body healed, but his mind never did.

"When rumor began to spread, he confided in me. I reassured him that it wasn't his fault, that he was outnumbered and there was nothing he could have done to stop them. Shame ate at him though. He chose a path of self-destruction and numbed his pain with liquor until he had nothing left. Eventually, he took his own life."

"Oh, Jacob. That's awful!"

"It is. He was an innocent victim, yet he wasn't viewed as one. If he'd been treated with mercy instead of ridicule, my cousin might still be alive. He was a kind, intelligent young man. It was a needless and terrible loss."

Rachel had tears in her eyes. "I don't want to die. I want to live. But I want to be a true wife to you."

"You are a true wife to me."

"Jacob..."

Stray hairs littered one side of her beautiful face, and he smoothed them away. "I know your heart wants this. But your body doesn't, and your mind is caught in the war between the two. I want you regardless."

"But–"

"An occasional kiss is enough. I don't need more than that from you."

Her lips tightened into a thin vexed line, then loosened and plumped back up as she sighed. "I still don't understand why you married me?"

He pressed a kiss to her worried brow. "I know something of warring hearts and minds and bodies, too."

Chapter Fourteen

Rachel smiled at the big brown lump that sat on top of the sideboard, weighting a letter. Jacob must've left it there while she was cleaning up from breakfast. She turned the item over in her hand and laughed. It was a carving of a fat brown bear standing on three legs with one paw raised.

> *My darling Rachel,*
>
> *Three days of the New Year have already passed. I had planned to surprise you with a trinket sooner, but my evenings have been monopolized by a lovely lady who enjoys lounging with me by the fire. She keeps me quite distracted.*
>
> *A bear is an odd gift, I suppose, and not very useful. But when I made it, I thought of you... of your strength and all you've overcome*
>
> *You are gentle and loyal and, at the same time, fierce. You are the partner I want by my side when I brave the trail, and you are the one I want to build a new home with in our very own promised land.*
>
> *With respect and much affection,*
> *Jacob*

Rachel read the letter a second time through, then tucked it safely away with the others. She hurried to his office and penned her reply.

My funny, thoughtful Jacob,
I am delighted by the carving. Your choice could not be more perfect.
I've never told you, but the first time we met, the time you walked up behind me in the garden, I feared I'd been cornered by a bear. Your shadow took on that form so thoroughly, I was convinced of my doom. It wasn't until you spoke that I knew you were a man. You'll probably laugh at me the remaining 362 days of this year, maybe longer, but the encounter made such an impression on me, I secretly named you The Bear-man.
I used to think you were fierce. Now I know you are a gentle creature who prefers to tempt ladies away from their chores and lounge near fires.

Your loyal helpmeet and partner in sloth,
Rachel

The floor above her creaked. Jacob was coming.

Rachel barely made it out of his office in time. She snatched the bear off the sideboard and pretended she was still admiring it as he lumbered down the stairs. "Someone's been sneaking about, whittling again."

Jacob held up his big, broad hands. "I still have my thumbs." He wrapped her in an easy embrace. "I have to jot a few things in the ledger before I go out. You?"

"I need to take stock of what we have left in the cellar. Will I see you at lunch?"

"Probably not. I'll be hunting."

She wished he didn't have to go. Jacob had done more than accustom her to his touch. He'd made her crave it. The security of his presence, too. Every time he left the house, she worried. And all through her day, she longed for evening, when she could join him by the fire and nestle herself in his protective embrace.

Rachel nuzzled his chest and filled her nose with his comforting, delectable scent. "I should get to work."

He patted her backside. "Bundle up when you go out. It's cold."

"You're risking more than your thumbs, Mr. Evans."

He grinned. Probably because she was already smiling.

Jacob slid his wayward hand up her back until it spanned the space between her shoulder blades. He braced her waist with the other. "Give me a kiss to carry me through my day."

Rachel gripped handfuls of his hair and pulled his face down to hers. His lips parted at her swift response, and she took full advantage. Rachel sealed her mouth to his and explored it so thoroughly, his whole body responded. Hers, too.

Ever since Jacob had *pleasured* her, as he called it, she could think of nothing else. He'd done so twice more, but with his hand, slipping it under her skirt as they kissed and cuddled by the fire. It brought about the same mind-altering euphoria and banked her desire for a time. But in the end, it only left her wanting.

Jacob tore his mouth away and rested his forehead on hers. "Perish the saints."

The effect her kiss had had on him emboldened her more. Rachel grasped his muscled fundament with both hands and pressed his burgeoning member firmly to her abdomen. "When are you going to teach me to pleasure you, husband?" She swiveled her waist and moved against him to put a razor-sharp tip on her point.

Face flushed and eyes clenched tight, Jacob grabbed her hips and held her still. "Soon," he ground out. "Very soon."

"Good." Rachel patted his backside playfully. "Let me go so I can pack your lunch."

She left him standing in a randy daze and wrapped up a Jacob-size pack of provisions, all the while fighting off a smile. Maybe she'd see him at noontime after all.

Jacob had escaped to his office by the time she was through, so she put on her coat and went to the cellar. By the light of a lamp, she surveyed everything there and made mental note of what they could take on the trip and what they should eat or gift before they left.

Braving the westward trail had been little more than a dream a few months ago. Now they were making lists and gathering supplies. The closer the date of their departure got, the more she acknowledged her fear. Jacob was wise and big and strong, but he was just a man.

The only way she'd make it through was on faith. And dreams. She'd given up on marriage—on ever having children or bearing the touch of a man—yet here she was, working toward those very things. Taking the risky chance that Jacob offered had set her entire dismal future on its end. Moving to California had the potential to do that and more.

Rachel blew out the lamp and closed up the cellar. It was silly, but she missed Jacob already. The barn door stood ajar, so she went to see him off. The ease with which she did so was proof of one more fear she'd overcome.

The first trip into Jacob's barn had been debilitating, even though it wasn't the place she'd been attacked. She was ready to bolt until she'd realized how different it actually was. The structure resembled the one on her father's land, but then, most barns did. What had set her on a course of change was the smell.

When it had first reached her nose, she'd retched, but then she'd swallowed hard and forced herself to stay... to pick out the subtle notes that made it unique. The scents of leather and hay were the same as any barn, but the mix of Jacob's feed was one all its own. So was the oil he used on his tack.

Now, when she went in, she focused on that, and the fact it wasn't the *place* that had harmed her, but an evil monster posing as an ethical man.

Rachel stepped inside. Goliath was still in his stall.

"Jacob?"

He must be inside the tack room in back. She started to go there but paused. Something was off. Something about the smell wasn't right. The room had a faint odor of... liquor. Liquor and tobacco smoke.

A hand shot out of the dark and closed around her arm.

Rachel gasped and struggled to get away.

A face emerged from the shadows. "Hey, pig lady."

"Earl, what are you doing here?"

His ugly, flat face screwed into an angry scowl. "Your mister took the job that should'a been mine and my brother's. Thanks to him and your pigheaded pa, we lost everything. I want res.. rest..."

"Restitution?"

"Yeah, that. I came to git what's mine."

She shuddered at the way he looked at her. This was not the simple, harmless boy she'd known as a child. "Let me go, and I'll get him," she said in the calmest, most convincing voice she could. "We can work things out."

"No."

Rachel wrenched her arm from Earl's grip and spun for the open door. A fist came at her and pain shot through her face. The second man struck her again, knocking her backwards and landing her hard in the dirt.

His familiar form loomed over her. "Hello, Rachel."

Rachel bit back a cry of pure fear. Once again, she was flat of her back, staring into a pair of heartless eyes.

Her lip began to tremble when the man who had raped her three years ago brandished his knife.

"You know the rules," he said as he flicked open the buttons of his falls one by one. "No fighting... No screaming."

She choked on the memory—on his name. Wesley. Wesley Rowe.

He grinned a sick, yellow-tooth grin. "Too bad your husband's such a big man. I'd've loved for him to watch."

The image made her retch.

Tears began to pool in Rachel's eyes. She couldn't go through this a second time, she just couldn't. Her hopes, her dreams—none of it mattered. If living meant being violated again, she'd rather die.

"Earl, help me," Rachel begged. "You're not like him—you're good. I know you are. I've known you all your life. Please, don't let him hurt me."

Earl shook his head. "My life was goin' to shit until I met Wes. He's showin' me I don't have ta live that way. He's helpin' me git what I deserve."

"What about Edgar? He–"

"Enough," Wesley barked. He gestured to Earl. "Keep an eye out, and you can have 'er next."

Rachel glanced around frantically, searching for anything she could use as a weapon. She would fight them off or die trying, but she would *not* be a victim again.

Wesley sauntered up to her, his trousers gaping and his arousal blatantly evident. "You gonna lift your skirts, or am I gonna have to rip them open?"

Her heart pounded and her mind raced. What was she going to do?

Whatever it was, she had to do it soon, before he got on top of her. He was lean, but he was strong, and he was armed.

With trembling hands, Rachel curled her fingers around the dusty fabric of her skirt and began sliding it up.

The monster smiled. "That's my girl. You liked it before, didn't you?"

Rachel fought the urge to vomit and inched her hems higher. By the time she'd tugged them to a level above her knees, he was standing over her legs, a boot on either side.

He lifted his right foot and nudged her ankle. "Spread your legs."

Rachel drew a slow, deep breath. Keeping her gaze locked with his, she bent her knees and dragged her heels toward her, keeping her legs mostly closed.

"C'mon," he said, looking smug. "Don't be shy."

She let her gaze drift down to his hideous appendage. Rachel marshalled her courage. She drew her legs back as if to clear his legs and open her knees, and then she kicked him as hard as she could in the groin.

Wesley coughed and lost his grip on the knife. He grabbed himself with both hands, then stumbled and fell over sideways.

Rachel leapt to her feet and ran for the door. Earl was still watching; he hadn't looked back. She shoved the clueless cretin aside as hard as she could and burst outside.

"Get her!" Wesley rasped. He had barely regained his ability to speak, but if she'd heard him, so had Earl.

Bounding through snow, she ran across the yard toward the house, screaming her husband's name. Someone gave chase. She didn't dare look, but it had to be Earl. He was gaining on her. She could feel it.

"Jacob! Help!"

The back door flew open.

Jacob leapt off the porch and aimed his revolver. "Rachel, duck!"

She dove to the side as a blast rent the air.

A body hit the ground behind her with a thud.

Rachel rolled to her back and sat up. Earl lay motionless in the snow, a knife in his lifeless grip and a circle of red spreading out from the center of his chest.

She clamped a hand over her mouth when a second shot put a hole in his skull. Rachel turned away to see Jacob stalking toward her.

"Are you hurt?"

"No, I'm–" Rachel flinched when another blast sounded.

Jacob grabbed his right shoulder and stumbled backward.

Blood seeped between his fingers.

"No!"

Another shot came, snapping his head back and knocking him down. He didn't move.

"*Jacob*," Rachel cried as she crawled over to him. His shoulder was drenched. His head was bleeding, too.

She shook him. "Wake up." Was he even breathing? She shook harder. "Jacob, wake up!" Rachel got no response. The man who'd given her back her life lay before her, eyes closed and face slack, with blood pouring out of his wounds and staining the snow.

"He can't help you," Wesley's vile voice said from behind her. "You're mine. You've always been mine."

Rachel swiped away her tears and twisted her upper body around. She glared up at him and knew the true meaning of hate.

Reality seeped through her blinding rage. Wesley had exchanged his knife for something more lethal, and her protector was gone.

She scanned the ground for the gun Jacob had dropped when he fell.

"Bad idea. You'll be dead before you can fire the first shot."

Rachel hung her head. She bent and kissed Jacob's cheek, and nearly lost her composure. As she prepared herself to rise and face her fate, her hand brushed over something—his hunting knife. She kissed him once more and whispered, "Thank you." Shedding a ruse of tears she didn't have to fake, Rachel slid the blade from its sheath and secreted it in her skirt.

Wesley Rowe would probably kill her. But she would fight until she drew her last breath, and if she had her way, he would die, too.

"That's enough," he spat. "Get up."

Rachel dried her eyes on the sleeve of her coat and pushed herself to her feet.

Wesley waved his revolver. "Back in the barn."

She stumbled along, going as slow as she dared and staying as far from him as she could. The smell of gunpowder hung in the air, mingled with the tang of blood. She was well acquainted with the odors of shame. Now she could add to that the stench of death.

"Quit stalling." He grabbed her arm and pulled.

Do something. Give yourself time to think.

Rachel dug her heels in. "Was it you who killed the chickens?"

Wesley frowned at her as if she were daft, and then he smiled. "They were tender and juicy, and they screamed when I cut them."

The man was Satan incarnate. She couldn't let him take her back to the barn. Rachel yanked hard against his grip. Her wrist slipped loose, but he still held the sleeve of her coat. She twisted and yanked some more until she peeled completely free of it.

Wesley threw the coat aside.

The ground rumbled with the beat of hooves as she backed away. Clarence must've heard the shots.

Wesley turned toward the sound, and Rachel rallied her wits—this was her chance. She took advantage of the distraction and dug for the knife. With a feral cry, she raised it over her head and charged.

A gun went off before she reached her mark.

Rachel skidded to a stop as Wesley fell. He didn't move.

The rider came closer. It wasn't Clarence. It was Edgar.

Was he one of them?

He stared at her, and then at the carnage. Instead of shooting her, he holstered his gun and dismounted. He picked up Earl's knife, then lifted his brother's body onto the back of his horse and swung himself into the saddle.

Amid the bitter cold and numbing silence, Edgar met her gaze. His bleak green eyes weren't the eyes of a lawless man. They were clouded with pain and shadows of what could have been.

"Go," she said, her voice shaky, but her words rock solid. "Don't get caught up in this."

Silently, he turned his mount and rode away.

Rachel looked down at Wesley's body. He had done more than

lie and rape and steal. He had taken lives and left others in ruin.

She collapsed on top of him and plunged the knife into his bloody chest. "I hate you!" she roared. She yanked the blade free and stabbed him again. "I hate you!" She stabbed him over and over until she couldn't lift her arms anymore.

Oh God, she was going to be sick.

Rachel scrambled off him and retched into the snow. She heaved until her throat was raw and her stomach was empty.

Leaving a trail of bloody handprints, she crawled back to where Jacob lay. Dark lashes fanned across death-white cheeks in a peaceful likeness of sleep. She started to touch his face but drew back her hand, refusing to taint his skin with his murderer's blood.

Hot tears ran down her face. "I'm so very sorry."

Rachel curled up next to Jacob's side and wished she were dead.

A few hours in the snow, and she would be.

Chapter Fifteen

"Dear God."

Boots crunched across the yard.

A hand shook her shoulder. "Mrs. Evans?"

Rachel clawed her way up from the depths of grief and opened her eyes. *Clarence.*

"Thank the Almighty. You're alive."

Clarence helped her to sit. "Sweet mother of– Where are you hurt?"

"I'm not."

His eyes roamed over her person. "You *must* be."

Rachel stared down at her clothes. Wesley's blood coated her hands and spattered her apron. Her stomach rebelled again.

She swallowed hard. "The blood isn't mine."

He reached for the left side of her face. She flinched back.

Clarence frowned and withdrew his hand. "Your cheek's red." He fished for his handkerchief, then packed it with a glob of snow and offered it to her. "This'll help with the swelling."

Rachel took it from him. She flinched again when the hard ball made contact with the place Rowe had struck her.

Her whole body trembled. "Jacob's shot. He– he's dead."

Clarence turned his attention to her husband, assessing his wounds and pressing two fingers to his neck. "Jacob." He patted his cheek. "Jacob, wake up." Clarence scooped up handfuls of snow and held it to Jacob's face. "C'mon, you stubborn oaf."

Jacob gasped. His eyes fluttered open, and Rachel choked back a sob.

"That's it," Clarence said, brushing the powdery crystals away. "I knew it would take more than a couple bullets to kill a man like you."

"Rachel!" Jacob thrashed and tried to sit up.

"Settle down," Clarence chided. "She's right here."

Jacob's eyes went wide when he saw her.

"I'm all right," she assured. She wanted to throw her arms around him, but she couldn't. Not until she washed off the blood. Her past had already tarnished her beloved enough.

Clarence looked over his shoulder at Wesley, at the knife still lodged like a paling in his flesh, then turned his keen gray eyes on her. "You did that?"

"He threatened me and shot my husband."

"He picked the wrong woman to cross."

Yes. Her chest shuddered. *He did.*

Elias galloped up and reined his mount to a skidding stop. "What happened!"

"I'm still sorting that out," Clarence replied. "Ride into town and fetch the doctor and the sheriff."

"No doctor," Jacob snapped. He struggled again to sit up.

Clarence tried to push him back down, unsuccessfully. "You're shot."

"I'm fine."

"You probably are, but–"

"I said no doctor!" Now he was trying to get to his feet.

"All right, all right. Stay put. You good with a needle, Mrs. Evans?"

She spoke as best she could through a tight throat and chattering teeth. "Good enough. Yes."

"Very well. Between you, me, and the coals in your fire, we should be able to get him patched up. Bring the lady her coat," he said to Elias, "then go for the sheriff."

Clarence put a staying hand on Jacob as Elias rode away. "Tell me what happened."

"I came out when I heard Rachel scream, and I shot a man who was chasing her. Then..." Jacob touched his shoulder and winced. "I don't remember."

"That's when Jacob was shot," Rachel said, aiming to reveal no more than she absolutely must. "I stabbed the man to make sure he was dead."

"What happened to the other one?"

How could he...? "What other one?"

Clarence pointed to the spot where Earl had fallen. "There's a second patch of blood."

Rachel looked from Jacob to Clarence and thought about Edgar—how he'd saved her, how he'd sacrificed his dreams to look after Earl and their wastrel of a father. Telling what happened might set the law on his trail. She didn't know what to say.

"I'm for justice, Mrs. Evans. Shall I explain the tainted snow to the sheriff or shovel it away before he gets here?"

Earl was lost regardless, but Edgar hadn't turned completely lawless. He deserved a chance to bury his brother and put his life to rights.

"There was a second man," she admitted. "Jacob shot him, too, but... he must've run."

"Do you think he's still a threat?"

"No."

"Fair enough. Let's get you two inside."

Clarence helped her to her feet, then Jacob. Rachel retrieved her husband's revolver and followed the men as they made their way to the house.

"I don't know what good this will do," Clarence grumbled as he steadied Jacob and acted as a human crutch. "If you faint, you'll take us both down."

"I won't faint. I'm fit as a fiddle."

Clarence harrumphed. "You're lucky, is what you are. Lucky the bullet that hit your shoulder went on through. Lucky the other one only grazed your head. And lucky you have such a fearless missus."

"I won't argue with that."

Clarence put Jacob in a wooden chair near the fireplace. He started to ask for hot water and towels, but halted mid-sentence when Rachel turned out her hands and looked down at her rusty skin in dismay. "I'll fetch the things I need, ma'am. Just show me where they are."

Rachel obliged him.

Clarence carried some of the heated water to her tub, blushing as deeply as she at the intimacy of the task. Thankfully, a clean dress already hung in the tiny room. "You go on and wash up while I tend to Jacob. Stitchin'll be the last thing we do. I've gotta stop the bleeding in his shoulder first, and I doubt he'll want you around for that."

Rachel nodded. She closed herself in the washroom and disrobed after Clarence's footsteps trailed away. As she knelt in the shallow water, a bout of weeping overtook her, and she let the tears come.

Jacob had barely escaped death, and it was her fault.

After the rape, she'd arranged things so she needed no one. Isolation was her refuge. All her new, drab garments fastened within her reach. Her corsets closed in front. She'd done it in a desperate, calculated act of self-preservation. Never had Rachel thought her past would wield anything but an arsenal of heinous dreams and private, shameful memories—that it would seek to harm anyone but her. But it had. *He* had.

Wesley Rowe was evil. And his return had revealed a worse truth: so was she.

So many times, she'd lamented her failure to act—to fight—and debated what she should have done differently on that fateful day three years ago. Lashing out and defying Wesley by running this time had felt good, but it had put the man she loved in harm's way and exposed a dark side of her that she'd never wanted to see.

Rachel wrapped herself with her blood-stained arms. She'd mutilated a man who might have still been alive when she'd plunged her blade into his heart. Possessing that much hatred for a fellow human being, no matter his crimes, was both frightening and disgracing.

As her weeping faded and her sorrow turned to resignation and numbness, Rachel picked up the soap and scrubbed her arms. She scrubbed and bathed and rinsed until her skin was white and pure, unlike her heart. Her corset bore no stigma of her sins either, so she fastened her undergarments back on and covered them with the faded blue house dress.

She paused at the entrance to the main room. She feared Jacob's opinion of her in light of her behavior, but his wellbeing was her main concern.

His hands gripped the arms of the chair, and beads of sweat littered his pale forehead.

Clarence looked up. He smiled, but it was strained. "We're ready for your talents. No doubt, Jacob has had his fill of mine."

The clench of Jacob's jaw eased some.

Clarence laid a knife with a narrow, charred blade on the hearth, next to a liquor bottle and a short glass containing an inch of amber liquid. "I've already cleaned the wounds." He pointed out locations of damage to her when she came closer. "I think one stitch here, at the entrance, and three or four in back will do." He rubbed his chin. "I'm undecided about the one on his head. It's fine now, but scalp wounds can be dubious."

"I'll put a couple there, too." Rachel swayed with a wave of nausea at the thought of piercing her husband's skin. It had to be done, but...

"If this is too much for you, Mrs. Evans," Clarence said gently, "I'm capable of stitchin'. Mine just won't be as neat."

"I can do it." She cut a length of thread and lined the end of it up with the eye of the needle.

Clarence lifted the glass and waggled it in front of Jacob. "Are you sure you don't want this?"

Jacob stared at it, then blinked slowly and shook his head.

"Suit yourself." He set it back down.

Clarence crossed his arms and observed Rachel's first stitch.

Jacob released a slow breath when she tied and cut the string, but he never flinched.

Apparently satisfied with both her technique and the fact she wasn't going to faint, Clarence lowered himself to the hearth. "I hope I didn't cause you any undue worry. At the sound of the first two shots, I lifted my gun to answer, but then I heard a third. I figured it was best not to give myself away. Eli must've parsed it out the same."

"Understood," Jacob said. He stilled when Rachel moved behind him and braced his skin with her hand. "I owe you," he added as she tied off another stitch.

"Nah. That's what neighbors are for." Clarence stood and brushed the wrinkles from the front of his trousers. "I'm gonna go watch for the sheriff. He'll ask what I saw, but I'll send him to you for the rest."

Jacob nodded.

Rachel finished closing and bandaging his wounds, unsure if silence was his way of coping with the pain or an indication that she'd lost his favor. He'd given her an odd perusal when she'd told Clarence her part of the story, and she'd offered Jacob silent entreaty that she'd explain later. Now she faced that moment of truth.

"Can you sit a little longer?" she asked, knowing it was partly to stall. "I'll get some linens so you can lay on the couch."

"No need. I'll sit." Jacob pushed himself up. He stood still, as if marshalling his strength, then walked the few steps to the couch and sat at one end.

"Would you like a fresh shirt?" Rachel asked, desperate for any reprieve.

"No. The sheriff can see me thus." A bit of color had returned to his skin. "Sit with me and tell me what happened—what really happened."

Rachel sat on the opposite end of the couch and clasped her hands in her lap. They had started shaking again.

Jacob frowned mildly. "Do you fear me?"

Yes—not your wrath, but losing your esteem. "No."

He held his hand out to her. "Come closer."

She moved and sat next to him.

"Now tell me, while we still have some privacy."

She focused on his deep blue eyes peering at her from under a lock of dark damp hair. "The first man shot was Earl."

"Earl Grimes?"

Rachel nodded. "He was the one chasing me when I yelled for you."

"I should know that; I saw him. Why don't I remember...?"

She shrugged and gestured to his head.

Jacob sighed. "So who was the other one? It wasn't Edgar—that much I know."

Rachel contemplated lying, but she'd already spoken more falsehoods than a decent person should in a lifetime. On this, the truth would certainly find her out. "The man I stabbed was Wesley Rowe... my rapist."

Jacob's eyes widened the way they had when he'd first noticed she was covered in blood. His nostrils flared, and he opened and closed his fists. He looked pained and furious and sick all at once.

"He—"

"Three years ago. Not today."

Jacob splayed his fingers and pressed his palms to his thighs. He looked as if he wanted to strangle someone, as if he was trying to gain control of both his body and his mind. "You told Clarence I shot him, but I couldn't have, could I?"

Rachel drew a deep breath and shook her head. "When I came out of the cellar, the barn door was standing open, so I went to look for you, to see you off. Instead, I found Wesley and Earl."

Jacob swallowed and grimaced as if his throat burned.

"Wesley hit me. He was going to rape me again, but I fought him and got away. Earl chased me. You shot Earl, then Wesley shot you."

Jacob glared at her. "You took a knife to a man who was armed with a gun?"

"It wasn't exactly like that." Rachel stared down at her hands. Jacob wouldn't turn her in for lying, but he'd shun her for murder. If he didn't already see her as ruined, he would.

She forced herself to look at him. "After you fell, I went to you. Blood was pouring out of your wounds. You were pale, and you didn't appear to be breathing." Her voice wavered. "I thought you were dead."

She paused and collected herself. "While my back was to Wesley, I slipped your hunting knife into the pocket of my skirt. It was the only chance I had. When he tried to force me back into the barn, I could see it in his eyes; he was going to torture me this time. He was going to kill me. I decided I would rather die there, fighting, than let him rape me again."

"Rachel..."

He wouldn't look at her anymore. It hurt, but she pushed on. "I ran at him with the knife, but before I reached him, somebody shot him."

"Who?"

"Edgar."

Clarity took the place of confusion. Sound memory or no, Jacob was putting the pieces together. "Edgar took Earl."

"His body, yes. And his knife."

"I killed him?"

She nodded. "You shot him twice, in the chest and in the head. His skull— I didn't have to get close to him to..." Rachel closed her eyes against the gruesome image. When she opened them, Jacob was staring at her.

"Have I made you regret your choice?"

"No. But once you've had time to think on what I did, you'll regret yours."

She wanted to kiss Jacob, to feel his lips on hers and rest in the safety of his arms one more time before she lost his esteem, but it wasn't to be. "I thought you were dead after Wesley shot you, but you weren't. What if he wasn't dead either? He'd only suffered one shot, and I stabbed him, Jacob, too many times to count. I'm a murderer."

Jacob's face twisted in disgust, and Rachel's heart prepared to split in two. "No you're not," he growled. "The miscreant was probably gone, but he would have died regardless—do you hear me? If I had been conscious, I would have shot him and stabbed him myself, and I would have forbade him aid. I would have watched the bastard bleed."

A sob bubbled up Rachel's throat, and Jacob's countenance softened.

"All killing is not murder, Rachel, and Rowe was already doomed. If not Edgar and you, it would have been a neighbor or a sheriff or a jury and a noose. Some men don't deserve to live."

"You say that now," Rachel murmured, swiping an errant tear from her cheek, "but I fear you will grow to hate me."

"I could never hate you." Jacob wrapped his arm around her and hugged her to his uninjured side. "You were defending yourself against a man who had wronged you, when you thought all was lost. If anything, I hold you in higher regard."

Rachel turned her face into his chest and inhaled the calming scent of his skin. She wanted to weep, but she refused to lose her composure.

"I'm sorry I wasn't able to help you," Jacob murmured, guilt thick in his voice.

"You did help me. If you hadn't stopped Earl... I'm sorry I put you in harm's way, but I didn't know what else to do."

"You did the only thing you could."

Jacob closed his eyes, buffeted by a storm of emotions and paralyzed by regret. Now he would be plagued by nightmares, too. Thoughts of what might have happened to Rachel had she not broken free and run to him made him ill.

His lack of vigilance had placed her in jeopardy, and she'd been forced to do things a woman should never have to do.

Boots clomped up the steps outside and thumped across the porch.

Rachel stiffened and sat up straight.

"If he asks," Jacob whispered before she pulled completely away from him, "tell the sheriff the same thing you told Clarence." He chanced a kiss, pressing his lips to hers gently, tenderly. Jacob lingered a moment, his gaze melded with hers, then he removed his arm from Rachel's shoulders and took hold of her hand.

The sheriff announced himself and entered, and Clarence followed him in.

Stroud came around the couch and stood, facing them. Newly fallen snow dusted his shoulders and filled the creases in his coat. His weathered blue eyes skimmed over them before he spoke. "Jacob..." He inclined his head in turn. "Mrs. Evans."

"Briscoe," Jacob replied. He'd only known Stroud a couple of years, but the sturdy, middle-aged man had policed the entire county since Rachel was small.

She cleared her throat delicately. "Would you like some coffee, Sheriff?"

"No, thank you."

Stroud hung his hat on a finial of the chair Jacob had occupied and took in the two of them again. The wrinkles fanning out from his eyes deepened with the perusal. He gestured to Jacob's bandaged shoulder. "How bad is it?"

"I'll live."

"And what about you, Mrs. Evans?"

"She's fine," Jacob said before Rachel could answer. "Just a bruise to the face." He was determined to shield her from as much interrogation as he possibly could. Briscoe Stroud was as far from biddable as a lawman could get, but he was fair, and he'd show a reasonable amount of respect, so long as he got what he needed.

Stroud took the hint. "Tell me what happened," he said to Jacob.

"Rachel was confronted by two men in the barn. She got away from them and ran. I went out when I heard her cries for help. They were chasing her, so I shot them. One of them got off a couple of shots at me before he died."

Stroud shifted his gaze back and forth between the two of them, then settled it on Rachel. "Is that the way you recall it, too, Mrs. Evans?"

"Yes."

"What happened then?"

"I don't know," Jacob said. "The shot that grazed my head knocked me out."

Rachel glanced at Jacob, and he squeezed her hand. "I thought Jacob was dead, so I took his knife and stabbed the man who shot him. The other one got away."

"That explains the tracks we saw," Clarence interjected.

Stroud glanced at him, then focused on Rachel again. The heat of the fire had begun to melt the snow on his coat, turning the white patches dark. "He didn't shoot at you—the man who got away?"

"He didn't have a gun, only a knife."

Stroud nodded slowly, as if he were mentally digesting her words. "And what about the one with a gun?"

"I waited until he was distracted."

"*He*...? The man you stabbed is Wesley Rowe. As I recall, he worked for your father a few years back."

Clarence's brows rose, and Jacob's blood began to a simmer. Rachel hadn't asked for this—not any of it. She'd been threatened and forced to defend herself. There was no reason to expose her past or shame her with innuendo. Jacob put his arm around her shoulders and glowered at the sheriff.

Stroud didn't miss that hint either. He visibly relented. "Do you know the identity of the man who got away?"

"It was Earl Grimes," Rachel said softly.

"So, Earl had taken up with Rowe?"

"Yes. He told me so."

"What about Edgar?"

She stared at her hands that were clasped in her lap. "He wasn't with them."

Stroud narrowed his eyes at her. "Did they mention the robberies in the area...? Say anything that led you to believe they were involved?"

Rachel lifted her head and glared at him so hotly, it melted the last of the show on his coat. "Wesley Rowe said our chickens were tender and juicy, and that they screamed when he cut them."

Clarence muttered something under his breath, and for the first time, Stroud wore an expression that wasn't suspicious or brooding. His eyes softened, and he grimaced in comprehension.

"No more questions," Jacob bit out, silently cursing Rowe and cheering Rachel's bravado. "My wife has been through enough."

Stroud reached for his hat and eyed the snow coming down thick outside the window. "I sent some men to see if they could pick up a trail, but they probably won't have any luck. Your neighbors have agreed to take turns keeping watch over your place and helping with chores until you're back on your feet."

"Got that right," Clarence growled.

Jacob blew out a breath and nodded.

Stroud shifted his attention to Rachel. "Mrs. Evans, I'll tell your parents you're safe, so they won't worry. Is there any other message you'd like me to give them?"

Jacob looked down at her when she didn't answer. "Do you want them to come?"

"No. I'm all right."

Jacob knew better. "Assure the Emersons that Rachel is well, but tell them that once the weather lets up, a visit would be appreciated."

"Will do."

Clarence paused from following Stroud out the door. "Do you need help getting upstairs?"

Jacob had grown weak, but he refused. He wanted Rachel to stay by the fire, but he didn't want to leave her. "I want to stay by the fire for a while."

"Call for me if you change your mind. I'll be, uh... seein' to things outside."

Jacob let go of Rachel long enough to clasp Clarence's arm. "Thank you. For everything."

"You're welcome." He turned compassionate eyes on Rachel. "If you need anything, Mrs. Evans, anything at all, you holler. I'll be here till nightfall, then Elias is gonna keep watch through the night."

"I'll fix you some soup and keep a pot of coffee on the stove for Mr. Guidry." Rachel looked to Jacob briefly. "Do I need to ready the spare room?"

"No, ma'am. Thank you for the offer, but you don't need to do any of that. The men have a makeshift camp set up about a half a mile from here. They'll keep Elias fed and warm. The most you'll see of him is a circle 'round your yard and maybe an occasional snoop through your barn. Speaking of which," Clarence said to Jacob, "what's the state of your cow?"

"She's dry."

Clarence nodded. "Just feed and water, then. Goliath, too."

Rachel sat forward. "Are you sure I can't fix you anything, Mr. Bishop?"

"I'm sure. You just worry about tending Jacob and keeping him in line."

Clarence bid them goodnight, and Jacob closed his eyes as the door pulled to. A low whirring hummed in his ears, and the floor tilted like a vessel at sea.

"Jacob...? Are you all right?" Rachel was staring at him, worry marring her delicate features. She reached out and felt his forehead, then brushed his cheek with her hand.

Tiny bumps had scattered across his skin despite the newly stoked fire. "I'm cold."

Rachel stood and draped the wool blanket around his shoulders. "You need to drink something warm." She brought him a cup of hot cider sweetened with honey.

Lifting his right arm hurt, so he managed with his left. After taking a few sips, he felt better. He must've looked better, too. She left his side long enough to make potato soup.

"I'm not hungry," Jacob said when she placed a steaming, cloth-wrapped bowl in his lap.

"I'm not either, but we need to eat something."

He liked that she'd said *we*. And she was right; they'd both missed lunch.

Rachel sat next to him, sipped her soup gingerly, and listened to the crackling fire as darkness fell. The need to sort through flashes of memory warred with the compulsion to take her into his arms. She stared into the fire as if she were replaying things, too, and he hated it.

Rachel glanced sideways at him. "I should have told Clarence about Earl. Those men went looking for him in vain, and now they're spending the night out in the cold."

"If you had told him about Earl, you'd have had to tell him about Edgar."

She sighed. "I know."

"I worried over it, too," Jacob admitted, "but the new snow likely hid the tracks and put a quick halt to the search. And, truthfully, we men enjoy an excuse to gather around a campfire from time to time."

Rachel looked up at him again, her guilt evident.

"Trust me. The men will keep watch over the farms, but they'll also tell tales and pass around a flask or two. They'll go home in the morning, tired but happy, feeling like sneaky, clever boys and valiant heroes."

Her slender fingers brushed a lock of his hair back from his face and lingered there as her gaze held his. "You're my hero."

Jacob swallowed past the denial that lodged in his throat. He wasn't a hero. He was a selfish, detestable man, and he feared the day she discovered the truth.

Rachel seemed to come back to herself. She withdrew her hand and her open regard. "I'll make up the couch so you can sleep by the fire."

"I don't want to sleep here," he said as she took the empty bowl from him. "I want the comfort of my bed." *And my wife.*

She frowned momentarily, then carried the bowls to the kitchen and washed them.

Jacob pushed himself up off the couch when she returned and tried not to lean on her as they went up the stairs. It was slow going, and he was grateful for the banister.

He fumbled with the buttons of his falls while Rachel retrieved some hot water from the stove. By the time she returned, he was down to his drawers and trapped by his trousers that had fallen into a heap around his ankles.

"I'll help you," she said, setting the basin on the bedside table. She freed him from his shackles, removed his boots, and offered to help him to the chamber pot.

"I can make it." He would damn sure make it, if it killed him.

Rachel bid him sit on the edge of the bed when he returned. She'd changed into her nightgown, but her hair was still up.

He started to take the rag from her when she wrung it out, but then she swabbed his skin with warm, gentle strokes that had him closing his eyes and sighing. He didn't deserve her admiration or her tender ministrations, but he was too tired to do it himself and too pathetically needful to stop her.

Rachel paused when she reached his waist, and color rose in her cheeks.

She would wash every inch of his body if he asked it of her, but he wouldn't. "That's good enough for tonight."

Jacob sat with his back to the headboard and waited for Rachel to brush out her hair. Her fine, auburn tresses fell in waves that reached several inches past her waist and gleamed like polished copper in the lamplight. Her hand made steady passes from the crown of her head downward, and as always, he found himself bewitched by the decidedly feminine act and the crackling slide of the bristles.

The spell was broken when she cursed and threw the brush.

"Rachel?"

"I hate him," she spat. Her shoulders slumped. When she turned around, her eyes were brimming with tears.

Jacob held out a hand to her.

Rachel's face pinched with emotion, but she rose and crossed the room to where he was. "I'm sick to *death* of Wesley Rowe," she gritted out through trembling lips, her hands balled into fists at her sides. "I'm tired of the nightmares and the memories. I hate that I can't be a wife to you—that he came here and hurt you. You don't deserve this, Jacob. I *hate* him. He ruined me—he ruined *everything*."

Jacob tugged her into bed with him and guided her head to his good shoulder. "He's gone now. He can't hurt you anymore." It was only half true, but he soothed her with it anyhow.

"I'm not supposed to hate," she muttered.

"You're human." *And so am I.*

Jacob expected Rachel's rage to turn completely to tears, for her to pour out her grief in a bout of choking sobs. Angry males fought and broke things. Angry females ranted, then crumbled and cried. Instead, she slid her arms around his waist and grew very quiet.

"I'm worried about you," she finally said. "I'm afraid for you to go to sleep."

He shared the same fear. "Talk to me, then."

"What about?"

"Tell me of Oliver's latest antics... or what kind of vegetables you plan to plant in your garden when we get to California. Tell me anything."

She got quiet again and stayed that way for several moments. "You're the bravest man I know. And the kindest. You're big enough to dominate by size and strength alone, and yet your gentleness shows no favoritism and knows no end." Rachel sat up and looked at him, her gaze straying to his bandages, then returning to his eyes. "I thought I'd never marry, and then you came along and..." Her lip trembled again. "I can't believe I almost lost you."

Jacob threaded his fingers into her hair and eased her face closer so he could kiss the dampness from her cheeks. His heart clenched as his lips made contact. He'd almost lost her, too.

The salty taste of her tears and the sweetness of her scent made him want to wrap her in his arms and never let go. He covered her soft face in kisses until their lips met.

Rachel joined in the kiss, her movements tentative and her posture taut and hesitant. Jacob nibbled some more and felt the moment her anxious mind gave way. Her hands slid along the sides of his head, and her fingers tightened around his nape. She explored his mouth so thoroughly, he nigh forgot his pain.

Her lips broke from his, with some effort, it seemed. "You're injured," she said mere inches from his mouth. "I should stop."

Hang his blessed injuries. "It'll keep me from sleeping." This wouldn't be the first time yearning for Rachel had kept him awake nights.

"Are you sure?"

A hungry, thorough kiss was her answer.

When she rose up on her knees, Jacob clasped her about waist with the hand of his uninjured arm and guided her until she straddled his lap and the hem of her gown rucked up to her thighs. The position put her head slightly higher than his, and it felt good to be tilting his face up for a change.

He ran a flattened palm up her side until his thumb grazed the underside of her breast. She didn't withdraw. In fact, she sighed into his mouth.

God's teeth—he needed to see her.

He felt along her chest until he located the placket of her nightgown. The tiny buttons were a poor match for his large fingers. He might've managed otherwise, but he was helpless to open them with only the one hand. "I want to see you," he murmured against her neck.

The lips pressing kisses to his temple went still. Rachel sat back and looked at him.

He hoped the lust in his expression didn't obliterate the sincerity. He plucked at her gown. "I want to take this off, but..." He turned his palm up, then lowered his arm to his side. "Will you remove it for me?"

She hesitated long enough to make him wish he'd never made the request. But, still, he waited. And prayed.

Rachel moistened her lips. The action conveyed her dilemma. It also stoked the smoldering fire in his groin. Her delicate hands lifted and grasped the placket, and his whole body shouted in victory. She loosened the buttons at a timid pace that would have had him knocking her hands aside and taking over, were it not for his vexing impairment and her past.

When she drew the billowing mass of flannel over her head and set it next to them on the bed, his eyes feasted on her bare form, and his heart swelled at her bravery. "Beautiful," he whispered.

She was. She'd been hiding curves behind her stays. Rachel was thin, and she wasn't greatly endowed, but neither did she have the flat, rangy chest of a schoolboy. A randy growl rumbled deep in Jacob's chest. He'd be loosening those damned laces the first chance he got.

Jacob banked his lust when he lifted his eyes and saw nervous uncertainty. Rachel's hand hovered at her waist as if she longed to cover her chest. He brought her fingers to his lips and planted a kiss on her dainty knuckles. "The sight of you pleases me. May I touch you?"

She nodded, her willingness unmistakable, but wariness still lurking in her eyes.

Jacob set her hand aside and slowly lifted his. He moved the column of her hair behind her shoulder first, then let his fingers trail gently across her collar bone and down the side of her breast. Her nipples had already peaked from the coolness of the air. With a light graze of his thumb, the right one responded even more.

After an upward glance to assure himself of Rachel's composure, Jacob placed his hand behind her back and drew her closer. He let his lips trace the same path his hand had, starting at the hollow of her shoulder and moving down until he was close enough to his goal that he could reach it with a slight turn of his head. Dragging his parted lips sideways across her skin, he found her nipple and closed his mouth around it.

She gasped and tried to pull away.

He loosened his hold and rested his cheek on the swell of her breast. "Do you want me to stop?"

"I... No one has ever touched me there before."

Praise the holy saints. "Tell me how you wish to go on. I enjoy touching you and kissing you here, but if you do not like it, I will stop."

She stroked his head, careful to avoid the spot where the bullet had nicked him. "I don't want you to stop."

Jacob praised every last one of the saints as he pressed light kisses to one breast while his hand gently kneaded the other. He made his way back to her nipple and smiled when she clutched him closer instead of pulling away.

"Teach me how to please you," she said on a sigh.

He smiled again and switched breasts, wondering how she'd found the wits to speak. "I will," he said as he closed his mouth around her other nipple.

Passion flared with every kiss and sigh and touch. Rachel's hips began to move, rubbing her delicate folds against his hardness and stimulating them both. Jacob groaned.

He eased them apart and placed her hand on the laces of his drawers. "Untie it, Rachel."

She held her breath and tugged at the string until the bow came undone.

Jacob nudged the fabric aside. He looked into her heated, cautious eyes. "Touch me."

Rachel paused for the briefest of moments, then brushed her fingers over the tip and grasped his shaft with a tentative curl of her fingers.

Jacob closed his eyes at the feel of her touch, skin on skin. He could spend from that alone. He wrapped his hand around hers and stilled her movements. Once the sparks in his bollocks dulled to a manageable roar, he moved her hand with his, showing her the way he liked to be touched.

He let go and watched as Rachel stroked him all on her own. Firmer. Bolder.

Yes, his mind hissed. He clasped his hand over hers and increased the tempo.

Rachel mashed her mouth to his in a hungry, disorganized kiss. "Do it, Jacob, please. Make me your wife."

He groaned, this time at his blasted dilemma. How could he say no?

Ignoring the voice of reason screaming in his head, Jacob tightened his grip and stopped her. Now his cock was screaming at him, too. "Let go and lift up." He levered Rachel's hips and positioned himself at her entrance. He would join with her, just this once, but he would go slow and withdraw.

As he began to slip inside, Rachel tensed. A pained look claimed her features.

Jacob stared at the deepening crease between her brows. The fit was snug but not overly much. He wasn't hurting her. She was battling memories.

"Look at me, Rachel. Open your eyes."

She did, with a tortured curve that weighted her whole face. It weighted his heart, too, but she needed to do this. She needed to make new memories, or the old ones would never give up their brutal domination.

"Look at me. Keep your eyes open." *Remember where you are.* He eased his right hand up her thigh.

Her lids fluttered when he brushed her curls and slipped his thumb between her folds, but she held his gaze. He massaged the spot, gently at first, then increased the pressure as passion took the place of fear. With an almost imperceptible flex of his hips, he encouraged her to resume their incremental joining.

Rachel took the lead. She took him inch by inch until he was gloriously deep in her heat and lunging at the leash of his restraint. After a long moment of stillness he desperately needed, he flexed his hips again and encouraged her to move on him. She rode him with small, even movements for a time, but then the steady stroke of his thumb pushed her pleasure to a point she lost her rhythm. Before long, she was poised half way up his shaft, completely still.

Her eyes drifted closed. Jacob studied her face and the state of her entire body. A sense of satisfaction tempered his lust. Her tremors were borne of passion, and the tension in her muscles, a sign of building pleasure and her body seeking release.

He rolled his hips and continued stroking. He kept his movements easy so as not to jolt her—the last thing he wanted was startle her away from the present and into one of her nightmares—but he was determined to drive her pleasure as high as he possibly could.

Rachel's hands closed over his shoulders, and her head fell forward. Her lips parted. She was close, so close. Jacob flexed his hips a little farther, a little faster. He clenched his jaw to keep from spending and forced his thumb to keep its steady pace.

Her nails dug into his flesh, and he was thankful for the pain.

Let go. Come for me, Rachel. He didn't speak it aloud, lest the simple words have the opposite effect.

Her mouth fell open, releasing a sweet, throaty sound as her muscles clutched him in waves.

Holy mother of— That was Jacob's undoing. He gripped her hip with his hand and bucked upward as a cannonade of pleasure shot through his loins, her body milking each and every explosion. He barely had the presence of mind to grit his teeth and stifle the shout.

He resumed a steady glide of his shaft as his wits returned, drawing out the pleasure of the joining until there wasn't any more to be had. Rachel loosened her grip and slumped against him.

Alarm and self-castigation rang out from all corners of his

mind, but he chose to ignore it. It had taken months for Sarah to conceive. And Rachel might very well be barren. Regardless, she had needed this.

He had needed this.

The ache in his shoulder returned, and a draft grazed the fine layer of sweat that coated both of their bodies. Jacob leaned his head back against the wall until he'd caught his breath. He lifted it up again and wrapped an arm around his precious, brave wife.

She remained boneless and molded to him, thank the Lord.

"I love you, Rachel Elizabeth Evans," he murmured as her breathing eased and their hearts continued to slow.

Her slender arms slid around his torso. With her face buried in the fold of his neck, he couldn't see whether she was smiling or crying.

"I love you, too," she finally replied.

It sounded like a little bit of both.

Jacob hugged her close and pressed a sideways kiss to her cheek. Her arms tightened around him.

He stayed that way until his eyes grew heavy. He'd hold her such as this all night, if it not for his blasted fatigue. Battle and injury stole a man's strength in large measure. Add to that astounding sexual satiety, and even a... a *bear-man* was done for.

Jacob smiled at the thought. He considered growling, but resisted the urge and mentally chuckled instead. She wouldn't have the first clue what he was about; and, damn, if he didn't feel more like purring at the moment.

He settled for a bit of teasing. "Am I to take it that you enjoy sitting on me so much, you plan to stay like this the rest of your days?"

Rachel lifted her head, completely nonplussed, with her hair in a glorious, disheveled muss and a most adorable blush tinting her cheeks.

Jacob feigned a serious bearing—*how*, he did not know—and

let her squirm, just a little. He finally grinned and put the poor girl out of her misery. "I'm joking, sweetling. I'm the one who likes this. You'll be lucky if I let you go."

That earned him a full-blown, fiery flush, and he couldn't help but laugh.

A sudden warmth spread its way through his chest and wrapped around his heart. Rachel hadn't come to him innocent, but she was inexperienced. That made him feel like her first. And he was, in all the ways that mattered.

Jacob cradled her jaw in his hand and kissed her tenderly, nibbling and brushing her lips at a languid pace. The heat around them was fading. He'd need to dress and bundle her soon. But his well-loved wife was finally soft and pliant in his arms, and, mawkish fool that he was, he wanted to savor the moment.

She shivered and pulled away. Tiny bumps dotted her cooling skin, and he silently cursed his selfishness.

Jacob hugged her to him as he tilted his pelvis and withdrew. Rachel's frame stiffened. Her eyes closed, and the rosy tint of her cheeks seeped away.

"Rachel?"

"Am... Am I bleeding?"

What? Jacob lifted her higher and eyed his lap. His groin glistened in the lamplight, but the fluids weren't even tinged pink. "No, there's no blood? Why–" A bolt of panic shot him straight through. "Did I hurt you?"

"No." The word calmed him, some, but her voice had the high, hollow quality of a frightened child.

He searched her eyes. "You can tell me the truth. If I did something to hurt you—if I ever do anything that hurts you, I want you to tell me right away."

"You didn't hurt me."

Then why had she–

Another bolt hit, but it was one of heartache this time. And rage. She must've felt the wet rush of his seed and assumed it was blood.

Holy everlasting God, what had that bastard done to her!

Jacob managed as pleasant an expression as he could with sickening images roaring through his head. He forced his breathing to slow and kept his voice level. "Sexual union shouldn't be painful, and nothing I do should ever make you bleed."

Such frank speech no doubt embarrassed her, but she didn't look away, merely nodded.

Thankfully, the cloth and basin was within reach. Jacob wet the flannel and squeezed out the excess. "Lift up." He cleaned her gently, then dunked the rag again and went to work on himself. He glanced up at her, the blush now on his cheeks. "Male passion, on the other hand, is messy business."

He tossed the rag aside and helped her on with her gown.

Rachel left him long enough to braid her hair and turn out the lamp, then climbed back into bed and nestled herself in the crook of his arm. Her warm breath stirred against his neck. "That was wonderful."

You were wonderful. "Yes, it was." He pressed a kiss to her forehead. "I'm proud of you." *And in awe of you. And so in love with you, I don't know what to do with myself.*

He'd blurted out a declaration of love in the midst of waning passion, and it was the superficial tip of a deep, deep truth. A dangerous, inconvenient, and staggering truth.

He'd fallen in love with his wife.

Lust was a powerful force. Mixed with love, it could bring a man to his knees.

They had barely reached the base of the stairs when sounds alerted Jacob to a wagon pulling into the yard.

Rachel left his side and opened the door.

Abigail came in, her face blanched and her eyes hollow and smudged. Lawrence followed close behind, gaunt and grim. He watched his wife and daughter cling to each other in a prolonged embrace, then wrapped his arms around them both.

Jacob waited quietly and gave the man some space for the sake of dignity. He doubted Lawrence knew he was present. His attention had been trained on Rachel from the moment he crossed the threshold.

Abigail was the first to pay him heed. "Oh, Jacob." She hurried to his side and looked him over. The bandage around his shoulder created a sizable bulge under his shirt. "I've been so worried about you. Should you even be about?"

Jacob smiled and took her hand in both of his. "I'm grieved to know you were troubled on my account. Rachel has taken quite good care of me, and I am on the mend."

Tears glistened in Abigail's eyes. "The sheriff told us what you did. Thank you for protecting Rachel."

He hadn't done near enough, but... "I'd give my life for her."

Lawrence cleared his throat. His eyes were as moist as his wife's. "We're grateful." It seemed he would have said more but cut himself off. The man needed an out.

"Do you need help unhitching your team?" Jacob wasn't sure how *help* would be accomplished, but the query was all that came to mind.

Lawrence regained some composure at that. "Thank you, no. Mr. Bishop met us when we drove up and offered to do it."

"Your team is in good hands, I assure you."

Jacob led Abigail toward the sitting area. "You're cold. Come sit while I stoke the fire." He needed to sit, too, and soon, but he would find the energy necessary to warm his guests.

Lawrence crossed the room with quick strides. "I'll tend the fire."

The urge to argue for form's sake was strong, but Jacob held the words at bay. He inclined his head. "Kind of you. Rachel, would you fix us some coffee?"

"I'll do it," Abigail said before her daughter could answer.

Jacob kept hold of her hand. "Your offer is appreciated, but you are a guest, and you are chilled from your journey. I will not have you taking ill." He also needed for her to see that Rachel was well, and Rachel needed the return to normalcy. "Have you eaten?"

"We had a light meal before we left."

Which meant they'd grabbed a few stale crumbs on the way out the door and had eaten less than that. "You'll join us for something more substantial, then." He looked back over at Rachel who smiled and nodded. Despite the gravity of the occasion, her countenance glowed.

He flashed an adoring smile in response and escorted Abigail to the couch.

Out of courtesy, Jacob remained standing until Lawrence was done building up the fire, but fatigue was a near thing. Lawrence chose to share the couch with his wife, so Jacob lowered himself into his oversized chair and tried not to groan his relief in the process.

The three of them conversed, skirting around the events of the previous day with euphemisms and subtlety.

Abigail's backward glances at Rachel grew so numerous, Jacob took mercy on her and suggested she join her daughter.

As soon as the women were deep in conversation and distracted with preparing the meal, Lawrence moved to the hearth and poked at the fire. "Stroud said Rachel was unharmed except for being struck. Is that true?"

"Rachel said she fought the men and got away before anything untoward happened, and I believe her."

Lawrence blew out a breath. "Thank God. When Stroud told me Wesley Rowe had returned, I could scarcely believe it. If I had known he posed you and Rachel any danger, I would have told you about him." His expression clouded with shame. "I should have told you regardless."

"Rachel told me."

"When?"

"The day I proposed."

"I should have been the one," Lawrence muttered. "I won't blame you if you hate me."

"For what?"

"For deceiving you. Although I didn't set out to. I just..."

"You wanted a future for your daughter, as any father would. I can't fault you for that."

Lawrence stared into the flames for several moments. "I wanted a future for my son, too, but he didn't come to me with his troubles. He just left." When he looked over at Jacob again, sadness and regret were evident, but also anger.

Jacob understood, but he felt no anger of his own. If Seth had left to hunt Rowe, he was probably dead. "He was young and witnessed something no boy should."

Lawrence's nod was weary. "You sound like Abigail."

"Your missus is a keen, insightful woman. As is your daughter."

"Rachel has blossomed under your care. Even so, I expected to find her in a much different state after what she endured yesterday. The fact she is going on as if it were any other day speaks well of you." Humility further weighted Lawrence's features. "Not many men would knowingly take a wife such as Rachel, and fewer still would treat her as well."

Jacob glanced at the ladies, who remained oblivious. "I love Rachel. Though I loathe what she went through for her sake, her past is of no moment to me. And truthfully, though I despise the events of yesterday, too, they allowed her to face her demons and defeat them. Would that we all have the chance."

Such was Lawrence's bearing, if he had held a drink, he would have raised it high. "Would that, indeed."

Chapter Sixteen

"I'm expecting." Every nerve in Rachel's body tingled with triumph and excitement. She'd finally said it.

Jacob looked up from his eggs and blinked. He frowned and stared at her as if she'd turned green and sprouted a head full of horns. "You're with child?"

Her smile broadened. "Yes."

"That's impossible."

His tone landed like fat drops of water on the glowing coals of her joy. Conception was unlikely—Jacob had only joined with her once—but it wasn't *impossible*.

"Are you sure? How do you know?" His tone was demanding, but his skin had started to pale.

Rachel fingered the smooth pewter of her spoon's handle. The blunt interrogation was as hurtful as it was embarrassing. "My monthly indisposition is nearly three weeks late, and... there have been other changes."

"Have you been nauseated?"

"Only twice." Though she could add now to the list.

"What other changes?"

Was he really going to make her list them? Her cheeks began

to heat. "I frequent the necessary, and my..." She gestured at her chest. "Parts of me are unusually sensitive." Her face had gone from warm to flaming.

His had gone gray and grim.

Rachel's mortification quickly turned into disappointment. News of a child was bound to stir mixed feelings in Jacob, but she'd expected him to receive it better than this. "You're not happy."

He finally looked at her with something other than barely restrained vexation. "I'm worried. We'll be leaving for Missouri in less than a month. Life on the trail is hard enough without the complication of pregnancy."

Compli– Rachel swallowed her indignation and her pain. He was right.

Jacob laid his napkin next to his plate and got up from the table. "I'll be hunting most of the day," he said softly. "I'll see you at supper."

Rachel muttered an acknowledgement and let him go. They needed to store up pelts and jerky for the trip, and the time he'd spent recovering had set him back.

She watched him through the window as he strode across the yard. Jacob was right about pregnancy being a hardship on the trip. But there was something else on his mind, something else he wasn't saying.

For the next several days, Rachel immersed herself in travel preparations and tried not to let her emotions get the best of her. Jacob had returned from hunting a bit more solicitous, but no more pleased. Other than encouraging her to eat well and rest, he barely acknowledged she was carrying his child. He'd also stopped showing her any kind of husbandly affection.

She had nestled against his side every night since revealing her news. Jacob didn't turn her away, but he didn't talk to her or kiss the top of head the way he used to.

After a full week of his subtle snubs, she gave up and kept to her side of the bed.

Rachel descended the steps and went to work building up a fire in the firebox. The heat of the stove didn't chase away the morning chill the way it normally did, and how apropos. Icy bitterness was taking root in her marriage, leaving her just as cold.

She straightened up and rubbed at a twinge low in her belly. Now she could add *odd aches* to her list of symptoms. Just to spite her brooding husband, she should scrawl them on a large piece of paper and post it on his forehead.

Rachel served Jacob when he came down for breakfast and sat, eating her meal in silence. She'd given up on making conversation, too. Food was difficult enough to stomach in her condition, and now each bite went down like a lump of damp sawdust. She finally set her fork aside and stopped torturing herself.

Teeth clenched, Rachel rose from the table with her half-full plate. She wanted to hurl it a Jacob's face. She wanted to howl and smash things.

He looked up. "Where are you going?"

"To do my chores."

"Are you ill?"

"No."

"You need to eat."

"I'm not hungry."

He gestured to her chair. "Then sit and keep me company."

"Why?"

His eyes flashed to hers at her sharp tone.

She shouldn't defy him, but she was too hurt and angry to back down. "What difference does it make whether I sit with you or not? You barely speak to me anymore."

Judging by his stricken expression, she'd scored a direct hit, one that was almost as satisfying as throwing the plate. Except she didn't want to fight. She wanted things to be the way they were before.

Jacob drew a measured breath, but not an angry one, the kind one drew when preparing to concede. "Would you please sit?"

Rachel swallowed her pride and lowered herself into the chair.

Jacob laid down his fork, the mundane movement somehow adding to the air of surrender. "I'm sorry if I haven't been myself lately. I lost a wife to childbed and I'm worried."

"I'm not insensitive to your loss, but... You got me with child, and yet you treat me as if I've betrayed you."

He looked truly penitent now. He looked defeated. "I am not angry with you. You are blameless in this."

Jacob left for the barn, fear gripping his heart and self-reproach chewing his gut to shreds. Rachel was blameless, but he was not. He'd known the risks, and he'd lain with her anyway.

Now he would have to treat her with affection—affection she rightly deserved—when his mind was screaming at him to distance himself, to remove every trace of her from his heart. How hopelessly impossible.

Giving birth to his baby could very well kill Rachel, and losing her would destroy him.

Jacob went about his work in a dismal, aching fog. The elation he'd felt over moving west was gone. Some *promised land* it would be. What good was it to possess the whole world if he had no one with whom to share it?

He returned to the house weighted by such regret and self-loathing, he could scarcely lift his feet.

The breakfast dishes had been cleared, but Rachel sat motionless in the same place she'd been when he'd left her three hours ago.

She looked up at him, and his heart broke; for, judging by the raw pain etched into her face, hers was breaking, too.

Had his sullen reaction to her news truly hurt her that much?

Her composure gave way like pebbles falling from a crumbling dam. "I lost the baby."

Jacob went to her side as her quiet weeping turned to sobs. He tugged her up from the chair, gathered her into his arms, and steadied her shaking body against his chest. Her grief tore at his heart, but his soul rejoiced in this cruel, blessed twist of fate.

He guided her to his big chair near the fire and settled her onto his lap. "Shh." He held her close and stroked her back. "It will be all right."

Rachel buried her face against him, and his shirt grew damp with her tears.

"Hush, my love, please. It grieves me to see you so upset."

"I w-wanted this baby so m-much."

"I know you did."

Jacob held her and soothed her until she finally quieted. "Are you certain the pregnancy has come to an end?"

Her cheek nudged chest as she nodded.

He used his next breath to temper a new worry. "Forgive my bluntness, but how heavy is your bleeding?"

"A little more than usual."

"Should I be worried?"

"I don't think so."

"You'll tell me if it worsens or if you feel in any way unwell. Are you hurting?"

"Not that much anymore."

Jacob leaned down and tilted his head to the side, so he could look into her eyes. They were puffy and red, and the sight of it gouged him anew. "Do you want me to send for your mother?"

Rachel released a slow sigh. "No. I'm all right."

"Are you sure?"

"Yes. My parents have had enough bad news."

He couldn't argue with that.

"I need to start lunch," she murmured, though she didn't make a single move to leave his embrace.

"Lunch can wait, and I'll fix it." He propped his feet up and resumed stroking her back and planting an occasional kiss on the top of her head. "You'll stay right where you are for now, and then I'll deposit you onto the couch for the remainder of the day."

And once she was peacefully napping with the aid of a strong toddy, he'd ride to the Bishops' house and seek Nettie's advice on just how worried he should be.

Rachel arranged the last of the flatware and table linens and closed the lid on the chest. Room by room, she and Jacob were packing everything they planned to take with them and separating that from what would be left behind. Her parents were doing the same.

In a matter of days, the four of them would load the wagons and say goodbye to Ohio forever.

Rachel's emotions were already fragile after losing the baby, and now they bounced from excitement to fear and from optimism to utter sadness. Leaving was made worse by the fact Seth was still missing. Her concern for him had become painfully acute in recent weeks, while her parents had dealt with it by hardening their hearts and refusing to speak of him.

She honored their wishes, but she refused to renounce her brother.

Rachel tapped on the doorway to Jacob's office. "Can I help with anything in here?"

He paused from examining the books on the shelf. "I'm almost done."

An open box sat on the corner of his desk. She crossed the room and peered inside. "Are these the things you don't want?"

"Mm-hm. I thought I'd give them to Clarence and Nettie."

Rachel dug through the random baubles and held up a carving

of a plump roasted turkey. Jacob looked over at her, and she raised a brow.

He shrugged. "I was feeling peckish that evening."

Rachel grinned and returned it to the box. She pushed aside some outdated copies of the Farmer's Almanac, and her smile waned. A wooden toy lay in the bottom of the box, a long rod with nobs on both ends and three smooth rings that were loose enough to slide along its length but too small to slip off. She lifted it and examined it in the bright morning light streaming through the windows. It was a rattle.

Jacob looked up again, his smile fading just as quickly.

So many questions filled her mind, Rachel didn't know which one to ask. Whatever she did, she shouldn't presume. "Did you make this?"

His tight expression eased a fraction. "No, my grandfather did."

Rachel ran her fingers over the smooth maple and tipped the toy from end to end, making the rings clack. Had she noticed the tiny bite marks on the nobs earlier, she would have known the answer to her first question. They did, however, guide her second. "Did he make it for you?"

"Yes." Jacob's attention was back on the crate he was filling with books.

"This is well made and still useful. Why are you getting rid of it?"

He packed the next book and the next. "It's just a toy."

"It's a remembrance of your youth and your ancestor, something to be treasured and handed down."

Jacob sighed, and his arranging of the books gained a little force. "We've been over this, Rachel. The wagons can only hold so much. We have to be selective about what we take."

Rachel resisted the urge to roll her eyes. If he was going to be stubborn to the point of ridiculous, so could she. "Very well, then.

I'll leave behind the bear and the hairpins you carved for me and take your rattle instead."

She was prepared for a scathing set down, even a flying book, but Jacob's reaction puzzled her as much as his choice to discard his childhood toy.

He stopped what he was doing and walked over to the window. Standing with his back mostly to her, he stared out over the fallow fields and the barren fruit trees that would soon be budding with new life.

The pit of Rachel's stomach tightened around a sudden weight.

Jacob wasn't focused on the orchard. He was looking in the direction of the graves.

After a silence so long, Rachel nearly lost her mind trying to parse it out, he turned around. The look on his face frightened her more than the sight of his blood in the snow. Whatever he was about to say would hurt. She could see it in his eyes.

"I didn't pack the rattle because we won't be having children."

Rachel bit her lip to keep from arguing—from crying. What purpose could he have for such a choice?

She'd sensed something was amiss when she'd lost the baby—that there was more to his relief than the fact she wouldn't be pregnant on the trail—and now she knew for sure. Her resentment had long festered, and Jacob's shocking admission lanced it wide open.

She tossed the rattle into the box and locked gazes with her husband. "Good. You're finally being honest. Don't stop there."

"What are you talking about?"

"You think I lied to you about Rowe—that I didn't fight him off. You think it was *his* child I lost."

"No, of course not!"

Rachel stood, fists clenched and nerves buzzing from the confrontation. His shock was too real and his retort too sincere for her not to believe him, but there was more to this than losing his first wife. And the only other reason she could fathom hurt so much, she could barely bring herself to speak. "It's because I didn't fight him off the first time, isn't it?"

"Rachel—"

"You claim you don't see me as ruined, but you're loathe to have me bear your offspring."

"That's not true."

"What is it, then? Why don't you want children with me?"

He raked a hand through his hair and dropped his arm to his side. "I told you. I lost Sarah to childbed. I can't go through that again."

Rachel studied everything about the man standing before her—his slumped, submissive posture; his humble expression; his pain-filled blue eyes. He wasn't lying, but he was holding something back. "You speak as though all women die giving birth."

Jacob just stood there.

"Death is always a risk," she pressed, "and I am not blind to your loss, but most women survive the process many times over. So if it is not because of my past, why are you are so averse to having children with me...? Don't you want a family? An heir?"

"I do, but it's not that simple." She started to speak, but he held up a hand. "My reasons have nothing to do with you—I would gladly have you bear my children. The fault lies with me. If I sire your child, there is a significant chance you wouldn't survive the birth."

Jacob stepped closer and cupped her cheek with his hand. "I'll pleasure you as often as you wish and in as many ways as I can, short of joining our bodies, but I won't risk a child. Please, don't ask it of me."

He left the room, and Rachel stood numb in his wake. She didn't know whether to cry or scream.

In the end, she did neither. Jacob had stolen her dream of motherhood as surely as if he was a thief, but he'd also given her something—a small but valuable insight—and she would most certainly use it.

Rachel held her peace and went about the rest of her day. Jacob glanced at her from time to time, probably wondering why she had accepted his dictate without further protest. She hadn't accepted it, but he was firmly planted on this. Changing his mind was going to take time and durable arguments.

The following morning, once enough time had passed that he'd let his guard down, she advanced on the first hill of their battle—the cellar—and fired a subtle warning shot. "It was kind of Nettie to come visit me." She didn't have to add *when I lost the baby*. Nettie had only visited once in recent weeks. "I'd like to give the extra food to her, if that's all right with you."

Jacob's gaze lingered on her a moment, then went back to the items he was packing. "It is. She's certainly fed me enough."

Rachel passed him things as he filled the next crate. "She spoke fondly of Sarah."

Jacob paused and looked at her again.

"Nettie said Sarah had a medical condition that made the baby overly large... that she was thirsty a lot near the end of her pregnancy, and her belly grew rapidly in size."

Jacob's expression shuttered, and he went back to packing. "The esteemed *Doc Bennet* spouted that nonsense to make me feel better. Or maybe it was to make Sarah's friends feel better. Ladies thrive on knowing the reasons for tragedy."

Rachel ignored the jab but stopped handing him things to force him to look at her. "Since when do doctors palliate anything, especially to another male? I haven't known of it." She'd overheard Dr. Bennet tell her father she was as good as dead, and the memory still caused a chill to slither the length of her bones.

For a moment, the barest of sanguine looks flitted across Jacob's miserable face, and then it was gone. "What was he supposed to say? *Don't get another woman with child, lest you kill her?*"

Offended fury had Rachel clenching both fists to keep from throwing a big jar of pickles straight at his insolent maw. Rather than accost him for his brash, blunt speech, she decided to best him at his own game. "Yes. And he would have."

Rachel turned abruptly enough to swish her skirts and stomped up the cellar stairs. Retreat was part of battle, too.

Jacob didn't follow, not right away. He finished packing the cellar, then worked for a while in the yard, glancing occasionally at her through the windows.

She pretended not to see him.

Her anger had turned to hurt and genuine despair. If she couldn't convince Jacob the doctor was right, she faced a future more dismal than the one she had before. Instead of lying in bed each night alone, she'd be lying next to a man who refused to love her fully.

Loneliness was preferable to a life unfulfilled.

Rachel put some leftover soup on the stove to heat and went upstairs to pack the clothes. Her hands stilled at their task when the stairs creaked one by one with heavy, familiar steps.

"Rachel?" Jacob stood just inside the door, looking much more civil than he had in the cellar. "I shouldn't have spoken to you so harshly. I'm sorry."

She set the garment she was folding aside and turned to face him. "I didn't set out to argue either," she admitted in the same apologetic tone.

He walked in and sat on the bed, putting himself in a submissive position to her by virtue of height alone. When she didn't join him, he drew a deep breath and let it out. "Sarah was a petite woman, and she did grow unusually large. She went into labor at the normal time, but her labor was long and hard, especially toward the end. By the second day, she became so exhausted, she stopped complaining of the pain, and it frightened me. Then she lost the ability to push. The baby got stuck and—" Jacob swallowed, hard. "The baby was gone, so the doctor put all his efforts into saving Sarah, but... I killed them, damn it."

Rachel gasped.

"It wasn't some illness, Rachel. It was me—my size is what killed them." He stood, his eyes like twin oceans churning with a rising storm. "It's a vile sickness with me. I choose women—*keep* choosing women—who are too small to birth my spawn."

"Jacob." She took a step toward him, but he backed away, toward the door.

"I'm no better than a murderer."

"Jacob, listen to yourself. You're—"

"I'm right."

"No!"

"For God's sake, look at me." He slapped himself in the chest. "I'm huge. How could I produce anything but a giant?"

Tears gather along the edge of Rachel's lids. "Don't speak like this. You're not to blame."

"Yes I am. Sarah died because of me. The baby was so big, the doctor had to break some of his bones to get him out of her body!" Jacob closed his eyes and cursed. He opened them again, but his gaze was fixed on the bed. "As soon as he did, her blood poured out like a river. He mashed his hand onto her empty belly and kneaded it mercilessly. He– He put his *arm* inside." Jacob cringed. "I couldn't watch anymore. I held Sarah's hand and stared at her face as the life seeped out of her, and there was nothing I could do. Our baby lay broken, the doctor was up to his elbows in blood, and Sarah was dead."

"Jacob..." Rachel's throat closed around the rest of her words. Jacob was a boulder—strong and immovable, yet he stood before her completely broken.

His haunted eyes met hers. "You are my life, Rachel, my peace... my very heart. I can't lose you."

Rachel slid her arms around her husband and held him tight. She pressed her ear to the space over his heart. Its steady beat calmed her, but she would never be the same now that the she knew the horrors he had endured.

Jacob lifted his arms and cocooned her in the sweetest of embraces that was all at once gentle and desperate.

After they'd held each other a while, Rachel took his hand and led him out of the room and down the stairs. They had two nights left in this house, and they would not spend it in the room where his wife died.

The following day, the atmosphere remained amicable but quiet as they packed the last of their belongings and took simple meals. When nightfall came, they bedded down in front of the fire, as they had the night before, and enjoyed the last hours of true privacy they'd have for the next eight months.

Rachel's heart ached for Jacob, for the pain she would inflict, but she owed him the same degree of honesty he'd given her. "I'm excited about tomorrow," she said, tracing random patterns on his chest, "and scared. But I'm glad to be going with you."

He drew her closer and kissed the top of her head. "I feel the same."

"The mountainous Jacob Evans is scared?" she teased. "I don't believe it."

His chest shook with a chuckle. "Contrary to popular illusion, I am not a bear."

"No, but you are my hero."

He kissed her again.

"You're also my savior. You championed me when the world dismissed me as unworthy, and you offered me a future I never expected to have, the chance to realize dreams I'd given up on."

"I wish I could fulfill them all. You deserve a proper marriage and a conventional life."

"So do you."

Jacob sighed.

Rachel rose up on her elbow so she could see his face. "Do you recall the time you fell from the loft?"

His brow dipped slightly. "My back will never forget."

"And the time you tripped and Pa's wagon nearly ran you over? Do you remember that?"

"Of course." He was humoring her, but only just.

"You could have been killed in an instant. Death could befall you in the midst of any number of your daily activities, but you still do them."

"I don't have any choice. The work must get done. How else can we live?"

"Loving each other and raising children is also part of living."

He frowned.

"When you asked me to marry you, I wasn't deluded. I knew it wasn't an offer borne of love. But I *did* believe you offered a real marriage. In all of the practical reasons you gave me, Jacob, you never said we wouldn't share a bed... that we wouldn't have children."

Guilt wilted his stern, strong features. "I didn't mislead you on purpose. I thought you'd prefer a marriage in name only."

"I know. You are too honorable of a man to do anything less. But the fact remains, I want more than your protection and your name." The fear in his beautiful blue eyes touched her, deeply, but she stayed the course. "Please, Jacob. So much has been taken from me. Don't take this from me, too."

She waited for him to argue or yell or look away in disgust, but he just stared at her. "How can you..." He swallowed so hard, it made his throat ripple. "You put flowers on their graves."

Rachel flattened her palm against his chest. "I want to put flowers on your heart. I want to wrap your heart with mine so nothing can ever break it again." She brushed a lock of dark hair from his forehead. "I want to give you children. I want to be a true wife to you."

Tears gathered in his eyes.

"Surely you want this, too—a family, a son to carry on your name and inherit your land."

"I do, but what I want and what is my fate are different things."

"Ah, Jacob. You blame yourself for Sarah's death because it gives you the illusion of control, but an illusion is all it is. She died because of illness, not because of you. We'll all die one day, and the time is not ours to say."

"Then I pray I go first, because losing you would kill me."

There was so much painful honesty in those words, it flayed her heart and warmed it all at once. It also made his motives clear. Whether Jacob realized it or not, fear of risking his heart was what was driving him, not fear of fathering some anomalous child. "Death is not the only thief of happiness. If we stay wed yet refuse to live as husband and wife, we'll grow to hate each other, and that would be worse than death."

He closed his eyes and blew out a breath.

Rachel sensed that victory was near, that Jacob waged a losing inner battle, but she kept quiet. He needed to come willingly to his surrender.

"You're right... You're right." He stared bleakly at the ceiling. "You probably hate me already," he muttered.

"No."

"I'll give you children. I want them, too." He locked gazes with her. "But not yet—not on the trail. It's too dangerous. Promise me, Rachel. At least wait until we get to California."

Rachel answered him with a smile, and then she kissed him passionately and loved him in a way that kept the promise.

Chapter Seventeen

January 1852
Two Years later

Rachel swiped away the mist that coated the inside of her parents' kitchen window. Clearhaven, California was beautiful in winter. When the trees budded and the flowers burst forth again this spring, it would be breathtaking.

The trail west had been long and hard—harder than she'd ever imagined. But the trip had been worth every risk they'd faced and every bone-tired day. The land here was as fertile as her father had said. It would sustain their family for generations.

Her ma sidled up to her and laid a hand on Rachel's round belly. "It won't be long."

"No, it won't." A month at most.

And thank heaven for that. Jacob had built them a spacious house on his half of the property, but he insisted she stay with her mother during the days. The birth and lying-in would take place here, too, if he had his way about it, and he would. She'd given up trying to sway him. These were small concessions to make for her husband's peace of mind.

Her ma held her hand there long enough to feel a good strong kick, then went back to setting the bread to rise. "Jacob seemed a little better this morning, not as fretful as yesterday."

"He frets."

Her ma looked up with a sympathetic set to her eyes. "He has cause."

"I know. I reassure him every chance I get, but..." Rachel threw a hand up in exasperation. It mattered not that every female in her family from her great grandmother down had had easy births. Nothing she said made a difference.

"A good man will fret over his gravid wife until she is safely delivered. We can't change them; we can only encourage them and love them in spite of it. Or maybe because of it. I'd rather have a man who cared than one who didn't."

Rachel raised a brow and tilted her head in concession. "What are they doing today?" she asked, referring to her husband and her pa.

Her ma had switched to chopping venison for stew. "They're riding the fence line. They said they'd be back by lunch, maybe before."

Probably before. Her father's health had taken an unfortunate turn, and he wasn't able to work a full day anymore. He'd sought the advice of several doctors, but they'd been of little help. Some blamed his heart, others blamed his lungs, but none of them had a cure.

While Jacob fretted over her looming labor, Rachel fretted over how many grandchildren her father would live to see.

The chopping stopped. "Did you hear that?"

"What?"

"It sounded like a wagon in the yard. Here." She handed Rachel the knife. "Finish this while I go look."

Rachel wrinkled her nose at the smell, but took over the task.

Curiosity got the better of her, though. She rinsed her hands and walked to the foyer just as her ma was coming back in.

A modestly dressed young woman came in with her. Before introductions could be made, the woman's mouth dropped open. Then it spread into a smile. "You must be Rachel."

"How do you know my name?"

"Rachel," her mother interjected, "this is Rebecca Emerson, Seth's wife."

Rachel's eyes flew to her mother's. "He's here?"

Her ma nodded. "He's stabling his team."

Seth was here. Her brother had finally come home.

Rachel grabbed her crocheted shawl off the hook and wrapped it around her shoulders. That and her calico dress would have to do. She hurried for the door, stopping long enough to hug Rebecca and welcome her to the family. "Forgive me but—"

"Go," Rebecca said with the same sweet smile.

She did. Rachel stood on the porch, her heart filled with joy, and her whole body tingling in anticipation.

Seth rounded the corner of the porch, and Rachel's heart leapt as sharply as the baby in her womb. He truly had come back! And he'd grown up! He was as tall as their father. His shoulders were broad, and muscles shifted beneath his clothes like those of a powerful mountain cat. Was his hair still as blond?

She could barely contain herself as Seth's wide-eyed gaze took her in from her head to her feet. Well, as far down as her belly.

His startled cornflower eyes finally lifted to meet hers. "Rachel?"

The joy in her heart spread across her face in a broad smile. If she weren't so heavy with child and Seth didn't look as though he was about to cry, she would have run at him full speed and captured him in a hug.

Regrettably, she checked the impulse. They both needed to spare their dignity.

His disbelieving eyes skimmed over her again. "You– You look well."

"I am." She glanced down at her burgeoning middle when his gaze wandered there again. "I'm Rachel Evans now. I married two years ago, before we moved west." She clutched the tails of her shawl in one hand and gestured toward the north side of the property with the other. "Jacob and I live in a house on the back half of the land."

Seth lifted his chin in acknowledgement, then shifted on his boots. She wished he would speak.

Rachel smiled at him again. "Welcome home."

The light in his eyes dimmed. "Thank you. But I'm not sure *welcome* is what I am. Ma's greeting was tepid, and she wasn't sure if Pa would even talk to me."

"You showed up out of the blue. Give them time."

Seth sighed. "I will, but I don't know what good it'll do. They hate me."

"No they don't."

"Yes they do. They barely spoke to me after— They blame me, and rightly so."

"No they don't. They blame themselves. I..." Images from the past stole her focus, but she wrestled them aside. She'd waited years for this chance. She continued in a softer voice, but she did continue. "I was in the barn alone because Ma sent me."

"Why would she—"

"Just listen to me. It's not your fault." Rachel led him to a grouping of chairs on the porch and urged him to sit, but he seated her first. She relished the simple touches... the feel of her brother's wrist in her grasp as she tugged him along... his gentle-but-steady hands on her arm and her waist as he lowered her into one of the chairs. The urge to hug him was even stronger, but now she might be the one to fall apart.

Rachel gathered her courage, chained her demons, and fortified herself to tell the story she hadn't spoken aloud to anyone in over two years.

"When Pa went out to call the men to breakfast, they were gone. Their horses, everything, gone. He was surprised they didn't stick around to eat—even checked to make sure they hadn't stolen from us. He finally admitted he was wrong about them and said they must have wanted to get an early start.

"Ma was perturbed because she'd cooked so much food. She started grumbling about how she was going to keep it all from spoiling before it got eaten and told me to find you. Pa didn't object. Both of them thought I'd be perfectly safe or they wouldn't have sent me. You have to believe that, Seth. You know how they are."

She spoke the truth, but it didn't appear to assuage his guilt much.

"I didn't even try to help you," he said.

"Yes you did."

Seth pounded the arm of the chair. "I should have tried harder," he growled. "I should have fought them."

"No." Fresh tears glistened in her eyes as she clasped her hand over his fist. "The man behind you was twice your size, and they both had knives. If you had fought them, they would have killed you."

"Do you wish they had?"

"Killed you?" How could he even think–

He nodded.

"No. Never! I didn't blame you then, and I don't blame you now."

Rachel's eyes closed briefly as the depth of his guilt magnified her pain. "For a while, though," she said, opening them again, "I wished they'd killed me. I thought my life was ruined and I wanted to die. I couldn't get those images out of my mind, no matter how hard I tried." Her voice dwindled to a whisper. "I didn't have to be asleep to have nightmares."

"And seeing me every day didn't help," Seth muttered.

"You're wrong. Having you with me when... Your presence helped me get through it. And then afterward, every time I saw you—"

"You relived the attack."

"No. But *you* did, and I didn't want you to."

Seth's brow creased. Rachel reached out and smoothed it away.

"I left because I thought you'd be better off without me," he said.

"I know. And in a way, I was." She rubbed away another crease. "When you left, it forced me to think of someone other than myself. I realized I was hurting the people around me by giving up. I started eating the next day.

"It hasn't been easy, and I'll never be the same, but I've made my peace with it. I have a man who loves me, and now a child. They give me a reason to keep going when the bad days come."

"Is your husband good to you?"

"Yes. Jacob's very kind, and he's the most patient person I know. He's had to be." She looked up at him through her lashes, heat filling her cheeks. "I'm not always the kind of wife I should be, the kind he deserves."

"You're a fine woman, Rachel. He's lucky to have you."

She didn't feel that way, but... "Jacob tells me the same thing."

"He'd better. And he'd better be good to you."

"He is." Rachel considered telling Seth that Rowe was dead, but that story could wait until later. She patted Seth's hand, then leaned back and pulled her shawl up around her shoulders. "Jacob lost his first wife when she gave birth. His firstborn, too. It was horrible and he still grieves, but it changed the way he views life." An introspective smile drifted across her lips. "We're an odd, broken pair, but we're good for each other."

Seth sat for a moment, looking thoughtful. "We should go inside. It's too cold out here for you." He rose and helped her up.

Before he could offer her his arm, she embraced him and

hugged him tight. "I'm glad you came back."

"Me, too," he murmured, emotion clogging his throat. "I've spent the last five years thinking you were dead."

Rachel drew away, smiling and looking at him through moist eyes. "No. Just learning how to live."

Chapter Eighteen

Seth exchanged a tired smile with his wife as she went about fixing a fresh pot of coffee, her honey-colored hair catching glimmers of lamplight as she moved. They'd only been here a few weeks, and Becca already fit right in as though she'd been a part of his family all her life. "Thank you for taking over the kitchen so Ma could stay with Rachel."

"I don't mind. It helps to have something to do." Truer words were never spoken.

"I hope, for Jacob's sake, Rachel's labor doesn't last much longer." It had started the previous afternoon and continued steadily through the night. All of them had taken it in turns to comfort the very fretful father-to-be.

Becca cut her eyes sideways at Seth, almost flinching. "How is he?"

"Not good." If Rachel didn't have the baby soon...

"Your father's not having an easy time of it either."

No, he was not, and that she'd noticed further showed how attune Becca was to his family. "Pa went to work in his office, so I'm going to sit with Jacob." Seth gave her a peck on the cheek and left to search for his charge.

He found him sitting at the top of the stairs, near the bedroom containing his wife.

At the sound of Rachel crying out in pain, Jacob hunched forward, his elbows on his knees and his hands grabbing fistfuls of hair on either side of his head. Seth wasn't sure whether the trembling giant was going to scream or pray or cry.

Seth paused on the quarter landing, filled with concern for his sister and deeper concern for his brother-in-law. Jacob was wrought with more than the normal anxiety of an expectant father, and he was a huge, tough mountain of a man. That his wife's confinement had reduced him to this... well, it wouldn't do.

"Don't tell anyone," Seth said as he climbed the rest of the way and joined Jacob on the step, "but your child will have a cousin in roughly seven months' time."

The poor brute didn't even lift his head. His fingers tightened. If he didn't let up, he was going to snatch himself bald.

Seth nudged Jacob's shoulder with his own. "What do you think of that?"

"Huh?" Jacob stared at Seth with a haggard look of puzzlement made worse by the cockeyed spikes of hair sticking out from the sides of his head.

For the love of all that is dignified, may I not be reduced to this when Rebecca's time comes. "Cousins," Seth repeated. "In a few months, your child will have a cousin."

"Rebecca's expecting?"

"I think so. She hasn't said anything yet. In fact, I'm not sure she's even aware, what with all she's been through over the last couple of months." He chuckled. "Of course, now that she's settled—and thick as thieves with the Emerson women—she won't be oblivious long."

"Goodness, no." Both men shuddered.

Seth shifted and leaned against the banister. "Becca will want to surprise me, no doubt. I'm holding my tongue. I'd appreciate if you'd do likewise."

"I will." Jacob clapped him on the arm and squeezed. "Congratulations, Seth. I mean that sincerely."

Ouch. Seth resisted the urge to rub the spot. "In a few months, the tables will be turned. You'll be calming *me* as I fret and pace."

"I suppose so."

A lusty little wail came from inside the bedroom.

"Thank the Almighty!" Jacob exclaimed, closing his eyes. Some of the tension abated his massive shoulders.

Jacob cocked his head to the side when the baby's wailing quieted. Several silent minutes passed, and his frame tightened again.

He pushed himself up and crossed the upper landing, turning his ear to the chamber. He eventually flattened his palms and rested his forehead against the door. A bearing so grave came over the man, Jacob could have openly sobbed or smashed the wood to splinters, and neither act would have been a surprise. "Rachel..." he murmured, "say something."

Jacob cursed propriety and threw open the door.

"This is highly improper," the doctor blustered from his perch on the side of the bed.

I don't give a damn. He would have sworn it out loud, were Abigail not in the room, and he would have punched the doctor had Rachel not been properly covered.

Jacob stalked to the head of the bed. The prim fool was blocking his view. "What's wrong with her?"

The doctor stood and jerked the hem of his vest down. Judging by his level of indignation, he'd have shot his cuffs, too, if his sleeves weren't rolled to the elbows. "Nothing is wrong with her. She's the picture of health."

Jacob resisted the urge to growl. Rachel was most certainly *not* the picture of health. Her skin was pale, and her face was deeply shadowed with exhaustion. He turned his back on the charlatan and eased down beside her where she lay half sitting and propped on pillows.

Her eyes fluttered open with the shifting of the mattress. A smile spread across her lips and speared Jacob straight through the heart. "Did you see the baby? You have a son."

A son.

Jacob shook his head. "I heard him, though."

"Is that why you came in?"

"No." He brushed a stray lock of hair from her forehead. "I came in because I didn't hear you."

She blushed, and he was glad to see some color infuse her cheeks. "I made enough noise for the both of us."

No she hadn't. For all her long hours of labor, she'd barely uttered a peep. "I was worried about you, Rachel. I'm sorry if I intruded where I shouldn't have, but I needed to be sure you were all right."

She pushed herself a little higher in bed and smoothed Jacob's hair in a maternal gesture. "I'm glad you're here." She motioned to her mother, who came over to the bed and handed her the baby.

Abigail placed a slender hand on Jacob's shoulder. "Rachel's well, Jacob. Both of them are."

Swallowing around a lump in his throat, he nodded.

"Dr. Strickland," Abigail said with the kind of smile that could calm beasts and end wars, "if you feel Rachel would be safe under the vigilance of her husband for a short while, I'd be grateful if you'd join me in the kitchen for a cup of coffee. You're the most skilled physician I've had the fortune to meet. I'd like to ask your opinion about a few matters, so that I might better care for my daughter in the coming days."

Strickland looked so conflicted, and flattered, Jacob could barely keep from laughing at the blasted fool. "Well..."

"I know it's a bit unconventional," she added, "but I value your knowledge, and I'd be remiss not to offer you some refreshment after the long hours you've spent caring for our family."

The doctor looked from her to them. "I suppose it would be all right." He refastened his cuffs and followed his delicate conqueror out the door.

Winning point to the mother-in-law, lovely woman.

Rachel handed over the tiny bundle.

Jacob stared down at the sleeping infant who barely filled his hands. "Is he all right?"

"He's fine. He's perfect."

Jacob cradled his son closer, and the tender reverence of the moment threatened to cut off his air. He gazed into Rachel's shimmering eyes. "When you finally got the courage to give yourself to me, I thought that was the greatest gift you could ever bestow." He stole another look at the precious, healthy baby in his arms. "I was wrong."

Jacob turned around and seated himself next to her with his back against the headboard and carefully handed the babe back, causing him to ponder how something nigh weightless could leave his arms so bereft. His loss was quickly forgotten. The sight of her holding their child filled his heart to bursting with pride and thanksgiving and love.

Wrapping an arm around Rachel's shoulders, Jacob rested his head on hers and finally let go of his fear.

Rachel ran her index finger lovingly over the infant's face. "What should we name him?"

He'd thought about honoring Seth with a namesake, but news of Lawrence's failing heath had changed that. And considering his immense respect for the man, it was really no contest. "I like Michael Lawrence Evans, for our fathers. Do you like it?"

She traced the infant's face again and tilted her head as if assessing his features. "I do."

"Then Michael Lawrence Evans it is."

A smile flitted across the infant's lips, and Rachel grinned. "He likes it, too."

The baby splayed his hand in an innate wave. Jacob touched his palm and marveled when tiny fingers wrapped around his much larger one. "Seth hopes our Michael will have a cousin to play with next year."

Rachel pursed her lips and didn't respond. She knew something. "Will he?"

"He will. But don't tell Seth. Rebecca wants to surprise him."

"I'll keep her secret. How far along is she?"

"Not far. Barely two months."

Jacob feigned an earnest expression, hoping the devilment in his eyes didn't give him away. "Advise her she should wait a while to tell him, a few more months at least. Wouldn't want to cause the poor fella any unnecessary worry."

The moment Rachel narrowed her eyes at him, he knew he was caught. "Jacob Evans, you are wicked."

"Oh, come now. Seth is a prankster at heart. He'd do it to me without a second thought."

She laughed. "Yes, he would."

"I've been warned that he delights in arranging dead snakes just so and leaving them for unsuspecting victims. But that's all right. I seem to recall a story Rebecca told about field mice."

Rachel rolled her eyes. "Have your fun, but you're in for a thorough thrashing if you teach such antics to our offspring."

Jacob chuckled. Her spunk reassured him of her health, but her comment made him think beyond the present. "In a year or two, we'll be doing this again, won't we?"

"God willing."

God might be willing, but he was reluctant. "Every time you bear a child, we risk disaster."

"And each time, we also risk joy."

Jacob studied the little fingers that were gripping his own and, in an odd way, giving him strength. "You must remind me of this,

Rachel, *keep* reminding me of this."

Her lips curved with the sweetest smile he'd ever seen. "I doubt Michael will let you forget it."

He peered deeply into candid green eyes that warmed him, anchored him—the eyes of the woman who had both snared him and saved him. "I love you."

"I love you, too. So very much."

Jacob kissed his brave, beautiful wife and began counting what he hoped would be a long list of blessings.

Thank you for reading my book!

I hope you enjoyed *Precious Atonement*.
If you haven't read *Come Back*,
the highly-rated novel that inspired it,
you can find it at major online retailers.

If you want to be notified of new books and special giveaways,
sign up for my newsletter. http://eepurl.com/P2EWL

Follow me on Twitter @MelissaMaygrove

A Texas-sized thank you goes out to my beta readers, my mom,
and the awesome members of Pioneer Hearts for helping me put
the final polish on *Precious Atonement*.

Get your happily ever after.
www.melissamaygrove.com

Printed in Dunstable, United Kingdom